Dedication

To my wife Ann, whose unwavering support and editorial assistance made this book possible.

Lingua Cosmica

Fred J Line III

Contents

Chapter One

A solitary figure clad in the bulky garb of a lunar spacesuit slowly moved across the grey landscape. The piercing light from his headlamp cut a swath through the impenetrable darkness. Off in the distance, a light shown, somehow providing reassurance that others were about. The bone chilling cold was ever present in lunar night. He could feel it on the inside of his visor. A stark reminder of this inhospitable world. The sound of air being drawn from his breathing air cylinder made for an almost hypnotic rhythm, each new breath a verification that at least for now, everything was working. The telemetry screen inside his visor gave a running commentary on his life support system; air remaining, $co2$ concentration, internal suit temperature, humidity level, accumulated radiation dose and more. He looked back and saw the trail of footprints in the fine dust of the lunar regolith, signs of his presence here in this godforsaken place, signs that would remain long after he was gone.

"Well, I certainly never get tired of the view anyway," Jake thought to himself as he stared into the vast expanse of space.

He'd only been doing this job for a relatively short time and still felt a thrill of excitement every time he looked at the millions of stars over his head. He had never really thought that he would become a lunar geologist. He had always seen himself as pursuing a more traditional geology occupation, but somehow the lunar bug had gotten to him.

He looked around and thought to himself how working on the moon never seemed very *natural*. The temperature extremes, the lack of atmosphere, the risk of meteors and cosmic radiation all conspired to make this a place where inattention could be fatal. He always tried to keep that in mind and never get too comfortable.

This was his second rotation on the moon and he was about halfway through this six month assignment. He felt a sense of satisfaction with what he'd accomplished so far, but he also was exhausted by the strain of spending so much time in a space suit. The alternating periods of intense darkness and blinding light on the lunar surface was something that took getting used to. He had spent the first assignment on the moon largely working in the South Lunar Base assay lab. That was certainly a lot easier than this field assignment. Now he was on a geological survey mission in the Van der Waals crater. It was about 60 miles in diameter with a notched and rugged crest on its northern side but almost no crest at all on its southern side. It was named after a Nobel prize winning 19th century physical chemist.

Jake carefully examined the outside of his multilayered composite space suit and noticed the usual buildup of moon dust that always had to be carefully removed when reentering the rover. He never realized when training for this mission how much moon dust would get into everything. It really took a toll on equipment and people. It's the one thing about the Moon he certainly wouldn't miss. He was looking forward to finishing this mission and heading back to the lunar station near the south pole. The South Lunar Base was really quite a facility, a place where one could experience a little taste of normalcy, maybe knock down a few drinks and trade stories with colleagues.

He was jarred back into reality by the voice of Jamison, the mission group leader in his headset.

"Are you going to spend the rest of the day contemplating your navel or are you going to get some work done?"

Jake felt a little chagrined by this friendly gibe. He really had kind of drifted off there for a moment, lost in thought. But now he was brought back swiftly to the task at hand.

"Ok chief, I was just thinking about a burger and fries at In-n-Out ."

He glanced over at their lunar rover and gave Jamison a salute and confirmed that the microwave antenna was fully deployed. It was the vital link in transmitting the spectral data he was gathering back to the lunar station. The robotic X-ray fluorescence unit he was monitoring plodded slowly across the lunar plain, sending a continuous stream of elemental data analysis, and leaving track marks in the gray lunar regolith. This monitoring was the next step after the satellite magnetometer results obtained from recent flyovers had yielded results suggestive of possible KREEP rich terrain.

In the absence of an atmosphere, the light from his helmet cut like a knife through the darkness, with virtually no visibility of the terrain outside its direct beam. He remembered as a kid thinking that the dark side of the Moon would be an area of eternal darkness. It was surprising to learn that it wasn't true at all. Great swathes of the "dark side" were bathed in intense sunlight for up to two weeks, with the corresponding temperature fluctuations seen generally on the moon. High temps up to 225 F. during the lunar day and lows down to -300 F. during lunar night. One more reason why great effort had gone into the design of their space suits. The multilayer construction included plies to provide thermal insulation, others to attenuate cosmic radiation, and several outer layers to provide protection against penetration by micrometeoroids. Joint design had been a difficult challenge but key to making the suits flexible. The joints had to allow broad range of movement, but not allow leakage or compromise thermal integrity.

But temperature extremes weren't the only hazard. Jake thought back to the disaster of '63 when an entire crew in transit to the moon was killed by a coronal mass ejection that enveloped their spacecraft. Lunar exploration had seen tremendous research done in ways to protect personnel from the constant cosmic radiation, but these measures couldn't really address those occasions when the sun "hiccuped" and sent out a seething cloud of plasma.

Jake rechecked the readout on the fluorescence unit. All the instrument performance parameters were showing green. The instrument creeped ahead slowly on its titanium tracks, designed to passively bombard the lunar surface with X-rays to cause metals present in the soil to fluoresce. Not disturbing the lunar regolith was critical. The fine lunar dust was death to any precision instrument and wasn't much better for humans.

"Jake, you're at your dose limit for the day. Time to head back to the rover." Jamison had been monitoring the data stream in the rover, and

3

spoke into Jake's headset.

"Roger that," Jake replied. Radiation dosimetry was a big deal and daily exposure rules had to be followed religiously.

He headed back toward the rover entry lock, taking care to secure the testing device before heading in. Once in the lock, he actuated the external door and then began the slow cumbersome process of desuiting. The first step, once the air lock was pressurized, was to dedust the suit using the vacuum nozzle. Using air for vacuum suction was its own technical challenge, since air is a precious commodity on the moon. The suction unit would clean off the suit's exterior surfaces, filter the air to collect any dust and then recompress the suction air for reuse.

Once this cleaning step was done, Jake cracked the seal on his helmet. It felt good to get it off. He always felt a touch of claustrophobia in the confines of the suit. He proceeded with removing the rest of the exterior suit, hung it in place next to the row of suits used by the rest of the crew, and opened the inner door to enter the crew compartment. Once inside, he removed the suit liner that circulated heating or cooling water to maintain his body temperature and the communication cap that allowed him to dialog with the rover while on the lunar surface.

After spending hours in the relativity sterile environment of the space suit, he always found reentry into the rover an interesting set of sensory experiences. The mixture of food odors, human sweat and burnt coffee always surprised him. He looked around the cabin and saw that Mallory had already donned his suit liner and was almost ready to go out and replace him. There was a steady hum of instrumentation.

The lunar rover was their home for the duration of a lunar mission. It was a large ungainly looking vehicle with steel tires, 50 feet in length, large polycarbonate windows in front, with an array of communication antennas and dishes on top. The vehicle included equipment bays, sleeping quarters, bathroom and shower, a miniature kitchen and dining area, small assay lab and tiny office area for Jamison. The unit was powered by an electric motor run off solar cells and batteries. During lunar days, the supply of energy was bountiful, but during lunar night the consumption of energy had to be more closely monitored to make sure solar batteries could meet their energy needs. The rover was pretty spartan but the crews could entertain themselves with video feeds from

4

earth and an occasional chess game.

Jamison was standing at the main control panel reviewing the latest data set from the florescence unit. Jake was pretty tired and didn't really feel like eating at this point. He headed back toward the crew quarters and found his sleep module. Suit work on the moon was always pretty exhausting, so he thought he'd fall right asleep.

But he didn't. Instead he found himself thinking about his dad. His dad had been a geologist too. Jake grew up in the Texas Gulf Coast. His dad, Scott Mackenzie, worked for one of the big petroleum companies. Early in his career, he traveled all over the world looking for the big untapped oil reserves. Later on as oil became harder to find, he found places in the US where fracking could squeeze the last traces of oil out of the rocks. His family had made a good living off oil, but toward the end of his career, when manifestations of climate change had become undeniable, his dad would say that it was "time to move on". His dad had passed away suddenly in 2066 almost 10 years ago and Jake still missed him. Hattie, his mom, still lived in the Houston area and he was thankful that she was in good health. He had a younger sister, Barbara, who had become an orthopedist and lived near their mom.

Despite spending his entire career in the petroleum business, Scott Mackenzie would have been gratified at the way the planet had moved on. The world went through a revolution with the advent of fusion reactors. Prior to fusion, the uneven distribution of energy resources saw many places in the world languish because of the lack of cheap, easily available energy. The predictions of doom from global warming at the start of the 21st-century had become a drum beat, louder and louder until they could no longer be ignored. The urgent need for action drove energy research including fusion until finally worldwide efforts to crack the "fusion" code were successful. Scientists and engineers succeeded in harnessing the power of the sun inside a reactor. It was technological development at its finest and it transformed the world. The last coal fired power plant went off-line in 2040, and the period of clean renewable energy was upon us. The change in energy dynamics could be seen everywhere. Places like the African continent, which had always suffered from the lack of cheap energy, became new centers of prosperity. Countries could no longer use energy as a weapon or a threat.

One of the few caveats, however, to this optimistic picture was rare earth elements. Everything from a fusion toromak to computer components consumed a lot of lanthanides, yttrium and scandium. The pursuit of rare earth metals remained a key area where countries competed to corner the resources. China had had a serious semi-monopoly in the early 21st century but that had ended once lunar exploration and mining started to bear fruit. The moon was now seen as a significant natural resource. There was a certain Wild West quality to lunar exploration. The International Treaty on Lunar Exploration was signed by all the major powers in 2052, but despite that there was still much jockeying for position among the different countries working to exploit the moon's resources. Occasionally it led to actual violence on the moon when disputes arose about who owned a particular section of territory and what rights they had to perform mining on that property.

Rare earth elements aren't really rare. They just occur in most places in concentrations that make mining processes economically infeasible

After tossing and turning far too long, Jake finally drifted off to sleep.

Jake reentered the control room after a good "nights" sleep. One of the challenges of a lunar exploration was maintenance of circadian rhythms. In the absence of the normal day/night cycle, artificially induced sleep wake cycles had to be adhered to to prevent crews from burning out.

"So, how do the readouts look," Jake asked.

Jamison looked up from the display screen, the reflection forming a colored pattern on his weary face. "It's starting to look like we might be on to something," Jamison replied. "These are the highest results we've seen for lanthanum and neodymium in some time. Looks like we might be on the fringes of a magma crest."

"That sounds promising," Jake replied. "Maybe we need to think about doing a gravimetric survey."

Jamison responded, "I've been thinking that, too."

The gravimetric survey was the logical next step. The satellite magnetic study conducted first had provided a broad picture of the terrain in the area they were studying. The on-site field study they had just conducted suggested that rare earth elements were present in the regolith at higher levels than were seen generally. Now the gravimetric study would be

6

focused on a smaller area of lunar landscape and provided a considerably more detailed view into the topography of that area. It was performed using a satellite in permanent lunar orbit which measured variations in lunar gravity across a 3 mile wide section of lunar terrain to get a view of the subsurface geology. These instruments had become so sensitive, that detailed images of subsurface topography could be generated.

In earth geology, efforts are made to find areas where metals had been concentrated typically as a result of water flow processes in subterranean grounds. Lunar geology was quite different. The almost total lack of water on the moon's surface meant that similar concentration processes did not occur. It was thought that most concentration of rare earth metals on the moon had occurred primarily during the period when the moon was molten magma. After the moon solidified, there were no ongoing processes that would concentrate rare earth metals to make recovery more economically viable. A KREEP (K-potassium, REE- rare earth elements, P-potassium) pocket was a lunar geology term to describe possible areas where the primordial magma cooling process had produced areas of concentrated rare earth metals. The gravimetric study would reveal whether the subsurface topography was a promising location to site a future mining operation.

"I'm gonna make a call into headquarters and ask them to review our latest data. If they agree I'm going to go ahead and order the gravimetric study," Jamison added.

"Do you think we can get that done before the end of this mission?" Jake asked.

"No, I've already told headquarters that we're headed back," Jamison answered. "We're overdue for our next furlough."

"Yeah I'm ready for a break at South Base. A little R&R would really be welcome," Jake said.

"I'm going to tell Mallory to start packing up the X-ray unit for a return to base," Jamison said.

Jake and the crew completed shutdown procedures within a couple of hours. They stowed all the portable instrumentation, recleaned the external surfaces of their spacesuits, did a general cleaning of the rover interior, organized and packed a number of samples that would be analyzed by the lab at South Base, and packed up their personal belongings.

They began the almost thousand mile return trip to South Lunar Base
. A good part of the trip was fairly easy going thanks to the Vallis Planck,
a valley that went almost in a straight line toward South Base, until it
reached the Schroedinger crater. The Schroedinger crater was more than
150 miles in diameter and provided some pretty challenging mountainous
terrain. Once past that crater, the path onto South Base was fairly smooth
and level. Jake felt a little flutter of anticipation. He'd been on this latest
mission for a couple of weeks and looked forward to getting outside the
confines of the rover back to the relative comfort of South Base. The trip
back would be fairly routine but required generally slow going to cover
the crater pocked terrain.

During initial lunar exploration, scientists were somewhat surprised at
the absence of "maria" or seas on the far side compared to the portion of the
moon visible from earth. During a full moon, the maria are readily visible
even to the unaided eye. The seas are actually large dark basaltic plains.
It was hypothesized that the cooler far side experienced condensation of
the magma sooner and so formed a thicker crust; meteoroid impacts on
the near side would sometimes penetrate the thinner crust and release
basaltic lava that created the maria, but rarely did so on the far side.

The trip back was largely uneventful. Jake and Mallory spent a good
bit of the time back in the equipment bay cleaning and maintaining the
various instruments used in their geological surveys. Jamison piloted
the rover most of the time with occasional relief from Jake. It was pretty
monotonous to cross an unending barren landscape. Making the return
trip in lunar night was pretty slow going. On the trip out from South
Base, they had periodically left electronic markers which during this
return served to confirm they were following the correct route. Certainly
for much of the trip they could simply follow their own tracks but that
became less reliable as you got closer to South Base. If they had been in
a period of full light, their progress would have been somewhat faster.
Occasionally they would have to backtrack when the selected route was
too steep or a rockfall had blocked their path. Despite the multi wheel
drive of the rover, its size made it somewhat ungainly and limited where
it could negotiate the lunar terrain.

Crews doing lunar geology tended to have technical degrees and
often advanced technical degrees. The complexity of lunar work and the

numerous complex systems required including life support, navigation, geological surveying instruments made technical skill sets a must for successful missions. Jake had an undergraduate degree from Purdue in chemical engineering and a masters from Stanford in Geology. Mallory, the instrument tech on this trip, was an electrical engineer from Duke University. Jamison, their group leader, was a PhD in Metallurgy but objected anytime someone used his doctor title. To work on the moon, all of them had gone through the Lunar Mission training program operated by NASA. This two month course covered everything from space suit basics to cosmic ray dosimetry to response to meteor emergencies.

This manned mission on the moon was an exception to the normally highly automated lunar processes. Artificial intelligence had grown exponentially during the last 50 years and now virtually any manual task could be more easily done by a machine than a man. The several lunar dig sites that had been established for mining of rare earth metals were largely run by machines. The typical lunar mine would have a human mine superintendent, a human maintenance superintendent and a crew of maybe 200 robots.

The threat that artificial intelligence would someday take over the world had been real and there was a period when there was some question if AI could be controlled. Eventually, a set of global programming standards were adopted which built into every robots central processor certain prohibitions on their activities. While more complex in its framing then Isaac Asimov's three laws of robotics, it was nonetheless extraordinary that a 20th century sciencefiction writer had anticipated both the issue and the solution.

The Western Consortium South Lunar Base was a joint project of the US , the European Union and England. It was a surprising mixture of industrial mining headquarters, space port and tourist destination. Many had doubted that tourism would flourish on the moon, but the doubters had been wrong. The opportunity to stand on the surface of the moon and watch an " Earth-rise " had proved to be an irresistible draw for many. From the moon, Earth was a huge blue and white orb in the lunar sky. The annual lunar tourist traffic amounted to more than 10,000 people per year. The developers of the tourist facilities had put together a savvy blend of the awe inspiring and fun. Incredible views of Earth and the Milky Way coupled with a four star hotel, games to experience the wonder of 1/6th gravity, hikes on the lunar surface and seminars on everything from lunar hydroponics to astronomy came together to make the lunar vacation a "lifetime" experience.

In the Atrium of the hotel, designers had reproduced a tropical rainforest with towering bamboo stands, and an amazing variety of orchids and many exotic plants. Quite a feat considering how precious water is on the moon. There was even a full service casino for those who had to gamble regardless of their surroundings. There were Las Vegas style productions featuring top name entertainers. Within the hotel, it was easy to forget where you were and how hostile this world was just on the other side of the dome. Perimeter lighting made the dome spectacular at night, and during lunar day, the dome panels would darken to reduce the otherwise blinding light of the sun.

An indoor track and field facility allowed people to test their limits in 1/6th gravity. Everything from high jump to broad jump to shot put and javelin allowed people to break terrestrial world records with ease. Track events were a little more challenging. Running in reduced gravity tended to produce an excessive hopping motion which made achieving fast lap times difficult.

Occasionally things went awry when an overzealous tourist on one of the outside the dome excursions tried something stupid like leaping off a tall cliff.

They immediately learned that lack of an atmosphere meant no terminal velocity: if you jump from a high enough point on the moon you still die.

The South Lunar Base space port served as both landing site for lunar visitors and stopover point for people headed to the Mars colony. In many ways it resembled an earthly airport but was more compact in size.

The Mars colony had been up and running for almost twenty years, but it was still a relatively modest size venture. The length of the trip along with the challenges of living in the harsh conditions of Mars had meant only the most daring souls were prepared for the level of commitment required.

Scientist had hoped that the development of fusion energy would also translate into benefits for space travel. However, it hadn't really worked out that way. The complexity of producing a miniature sun inside the fusion reactor had revolutionized power generation but had thus far proved too daunting to achieve the degree of miniaturization required to power a space craft. But space travel had nonetheless made awesome advances. Both lunar and Mars bound space ships were powered with plasma-based propulsion systems. These plasma systems required hydrogen as a fuel but in quantities far less than conventional rockets, which meant that it was no longer necessary to transport massive quantities of rocket fuel from the earth. Hydrogen in various forms was widely available either as an electrolysis product of lunar water or from the solar wind. This had been the breakthrough that finally made travel to Mars practical. With the plasma propulsion system, velocities significantly higher then had been possible with liquid fuel rockets were attainable. What had originally been a trip of over a year now had been reduced to a little over 60 days. Once on Mars, the craft was able to refuel with hydrogen extracted from the thin Martian atmosphere for the return trip.

Jake looked up from the instrument panel and could just make out the outline of the South Base dome in the distance. During periods of lunar night, the South Base dome lit up the night sky, could be seen from great distances and was truly spectacular. After spending weeks in the almost suffocating darkness of the moon, the dome was like a beacon calling out to weary travelers. It wouldn't be long now until they were back among the comforts of the base. He saw that both Morrison and Jamison had seen it too. They had this look of anticipation that he was sure was reflected in his own face. Two weeks out in the rover was a long time to be cooped up. He planned to have a real dinner tonight at the spaceport 4-star restaurant with Janice, the lab director from the spectroscopy lab. They had had a couple of dates recently and found themselves very attracted to each other. Janice was a PhD geophysicist and assistant professor in Stanford's Geology School and was nearing the end of her lunar assignment. Jake still had another 3 months on his lunar assignment. He was enrolled in the geology PhD program at Stanford and was anxious to resume his dissertation research. While a lunar assignment was considered a plum assignment, and was an important box to check off on your resume, it was nonetheless an interruption to his career plans.

They were just passing the space port. A row of sleek star cruisers were lined up at the main terminal building. One off in the distance had been brought into launch position and was clearly going to depart soon. Probably the biweekly Mars shuttle, loaded with provisions, spare parts and replacement crews for Mars Base. Jake had never done a Mars rotation. He wasn't really sure he had what it took to be successful on a Mars mission.

While the Moon had become a popular tourist destination, an assignment on Mars required hardier souls who could endure the suffocating confines of a starship for the 2 month trip, and then on arrival tolerate the spartan trials of life on Mars. Mars was really a research and mining facility, with no hint of the play activities found on the moon. Just as with the moon, cosmic radiation on Mars limited surface activities. The base on Mars was almost entirely subterranean with only the rover building and communications center visible on the rust colored terrain.

Up ahead Jake saw the access ramp for the main underground facility at South Lunar Base. Jamison called the control tower and identified the rover and requested hanger access. It was immediately granted and the huge outer airlock door slowly started opening. Once it was fully open, they drove in and the powerful airlock door slowly lowered into place behind them. The inner lock door opened and they drove the rover into the main lunar vehicle hanger. Jake always found the size and scope of this underground facility pretty mind boggling. It had been a massive effort to establish this underground base that had required 10 years, the labor of over 500 workers and engineers, and had cost a few people their lives in this environment where mistakes were often lethal.

Jamison turned to Jake and said "As soon as we get the equipment bay unloaded, you and Morrison can head up to the dome." That was good news for Jake. Sometimes a return from a mission could drag out if the mission leader insisted on strict adherence to mission debrief procedures.

Once the critical instrumentation had been removed from the rover, a maintenance team would take the vehicle, do a thorough cleaning to remove the lunar dust that got in and on everything, and go through an extensive testing and maintenance protocol. The difficulty of dealing with mechanical breakdowns while out on a mission made rover reliability critical and they were therefore handled with almost the same level of care seen for spacecrafts.

Jake gathered his gear and felt a swell of excitement exiting the confines of the rover. While the lunar hanger wasn't open air earth, it almost felt like it. Being able to walk long distances, breathing lunar manufactured air without a suit was refreshing. The hanger bustled with activity. There were 20 or 30 rovers similar to theirs. There were a number of the lunar tourist buses in various stages of trip preparation. They looked similar to rovers, but were larger and featured oversized portholes to enhance viewing. At the rear of each bus was an airlock to facilitate extravehicular activities. Jake had never been on one, but had often seen them out entertaining tourists with interesting rock formations or spectacular views.

"You'd almost think you were on earth if not for the slight spring in your step that comes from only weighing 30 pounds," Jake thought to himself.

Jake rang up Janice and she answered immediately. "Hey there stranger, back from the badlands I see. How did it go?"

"Oh it was all pretty dull and routine," Jake replied. "But we did come across a possible magma crest. Could turn out to be a rare earth excavation candidate."

"Well that's good news ! From your descriptions of these rover missions, seems like decoding lunar geology can be a challenge," Janice said in that soft Georgia flavored accent that Jake had found so alluring.

Janice had grown up in the outskirts of Atlanta. Her parents had both been PhD biochemists who met while doing pharmaceutical research. She had two sisters, both of whom had also become biochemists. They always teased her about her geophysics career choice, saying "you have to have rocks in your head to do geophysics."

She was a star athlete in high school and lettered in both softball and volleyball. Her senior year of high school she was the starting catcher when her softball team won the state championship. Her dad was so proud he could hardly contain himself. At one point in the semifinal game, her team had been one ball away from elimination. She and her best friend Heidi, who was also the pitcher, threw 20 strikes in a row until the batter finally didn't hit a foul tip and struck out. They went on to win that game and the one after. She considered going on to Div 1 sports in college, but decided the commitment required for sports would affect her academic performance.

13

She graduated summa cum laude from the University of Georgia and then proceeded to get her masters and PhD in Geophysics from Stanford. Stanford had immediately offered her an assistant professors job and she had been there for 3 years now and loved university life.

The lunar assignment hadn't been part of her plan, but one of the tenured senior professors had convinced her that a short term lunar assignment would round out her resume and enhance her pursuit of a tenured position.

"It's true," Jake responded. "Research crews have on several occasions selected mine sites that ultimately didn't yield much. There is some pressure on us to make a big breakthrough since the Chinese base had reported out a major rare earth site in their lunar zone. We need to come up with a candidate excavation site soon. But enough about work. How about that dinner I promised you? Does tonight work? " "You bet!" Janice replied. "I've been looking forward to this every day since you left on your mission."

"Pick you up at 7:00?" Jake asked.

"Sounds great," Janice replied. "See you soon."

Jake got on the lunar tram and headed to the main base quarters. He mused to himself how habits from earth life persisted on the moon. He and Janice were meeting this "evening", but of course there is no real evening on the moon.

Jakes quarters were part of the South Base Hilton. Jake thought it had been foresighted to design a single hotel unit that catered to both tourists and technical crews on lunar assignment. The luxuries that tourists found appealing also made the rigors of a several month lunar assignment more bearable. Jake enjoyed passing tourists in the hallways. They always had that "star struck" and excited look that comes with a person's departure from Mother Earth. They would eye his Western Consortium uniform with awe. Spacemen were still viewed with some amount of hero worship.

Jake entered his quarters. Everything was in its usual spotless state of cleanliness and order. The cyber maid came through daily when he was in and weekly when he was on a mission. He just had a short time before he was due to pick up Janice, so he spent a few minutes browsing his email and turned on the window. The window was actually a television monitor that in its screensaver mode looked like a window looking out over the lunar landscape with the dazzling geodesic dome in the foreground and the gray lunar landscape stretching off into the distance. In reality his hotel room was located 50 feet below grade. The layer of regolith, the term used to describe the outer surface layer of the moon, under which the hotel was built, provided crucial attenuation of radiation from cosmic rays, solar wind and solar flares. Without this protection, the time that lunar visitors could safely spend on the moon would have been greatly reduced.

The design also provided protection from meteor strikes, a hazard ever present on the lunar surface. Early in it's history, the moon was bombarded for millions of years by countless meteors. That accounted for the composition of the regolith, a loose layer of debris up to 10 meters thick in some places, the result of countless pulverizing impacts. While the modern lunar landscape is subjected to far fewer strikes than the primeval moon, when they occur, the results could be devastating. Back during the original South Base construction work, a meteor about the size of a basketball had penetrated one of the temporary pressurized construction buildings, resulting in depressurization and loss of everyone in the building. Since that time, considerable improvements in the protection against such strikes had been made. Besides the main safeguard of subsurface construction, additional measures included a radar net to locate and track incoming meteors, and a surface to air missile defense system that could destroy a high percentage of meteors threatening the base. In addition, there were extensive procedures in place to address depressurization events. Everyone was drilled constantly to be able to find and don emergency air supply on a moments notice.

Jake tapped on Janice's door and he heard the sound of her footfall as she approached. The door opened, and Jake felt a quiver of excitement as he was reminded of this lovely and brilliant creature with whom he was to spend a delightful evening.

"Don't you look lovely, Dr Barnes !" Jake blurted out, feeling his usual awkwardness in her presence. She was lovely, and an accomplished geophysicist. For a short time on earth, she had been his thesis advisor, but they had both agreed it wasn't a good idea, once the attraction between them had become clear. Besides that, he had also decided to focus on geology rather than the more academically oriented area of geophysics.

15

"Looking pretty good yourself there, soon to be Doctor Mackenzie ," she replied. They immediately embraced and spent some time in a long passionate kiss. "I've missed you so much Jake," Janice whispered in his ear.

"Me too" was all Jake could muster. He was too distracted by her scent, her feel and her presence to be able to say anything very brilliant. She broke the moment of tension

"But enough of this for now. I'm starving! Let's go eat."

They boarded the space tube to the dome where the restaurant and numerous tourist attractions and observation platforms were located. They then took the main elevator. Once the elevator cleared the subsurface levels, they were treated to the dazzling view of the lunar geodesic dome. The structure consisted of thousands of clear glass polyhedrons in a titanium framework. It was over half a mile in diameter and had been the brainchild of Elon Musk, one of his last inspired recommendations before he finally passed away at age 95 in 2066. He had argued that bold and audacious was what was required to make lunar tourism work, and of course he had been right. Both the glass polyhedrons and the supporting titanium frames were manufactured from lunar materials. The silicates for the glass were abundant everywhere on the moon, and several rich deposits of ilmenite had been found not far from South Lunar Base, from which titanium was smelted.

The restaurant was located mid level in the dome. They exited the elevator and were immediately greeted by the maitre de. "Good evening, Dr Barnes. Welcome to Over the Moon. So good to see you again! And Mr McKenzie. Back from your mission I see! We been saving some special dishes just for you two." Henri the head waiter was of course the latest generation of robotic wait staff. He had a name recognition library of every guest and mining worker on the moon and was programmed with that poise and suavity seen in maitre des since time immemorial . Henri snapped his fingers and adopted an irritated tone as he called out to one of his waiters "Table #7 for our honored guests. Don't keep them waiting!"

No expense had been spared for this Michelin four star rated restaurant.

Celebrity chefs did assignments here to bring top notch cuisine to its patrons. A world class wine cellar had been assembled. Weekly shuttles from earth ensured fresh food was always served.

Jake and Janice spent a few minutes staring in awe struck wonder as the Earth, floating above them in the lunar sky. It appeared 3 or 4 times bigger than the comparable view of the moon from earth, and was this beautiful blue and white orb. For those who had been on an extended assignment, this view of Earth evoked strong emotions and thoughts of home. Many who visited the moon considered this view to be the most moving experience of the whole lunar trip. A close second of course was the dome. The entire dome was surrounded by spotlights that bathed the structure in light and reflected off the burnished titanium frame.

Jake pointed out several interesting landmarks to Janice and Janice commented on how romantic it was to dine by…earth light.

The dinner was of course divine.

Chapter Two

"This is exactly what I needed," Janice thought to herself. She had only been back from the lunar mission for approximately two weeks and now here she was in the middle of a jungle involved in a very interesting archaeological dig.

Initially being back on earth required some acclimation. Suddenly weighing 120 pounds again seemed very difficult. For a few days she had felt really sluggish. However that all passed with time. Now she was readjusting to life on earth and in the last few days had started to feel herself again.

Her participation in this project had been in the works for sometime. While geophysicists didn't typically work on archaeological projects, it was an area of interest for her and she was seriously considering further academic work to develop a credential as a geo archaeologist. Geo archaeologists study the natural physical processes that affect archeological sites such as geomorphology, the formation of sites through geological processes and the effects on buried sites and artifacts post-deposition. Geo archaeologists' work frequently involves studying soil and sediments as well as other geographical concepts to contribute to an archaeological study.

She was at Coba, a Mayan archaeological site located on the east coast of the Yucatán. She had secured a summer assignment here through one of her contacts in the Stanford Archeology School. While this site wasn't new in terms of archaeological explorations, the project she was now involved in was attempting to fully map this large complex. Serious excavation of the site had begun more than 100 years ago, but a large portion of the city still remained to be explored.

She had flown into Tulum Airport last week, which in recent years had experienced explosive growth in tourism and now rivaled Cancun as the Mexican resort town of choice. The area was beautiful, lush and green with white sand beaches, emerald blue water and Mayan ruins dotting the landscape.

The archeological team were all staying at a beachside hotel which featured direct beach access and a rooftop terrace, where many of the team would meet after dinner to talk and socialize. When Janice checked in, she found a fruit basket in her room, left by the project lead as a welcome gesture. On her first evening in Coba, she ran into several members of the team at dinner, and they invited her to join them and made her feel very welcome. She had been a little anxious about how this Summer work would turn out. Sometimes academics can be a little *intense* but she found this group to be warm and friendly. They spoke positively about the project leadership and it left her feeling good about her decision.

The culture shock and transition from the moon to Palo Alto to Tulum was quite something. She was sorry that she had been able to spend so little time with Jake before having to head home, but she felt sure she would see him again.

The next day, she rode with several of the team members out to the dig site and checked in with the project administrative head, Dr Karen Parker. She was given a tour of the site, driving around in a jeep.

"So here's an example of a stelae, a stone slab that records Mayan dynastic information. These are scattered throughout the site. Unfortunately, many are too eroded to allow accurate deciphering," Dr Parker pointed out a stone which Janice would have missed.

"Using the ones which are readable, our team has been able to identify some of the Mayan rulers and their dates of ascension,". Dr Parker continued.

"When was Coba at its peak, in terms of this site as a trading center?" Janice asked.

"Coba was first settled in the Pre-Classic around 300 B.C.-200

A.D but all that remains are pottery shards to tell the story. It began its development into a local power in the Early Classic from 200-600 A.D and achieved its height as a regional capital during the Late Classic about 600-900 A.D when most of the buildings, sacbe , and the erection of the numerous stelae took place," Dr Parker replied.

"Straight ahead now you're looking at the Ixmoja Pyramid. This is the tallest Mayan structure in Coba and in fact in northern Yucatán," Dr Parker continued.

"Wow, that's pretty impressive!" Janice said. "How tall is it?" She craned her neck to lean out of the Jeep for a better view.

"It's 42 meters," Dr Parker answered. "Up ahead there on the left, you can see one of the ball courts.The ancient Maya ballgame called pitz was part of Maya political, religious, and social life. Played with a rubber ball ranging in size from that of a softball to a soccer ball, players would attempt to bounce the ball without using their hands through stone hoops attached to the sides of the ball court."

"And coming up on the left there you can see Xai'be plaza. It is from the Xai'be plaza that the 62mile/100km sacbe, Sacbe 1 the longest in the Maya World, leads off from the southwest corner westward to Yaxuna. The sacbe are the Mayan roadways and are really engineering marvels," Dr Parker explained. "Right around Xai'be plaza is where Dr Wilson has been concentrating his focus for this dig season."

They just sat for a few minutes and took it all in. The heat was oppressive and both Janice and Dr Parker were drenched in perspiration. In the background, the sounds of bird life in the jungle was a constant cacophony of sound, with parrots and numerous other bird species joining in.

"So how long have you been on the dig, Dr Parker?" Janice asked.

"Please, just call me Karen,"

"And please call me Janice"

The two ladies smiled at each other warmly.

Karen continued, "So back to your question, I've been here about 3 years, every since Dr Wilson took over"

"I've really been impressed with how friendly all the team members are. Everyone has been very nice," Janice said.

"It's all about the tone at the top. Dr Wilson is a terrific leader and he expects people on the team to work together in harmony. I've been on other digs, where petty rivalries and academic snobbery have created strife, and I'm so glad that's not happening here. I think you're going to like it here, Janice."

"And be sure not to miss the biweekly beach barbecues!" Karen gushed.

They drove around a little longer and finally arrived back at the project headquarters building.

"So Janice , I'm charged with helping team members get oriented and addressing any needs you may have. Please don't hesitate to come to me if you need anything." Karen said.

"Thank you very much," Janice replied. " And thank you for the tour, Karen. After your great explanations, I feel like I can get up to speed quickly."

"You're quite welcome, Janice. We're excited to have a geophysicist on the team!"

She was soon put to work performing ground penetrating radar runs along the perimeter of the Xai'be plaza.

She had been at it for several hours. The oppressive heat took some getting used to, but she tried to pace herself and keep hydrated.

In the middle of one of her runs, she looked up and saw that Dr Wilson was waving at her.

"Dr Barnes, I apologize for not meeting you sooner. Welcome to Coba! I hope Karen gave you a good initial orientation. Do you need anything from me?

"No, thank you Dr Wilson, everyone has been terrific, Karen gave me a great overview of Coba and I'm ready to do whatever I can to help."

Dr Wilson smiled at her and said "So glad to hear that! So let's get you in the thick of it! It looks like you're already completed grid 241.

21

Could we meet this afternoon to discuss what you've found?" he asked.

"Of course," she replied. "I should be able to complete the grid 242 GPR run by 2 o'clock. Could we meet after that?"

"That works for me." he replied.

Dr. Graham Wilson shambled off, as usual looking lost in thought. He was a 60 something archeologist of world renown, famous for the work he had done to bring the Mayan culture to life. He had spearheaded the project that found the major Mayan trade center at Tikal and through his research had demonstrated that the Mayan cities were highly integrated and urbanized, featuring marketplaces and market economies to exchange many goods including obsidian. Now he was convinced that Coba held the key to finally determining what happened to cause the collapse of classic Mayan society.

Janice returned to her work on the GPR unit. She was currently mapping out a section of terrain where it was suspected that a large market area had been during Coba's period of peak prosperity around 800 AD. The GPR run would detect subsurface features that could be used to guide subsequent digging efforts.

The small tracked vehicle lumbered slowly along the path that had been cleared through the dry tropical forest. The trees here had a canopy height up to 20 m. Woody vegetation types abounded, including mangroves, petenes and pine savannas.

"I'm a pretty lucky lady," Janice thought to herself. The project was interesting and furthered her academic ambitions. And weekends on the beaches at Tulum were an added bonus.

Dr Wilson poured over the photographic evidence from the latest finds at the Coba dig site. He was sure they were getting close to what he suspected was the royal palace. He'd been closing in on it for some time, but it had proved to be elusive. His hope was that this could become a major find for additional glyphs that would help to definitively resolve the question of what had ultimately led to the decline of this vibrant Mayan society around 900 AD.

The ultimate decoding of the Mayan hieroglyphics or "glyphs" as they were known, had been one of the great success stories of modern archeology. Progress went slowly in the early 20th century, with disagreements among leading linguists of the day concerning how to translate the Mayan language. A major breakthrough occurred in the 1970's when a working group at the Mesa Redonda de Palenque were able in a single afternoon to translate the first dynastic list of Mayan kings. After that, the progress in translating Mayan codices had been stunning. By 2020, more than 90% of the Mayan texts could be read with reasonable accuracy.

But the kicker of course was the fact that so many of the Mayan codices had been destroyed. Under the direction of Bishop Diego de Landa in the 16th century, an untold number of Mayan codices were collected and destroyed, as part of a campaign to eradicate pagan rites. Now researchers like Dr Wilson held out hope that somewhere an undiscovered cache of Mayan writings would come to light.

Dr Wilson looked up as Janice arrived for their 2 pm meeting. " So are you finding our project here to your liking, Dr Barnes?" he asked.

"Oh, absolutely!" she replied with enthusiasm. "The team here is great to work with and the progress you're making in mapping out Coba is impressive.

I really appreciate this chance you've given me."

"Well, adding a first rate geophysicist to our group is a real plus for our research," he replied. "So let's take a look at grid 241."

Janice began. "The mapping shows what looks like it could be an extension of the main market place, with stalls like we've already seen. At the far eastern end of the grid however, and at a slightly deeper elevation we see signs of a more substantial foundation. This could be the edge of a more massive structure" Janice paused for a second to see Dr Wilson's reaction. "Based on the layout of other Mayan cities that have been extensively mapped, a central temple adjacent to the main market area would definitely be possible."

Dr Wilson couldn't quite hide the excitement he felt. He knew it was premature to get his hopes up, but then moments like this were what made the work rewarding.

"Thank you , Dr Barnes. I think I'll get the team to start a new trench looking for this structure asap. I'm convinced we may be on the verge of finding a new key city facility," Dr Wilson said.

"Well the GPR data for grid 242 should help to confirm whether more of a large foundation is present. I can have that for you tomorrow morning." Janice felt Dr Wilson's excitement and wanted to help.

"That would be great." Dr Wilson smiled.

Dr Wilson pulled out the draft of the latest paper he was working on. He felt this could be the breakthrough that delivered definitive evidence concerning the final decline of the Mayans. Around the year 900 AD, the vibrant widespread culture of the Mayans seemed to almost vanish. Archeologists had tried to investigate what had happened. It was known that a sustained period of drought had been a factor in the Mayan decline, but by itself wasn't seen as an adequate explanation of the dramatic collapse. Some years back, researchers had formulated a theory that poisoning of the water supply in Tikal in Guatemala had lead to the decline of that town. The pigment widely used in Mayan culture to adorn buildings and other structures contained cinnabar which is a mercury sulfide compound with an attractive reddish orange hue. Additionally, the water supply in Tikal was contaminated with Cyanobacteria. Dr Wilson believed this water quality issue went beyond Tikal and was in fact to be found among other Mayan cities. The chances however of finding widespread physical evidence of this were not promising. Most Mayan reservoirs had long since disappeared. But Dr Wilson was convinced that there were more Mayan codices to be found which could shed light on the final fate of the Mayan culture. And Coba was where he had determined that the best chance to uncover additional Mayan hieroglyphs existed. In other Mayan writings, the temple at Coba was often mentioned. The implication was that it had been a center of cultural activity in the time leading up to the sudden decline.

Janice joined the other members of the dig team at the beachside cabana. She looked forward to a weekend lazing on the beach and catching up on her reading. Although she was just a recent addition to the team and really only temporary, the crew treated her like she belonged.

"Hey Dr Barnes. Feel like trying a little wind surfing this afternoon?" Bill Smothers, the forensic anthropologist was standing over her, looking relaxed in his oversized straw hat. "I'm heading over with several of the team around 2 if you'd like to go"

"Thanks Bill, but I think I'd rather just stay here and knock down a pina colada or two. Still trying to get my sea legs back " She replied "And please call me Janice."

"Oh that's right. You're pretty recently back from South Base. How was that? I've always wanted to go, but there isn't much demand for anthropologists on the moon, Janice" Bill replied.

"It's definitely a life experience. Maybe you should just go as a tourist. The things to do on South Base for tourists are pretty awesome" Janice responded

"Yeah, that's what I hear. Well, got to run. I'll check back with you tomorrow about windsurfing." Bill turned and headed off down the beach.

Janice watched him go and thought how pleased she was to be on this project. She looked forward to a pleasant summer before returning to Palo Alto in the Fall.

The next day, Janice walked into the dig site artifact processing lab and saw Dr Wilson was hard at work, hovering over what appeared to be a Mayan glyph.

"Good morning, doctor." she greeted him.

"Ah good morning, Dr Barnes. Sorry I didn't hear you come in."

"Is that a new find from the dig?" she asked.

"Yes," he replied. "Just brought in this morning from the north perimeter trench. Looks like it might have adorned a structure there, possibly a residence of one of the scribes."

"Are you able to translate it?" She asked

"I wish I could. " he replied. "I think the study of ancient languages was my real true love, but I just didn't have what it takes to really excel at it. Being cloistered away in a library of ancient texts was just too academic. I found I needed the stimulation that comes with real field work. But I have the utmost respect for those who can do it. I wish I could have been at that conference in the 1970's at Palenque when Linda Shele and Peter Mathews almost singlehandedly translated the Tablet of the 96 Glyphs. It completely opened up Mayan culture for us. Now with the advances made in machine based decipherment, I can run this inscription through the Mayan translator and have a good assessment of the content in minutes. In some ways, it's almost a shame. I used to be pretty good at reading Mayan codices, but now it's an outdated and unnecessary skill set."

"Yeah, I've read the whole story of how the Mayan language finally came to life. Pretty amazing," Janice replied. " I brought over the GPR readouts from grid 242. Do you have time to go over them now?"

"Of course," Dr Wilson answered. He replaced the protective cover on the glyph he'd been studying. "Let's go into my office."

They moved into his office, and Janice unrolled the printout from the radar study.

"Here's where the grid 241 study ended. You can see that the structural item we detected there actually continues in 242 and if anything has grown more substantial. Unfortunately, the layout of the grids has only revealed this one linear structure, so it's still unclear whether it forms part of a building foundation or is something else." Janice looked up to see Dr Wilson was rummaging through a stack of papers.

"Sorry, Dr Barnes. I am listening. I just wanted to pull out the grid map to see whether we should alter the GPR schedule in light of this finding. Hmm, here it is. Looks like maybe if we changed the schedule to give grid 262 priority, we might get a picture sooner of what this buried wall may be part of."

The work at the dig site proceeded throughout the summer. Janice found the work stimulating and was impressed with the dedication of the dig team. The mapping work she had done had been instrumental in revealing the outline of what did in fact have characteristics of other temple sites found in Mayan cities. Over the summer, Dr Wilson was able to get approval to enlarge the dig team, and had focused a good bit of his available resources on the potential temple site. Nonetheless, the work proceeded slowly as good science always must. The two additional trenches they had added in the temple area had yielded a few artifacts-clay pottery and a brooch possibly from the ornamental garment of a temple priest. But so far nothing really extraordinary.

Janice also enjoyed her summer on the beach. Bill Smothers, Lana King and John Carvey were dig team members with whom she had really bonded and with whom she thought she would stay in touch. Shortly before she would be heading back to Stanford, the beach crew organized a beachside barbecue. While it hadn't been specifically designated as a send off party for Janice, she knew it really was. She would miss them all and would miss this life, close to the earth in touch with an ancient culture. Her work as a geophysicist wasn't as relaxing as archeology. To support the corporate sponsors whose main interest was locating valuable ore bodies, she always felt some degree of pressure to produce results. "I guess Dr Wilson has his own pressures to produce," Janice thought to herself. "But at least for me just being a worker bee on this project, it's been a pretty relaxing summer."

Just a week before Janice's scheduled departure, Dr Wilson called a sudden meeting of the entire dig staff. Rumor had it that something big had been found, but whatever it was had been kept under wraps.

"Come on in everyone". Just squeeze in and find a seat." Dr Wilson was beaming, and it was clear that he had something noteworthy to report. " I wanted to let all of you know right away that we've had a major find in the second trench in the temple area. John Higgins and his crew last week uncovered what appeared to be a possible altar stone. This week as more of the altar stone emerged, it became clear that the top stone was in fact a cap on what we believe is a burial chamber. But enough from me. I don't want to steal John's thunder. John please come up and proceed with filling the group in."

"Thank you, Dr Wilson," John Higgins replied as he made his way to the front of the room. He was in his late 30's and had been working with Dr Wilson for the last 10 years, every since he got his PhD.

Janice had met Dr Higgins at one of the beach barbecues. He was interested to hear about her lunar experience. She thought back on that evening.

"Probably my only regret in going into archeology is having absolutely no opportunity to do any space travel," Dr Higgins said as they shared a couple of beers and sat by a glowing campfire on the beach.

"It's truly a life experience," Janice said. "I'm really glad I got the opportunity."

"Well maybe someday I'll get a chance." Dr Higgins gazed thoughtfully at the surf.

Janice returned her attention to the suddenly convened meeting.

Dr Higgins began. "Thanks to everyone for coming together on short notice. So Dr Wilson has given you a hint of what we've found. It appears that we've unearthed a burial chamber. We've found a sarcophagus made out of stone. It appears to be undisturbed. So far we haven't attempted to open it. We're going to do a number of noninvasive examinations first including X-ray analysis. We don't have any clues yet as to who may be buried there, but we think based upon its size and previous Mayan digs, that it may well be the grave of a king or chief priest."

Dr Higgins added: "But perhaps just as exciting as this find is, we've already found something else that's pretty stunning. As many of you are aware, some of the most impressive finds in Mayan archeology have involved codices, Mayan hieroglyphics recorded on bark paper. The most famous of course are the Dresden Codex, the Paris Codex, and the Madrid Codex. Together they represent more than 90 % of the Mayan text that's survived. The efforts by Spanish priests to destroy these priceless cultural relics in the 1600's was largely successful. We'll never know what was lost."

Dr Higgins looked around the room to emphasize his next point. "But I'm here to report today that adjacent to the sarcophagus we found a stone bin. When we opened up this bin, we discovered layer after layer of Mayan books that are in an extremely high state of preservation. We only looked quickly inside two of the books, but found them to be readable and undamaged. We immediately moved all of the books to a nitrogen chamber to head off any chance for sudden degradation. Until we are able to actually study the books extensively, we won't know their full significance, but I can tell you that in terms of volume of materials, they may well exceed all three of the major codices combined."

A murmur went through the room as the enormity of the find began to dawn on the assembled group. No one spoke for maybe thirty seconds. Then spontaneously, people started slowly clapping. The clapping gathered steam and everyone stood up, looking around the room to see the reactions of others. For many of the people in the room, a moment like this had been something they had always envisioned, but never expected.

Janice noticed there were definitely a few tears being shed.

"Thank you, John. You definitely brought the house down with this news," Dr Wilson said with obvious relish.

Dr Wilson continued, "But now that you're all in the know, we need to discuss a few things about security."

"Firstly, as hard as I know it will be, I need to request that all of you at least for a few days resist the urge to tell friends, family and colleagues. We're in the process of implementing more stringent security measures to protect this find. Once the word gets out, every treasure hunter within a 500 mile radius will have their eyes on us."

"Secondly, round the clock security will be established on the artifacts lab and that will include round the clock staff archeologists manning the artifact desk." With this last comment, a muffled groan went through the room, since they all would have to take their turns. "I know, I know, people," Dr Wilson sympathized. "But major achievements require major efforts. The days of Coba as a sleepy little dig site are over!"

Janice felt serious regret that her time on the project was coming to an end. The buzz of excitement among the project team continued. X-ray examination of the sarcophagus revealed what appeared to be a fully intact mummy along with what looked to be an extensive collection of artifacts. One of the Mayan bark books had been examined and digitized all the while keeping it in an inert atmosphere. The digital replica had been sent off to the world's leading Mayan language scholar to get his initial appraisal. Of course, Dr Wilson's request to keep the find under wraps didn't go as planned. Within a few days, the whole world knew about their find and as Dr Wilson had said.

"It was no longer a sleepy little dig site."

Chapter Three

Jake and Jamison were in the central Satellite Control Lab for the Western Consortium, seeing the image beamed back from the Landsat satellite. They had gotten final approval to conduct a limited scope gravimetric study of the Van der Waals crater. The satellite was in a polar orbit around the moon at an altitude of 150 miles which meant it passed over the moon's north and south poles and passed over a different lunar longitude on each revolution. They had been required to wait several days until the satellite orbit would be optimal for mapping the crater.

"Looks like this pass will work for us," Jamison commented nervously. There was a certain amount of pressure on lunar exploration leads to get results. Jamison was clearly hoping that this study would yield positive findings.

Jake watched him with interest. "I could be in his shoes in a couple of years," he thought to himself.

Jake saw that the satellite had automatically begun executing the gravimeter run over the crater. The Van der Waals crater was located in the southern lunar hemisphere about 950 miles from South Base. It was named after an early 20th century physical chemist from Holland who won a Nobel Prize for his work on one of the fundamental attractive forces within molecules. The crater is about 60 miles in diameter with some ridges along the north side but almost level on the south side. This is where they had found promising X-ray fluorescence results during their last mission with the lunar rover.

The gravimeter study would reveal the topography of the lunar terrain underlying the regolith. This type of measurement of variations in gravity had been performed for quite a while, but the introduction of quantum technology in the early part of the century had really revolutionized its use for examination of subsurface topography.

In this area of the moon, the regolith, the unconsolidated loose gravel-like covering over bedrock was thought to be about 10 meters thick. The hope was that the gravimeter study would show a so-called magma crest, where the configuration of bedrock formed almost a hidden mountain peak where potentially rare earth metals would have concentrated during the period when the magma was cooling off several billion years ago.

"Well there's really not anything more we can do at this point," Jamison said. "It looks like the satellite flyby was successful. We'll just have to wait for the computer analysis to be completed."

"How long does that typically take?" Jake asked.

"It should be done by tomorrow I expect," Jamison replied.

The next day, Jamison, Jake and the rest of the team met in the Control Lab conference room to review the satellite analysis.

The meeting was chaired by Dr Thornton Bryerton, the resident geophysicist on the team. He had replaced Dr Barnes whose lunar assignment had just ended.

I'd say all in all, the results are pretty positive," Dr Bryerton started. "The subsurface topography does show a clear magma crest running through the center of the crater. It would appear to offer a good chance for rare earth concentration effects to have occurred during magma cooling. I think we can recommend proceeding to the next phase."

Dr Bryerton pulled up a lunar map showing the Van der Waals crater. "I think we should target our core sampling on a zone from about here" He placed a digital mark on the map "Up to about here". He placed a second digital mark on the map.

"As you can see, this covers a lunar surface distance of about 10 miles, so I think we need to be thinking in terms of about 200 core samples. Based on the terrain, I would suggest the mean depth to be about 1000 feet. As always, the core sampling will be done incrementally, assuming

31

initial results provide the expected concentrations of rare earth in the core samples."

He hesitated for a second and then proceeded. "There was one thing in the results I found a little odd. At the east end of the zone covered in the gravimetric study, there was something at a depth of around 500 feet that almost looks like a structure, which is of course impossible. I'm going to forward the results on to headquarters and ask them to take a look. Probably just a recording error, but I'd like a second opinion."

"Maybe some space pirates buried treasure there!" Morrison interjected. Everyone laughed and then Jamison, in his usual business like way, proceeded to start discussing planning for the next phase.

Lunar mining had been the perfect candidate for greatly expanded use of robotic technology, given the harsh environment and the threats from radiation and meteor strikes. The several lunar mines currently operating were essentially all robots, with typically just a single human mine supervisor plus several maintenance superintendents present at the site. The same was true of the core sampling that was used to site a mine. The drilling rig resembled a miniature version of 20th century oil rigs, but without a single roughneck to be seen. The core sampling didn't require drilling a large diameter bore hole. Three inches was pretty much the standard. The cores that were obtained would be analyzed in the lunar control lab to develop a three dimensional profile of rare earth concentrations.

"With this number of core drillings required, I've ordered 10 drilling units to be sent up on the shuttle. Along with the 5 units we already have, that should allow us to complete the core sampling work in about 6 weeks. Two of the units will be dispatched immediately to get some preliminary data. There is about a one month wait to get the additional drilling units. So I'm hopeful that with luck and positive results, we can be looking at potentially actually commencing mine groundbreaking in 4 months." Jamison looked up from his notes and continued.

" As we have done on previous coring work, I'm envisioning three man teams consisting of a geologist, rover technician and a robotic mechanic to be present onsite during the drilling. Standard two week rotations with one week back at South Base. Jake, I'd like you and Morrison to take the first two week shift. Any questions?"

Jake raised his hand. "How soon do you expect we can start, Conrad? The rover is still undergoing maintenance from our last trip and I think it's not scheduled to be done for another week. Also, we probably need to make sure the analytical lab here is prepared for this volume of sample processing. I think it's been a while since they've been called on for this level of support." "Both excellent points, Jake," Conrad Jamison smiled. "I think we can commence as soon as the rover maintenance is complete and I've already given the lab a heads up. "

Jake walked out of the meeting relieved that they had a few days to spare before the next rover mission. It felt like he had just gotten back from the last mission. He really hadn't had much opportunity for R and R since his return to South Base. Sure, there was that wonderful dinner with Janice, but she had returned to earth a couple of days after that. He decided he was going to spend a few days trying out some of the things that brought tourists up here while he had the chance.

He had signed up some time ago for a trip to the Sea of Tranquility and he was pleased that he was going to be able to squeeze it in. One of the big attractions on the moon was to go look at the space vehicles and other junk that were left behind by our forebears during the golden age of lunar exploration. He also was looking forward to some telescope time. Free of the Earth's atmosphere, the moon offered the chance for spectacular viewing of the cosmos and of earth and he intended to do both during these next few days. But first he was going back to his apartment and get some much needed sleep.

Several days passed during which he mostly relaxed, caught up on some of his reading and did some planning work for his doctoral thesis.

Jake awoke with a start.

"Today was the day". He thought to himself. He looked at his watch and saw he had a couple of hours before launch. He had packed an overnight bag with what he thought he would need. He headed over to the spaceport and located the gate for Lunatours. He saw that a number of other people had already arrived and he got in the line leading up to the ticket counter.

After a short wait, it was his turn. " What's the name on that reservation?" the friendly ticket agent asked. "Jake er Jacob Mackenzie,"

Jake answered.

"Ah here you are ! Oh, I see you're actually a Western Consortium employee. We don't see too many of you here."

Jake blushed slightly. "Well I always wanted to visit these sites, so much history."

The ticket agent raised her hand. "You don't need to explain. We're just glad you decided to join us today. I have you down for the three day package. Is that correct?"

"Yes," Jake replied.

"The ship will be departing in about 30 minutes. Just take a seat in the lounge 'til we call you."

Jake took a seat. This was his first real chance to play total tourist and he was excited. After a short while, boarding was announced. He entered the spaceship and found his designated seat and strapped himself in.

"Welcome aboard Lunatours everyone ! We'll be departing for the Sea of Tranquility in just a few moments. Before we go, just a few safety announcements. In the event of a loss of cabin pressure, please note the row of compartments to your left. There are pressure suits available for each passenger and you have already provided your certification certificates showing you've been trained in donning the suits. Once we arrive at the park, please note that all of the artifacts you'll see are protected under the Lunar Artifacts Act, so pictures are fine, but touching is not allowed. Also, in the unlikely event of an unexpected solar flare or meteor storm, we will advise you using this warning light. If you see it go off, head immediately for the nearest shelter kiosk.

Jake watched the reactions of the other passengers. As an experienced lunar worker, he was well aware of these hazards, but felt sympathy for the tourists in the group. It probably all seemed a little daunting to some of them.

Once the safety orientation was completed, the flight attendant took her seat and shortly thereafter Jake felt the ignition of the liquid propellant rocket and the slight G-force of the acceleration as they headed for low lunar orbit. After a short burst of the rockets, he heard the hum as the plasma engine took over. It was just a short trip and soon they were landing at Tranquility Base.

Tranquility Base was of course the name made famous by Neil Armstrong when he first set foot on the moon over 100 years ago. Once lunar habitation had become a reality, the Lunar Artifacts Act had declared all of the various crafts, rockets and in some cases debris that had a been a part of man's initial lunar exploration as protected world heritage items. The actual location where Neil Armstrong and Buzz Aldrin landed was made a world park, modeled in concept after the national parks originally established in the United States. It was all still there of course: lunar historical objects were a museum curators dream. Objects never aged or rusted or decayed in the wonderfully inert atmosphere free environment of the Moon. Everything down to astronauts footprints and Alan Shepard's golf balls were still there in virtually pristine condition.

At the Tranquility Base Park, an underground hotel was constructed to allow tourists to visit in comfort. Attached to the hotel was a huge underground museum in which artifacts from more distant lunar sites had been collected. It included all of the descent stages from the Apollo missions, a couple of the Apollo ascent stages which had decayed from lunar orbit and crashed back on the Moon, the lunar rovers (moon buggies) from Apollo 15 and 16, several of the unmanned Soviet Luna series craft, two of the Surveyor unmanned craft which the US sent up prior to the Apollo missions , the Chang'e 5 descent stage from the Chinese missions and even probes that had been sent from India and Japan.

But of course, the centerpiece of the entire park was the perfectly preserved lunar landscape of Apollo 11. That was all preserved on the lunar surface, where thousands of tourists had flocked over the last 10 years to breathlessly ohh and ahh over the sight of Apollo 11's descent stage still sitting in the lunar regolith, surrounded by Neil and Buzz's space suit footprints and of course the American flag they had left behind.

Jake found the tourbus ride around the Apollo 11 shrine exhilarating. He enjoyed this moment of just being a tourist and watching the reactions of his fellow bus mates. Many remarked on how small the descent stage was and marveled that two men had been able to survive on the Moon in something so fragile looking. Others were stunned with how little evidence one saw of the passage of time. It almost looked like the hatch could open at any moment, and Neil would start slowly ascending the ladder. "One small step for man....."

The copper colored foil designed to protect parts of the descent stage from temperature extremes shone as brilliantly today as it had over a 100 years ago.

Hard to grasp that the heroes who landed here were long since passed away.

The footprints in the lunar soil were crisp and unaffected by time. While everyone who came there knew what to expect, it was an emotional experience to think about the whole lunar exploration thing reaching this pivotal moment right here. Jake thought to himself, "Just one failure on this mission and the whole thing might never have happened. If one rocket had fired just a second too long and Neil and Buzz had careened around the moon and off into an eternal orbit of the sun, it's hard to know if we would have continued to pursue this dream."

So even as an experienced space traveler, Jake had never lost his feeling of how big a deal this had been.

After a couple of days at the museum, it was time for Jake to get back to South Base. He had one last thing he wanted to do before he was scheduled to head back out to supervise the core drilling activities.

Once back at South Base, he headed to the Carl Sagan Observatory. He had made a reservation to join a small group of observers as one of the resident astronomers put the 200 inch Hale telescope through it's paces. The Hale telescope at one point was the largest optical telescope in the world and for years had been the centerpiece at the Mount Palomar Observatory in California. Eventually more powerful space based telescopes including Hubble and James Webb I and II supplanted it. But the developers of the South Base tourist attractions had seen an opportunity and had purchased it, had it disassembled, shipped here and carefully reassembled. Now tourists could be treated to live views of a dazzling array of sights in our galaxy and beyond. Jake found the astronomical program absolutely dazzling.

The astronomer continued. "And here you see the exoplanet Proxima B, 4 light years from us, the nearest planet to us found in a habitable zone orbit, orbiting the red dwarf star Alpha Centuri. The planet has an orbital period of only 11 days, so if you lived there the years would add up fast." The astronomer laughed at his own joke, but no one else seemed to get it.

36

The astronomer stepped them through some of the most iconic and dazzling views in the Milky Way and surrounding galaxies; the Pillars of Creation in the Eagle Nebula, the Horsehead Nebula, the Crab Nebula, of course the gas giants Saturn and Jupiter, and a host of other amazing sights.

After seeing most of the program, Jake decided it was time to head back to his apartment. He had enjoyed his brief stint here as a tourist, but was now looking forward to getting back to work.

The next morning, Jake once again found himself in the lunar rover, headed out to the core drilling area they had identified at the Van der Waals crater. This time the rover was towing a lunar utility trailer packed with several of the robotic core drilling rigs and several hundred feet of drill piping. The addition of the utility trailer made navigation of some of the steep terrain more difficult and consequently lengthened the trip back to the crater. They were underway for a full 24 hours before they started getting close.

Navigation on the moon had been greatly simplified back in '66 when lunar orbiting satellites had been launched to provide GPS capabilities for the Moon.

Jake looked over at Morrison, sitting beside him in the copilots seat and asked. "Can you recheck our current position and give me an estimate on when we'll get to the drill site?"

Both Jake and Morrison were pretty exhausted at this point. They were required by company policy to keep both pilots chairs occupied during the trip out, so there was really no opportunity to sleep for either of them.

"Roger that" Morrison responded. "Looks like we're less than 100 kilometers out, so we should arrive in about 3 hours. The topography doesn't show any major craters we'll have to avoid, so it's pretty much a straight line."

Prior to their departure from South Base, Jamison had filed the necessary paperwork to stake a claim to the area they were interested in on the Van der Waals crater. A so-called "Notice of Intent to Initiate Lunar Mining " was required once any lunar groundbreaking would occur.

The procedures to allow for an orderly process by which individual countries or country groups like the Western Consortium could pursue commercial mining operations had not come easily. Long ago a number of countries had signed the Artemis Accords, which set about to develop a framework for such an orderly process, but it had been deeply flawed from the beginning, with major players like China and Russia not being signatories. There had been a period in the 2050's, in the Wild West days of lunar mining operations when it had actually come to bloodshed between mining crews from the Consortium and Russia. Finally, after much finger pointing and serious diplomacy, the "Global Accord on Utilization of Lunar Natural Resources" had been established. It had required some serious concessions from the Western Consortium to get the Russians and Chinese on board.

Most notably, South Base which had originally been totally owned and operated by the Western Consortium became a multinational facility, with all of the major players getting the opportunity to set up mining bases there. Up until this point, Russia and China had had separate bases set up, but the location of South Base, in close proximity to the meager lunar sources of ice had made it the optimal place to be.

While South Base had flourished, and had become not only a mining center, but also a budding tourist destination, the same could not be said for the Russian and Chinese bases. They had languished and were pretty spartan facilities and were finally shut down once the accord was signed . In return for this major concession, the Western Consortium got the two main things they had pushed for: 30 year exclusivity on mining claims, and the ability in a single claim to gain control over a 30 square mile region of the moon. Of course, claims didn't come cheaply. Each time a country filed a lunar mining rights claim, they had to contribute 50 million dollars to the Lunar Exploration and Mining Fund, which had become the main revenue source to support the ongoing expansion of the South Base infrastructure.

"That's why Jamison is so uptight right now," Jake thought to himself. With the limited information they currently had on the Van der Waals crater site, they had needed nonetheless to initiate the claim process, meaning if the site didn't turn out to provide the level of rare earth metals they expected, the Western Consortium was out a big sum of money.

Several mining exploration superintendents like Jamison were now enjoying early and unplanned retirements as a result of bad hunches. And Jake knew the pressure was really on all of them, because when these projects failed there was always plenty of blame to go around.

Jake expected they would be running across some of the mining personnel from some of the competing countries. As soon as any country filed a claim, it immediately became a source of intense interest. Crews from Russia and China and possibly even Saudi Arabia were probably already out there, sniffing around the boundaries of the Western Consortium's new claim.

They arrived just when Morrison had predicted, although of course nothing really confirmed it other than lunar coordinates on the mapping system. They had crossed into lunar night during the trip up. Jake would have preferred to have done initial setup of the drilling equipment during lunar "daylight" but now they would be working in darkness for the next two weeks. Off in the distance, Jake could see the twinkle of lights from another lunar vehicle.

"There are our friends as expected," Jake said to no one in particular. He would have to make it a priority to tour their claim area periodically to make sure the boundaries of their claim were being respected.

Jake checked the clock and saw it was lunchtime. Crews were always working hard to maintain their daily cycle, despite having to deal with alternating periods of light and darkness. . He and Morrison broke out the ration packs and heated up the freeze dried food that was standard fare during rover trips. Jan Ingstrom, the German robotic maintenance technician joined them.

"Gutes Essen, meine Herren," Jans smiled and greeted them. He of course spoke perfect English, but enjoyed reminding them of his German heritage. He was the main man responsible for keeping the robotic drilling rigs functioning. Jake had worked with him before and knew he was excellent at his job. It wasn't an easy task. The high silica content of the regolith really chewed up equipment. The rover was crowded now with tools and replacement parts Jan would need.

"Jan, do you want to try and get the first rig out this afternoon? I just need to report back to South Base that we're in position and then I'm available if you need me." Jake smiled at Jan.

"Probably not right away," Jan replied. "First priority for me is to pick a location for the equipment trailer which is reasonably central to our first batch of planned core drillings. We need to be at a location that's reasonably close. Once those are completed we can relocate the equipment trailer one or two more times."

"OK that sounds good. Let me know when you think you've selected a location and we'll go check it out," Jake replied.

After lunch, Jake started programming the asteroid detection and warning system. The system coupled a local upward searching radar system with the lunar asteroid tracking program. The tracking program kept track of several thousand celestial objects ranging in size from 50 meter diameter behemoths to grapefruit size rocks and based upon your current lunar position, told you if any were headed your way. The local radar system looked for smaller objects. With its range of about 1000 km, the radar was a marvel of technology but unfortunately in the event of small fast moving objects, didn't really give them much time to respond.

The whole issue of meteor strikes was a conundrum. On the one hand, while the moon was struck every day by thousands of chucks of rock of varying sizes, the chances of being struck by one were very low. On the other hand, the extreme velocities of some of these objects meant that they could do lots of damage. A 10 pound rock traveling at typical asteroid velocities can produce a crater 30 feet across and shoot more than 150,000 pounds of lunar regolith into the air. The record so far had been pretty good. There had never been a lunar fatality directly from a meteor strike, but there had been a couple of vessel breaches one of which killed several members of a crew. More issues had actually occurred with space junk in low earth orbit. An entire crew had been taken out in '68 and since then a serious effort to retrieve and return obsolete equipment and other junk to Earth had been undertaken.

Jake confirmed that nothing big was headed in their direction, and verified that the radar was scanning the airspace. He saw that Jan was looking at him.

"Are you ready," he asked.

"Yes," Jan replied. "If you're ready, I can show you where I think we should go."

Jan joined Jake in the rover pilot seats and typed in coordinates to the navigation system. Jake heard the hum as the servo motors began to rev up. The rover started slowly turning, the headlights cutting a stark swath through the lunar landscape. The landscape here was pretty flat. Occasionally they would have to make a jog to avoid a crater, but none of it was very remarkable. It took them about an hour to reach the location Jan had selected. Jake could see that the lights from the other vehicles he had seen earlier were much closer now, but in his judgement they appeared to be respecting the boundaries of the claim Western Consortium had filed.

They were all pretty tired from the long drive from South Base and agreed to have another bite to eat and then turn in for a 6 hour sleep period. After the planned sleep, the interior lights in the rover gradually brightened and everyone slowly awoke.

"Ok, I'm ready to get started," Jan told Jake. Jan sat down at the portable control console that had been loaded onto the rover for managing the drilling rigs. He hit a couple of buttons on the control panel. Jake saw the hatch on the equipment trailer open and the robotic drill rig rolled out, towing a piping trailer loaded with the 3 inch pipe that would used to extract the lunar core samples.

"OK, we're ready to proceed," Jan reported.

"You may proceed," Jake responded. As site supervisor, he held overall responsibility for the site. He was ultimately responsible for everything that occurred on this worksite, hence a certain formality was the normal protocol.

While it wasn't essential, Jake had positioned the rover so that they could easily observe the drilling robot in action. Jake had done core sampling before, but he never ceased being in awe of this highly automated process. The robot already knew exactly where it was heading. It reached the first planned drill location, and immediately deployed hydraulic outriggers to provide stability for the drilling action. The rig was equipped with a large boom arm which on its end had an appendage that almost looked like a human hand. The boom arm appendage picked up what was clearly the drill bit, and proceeded to screw the first section of piping into the drill bit. The drill bit and first pipe section were then brought to a vertical position and inserted into the annular opening of the drilling rig. The drill bit slowly started to rotate and then gathered speed.

Jan hit another button on the robot control panel and Jake saw the drill bit was descending. The first lunar soil started to get kicked up by the drill. Slowly, the drill disappeared into the regolith.

The first 3 sections of piping went quickly. This initial phase was just regolith, soil with a gravel like consistency, so the drill met little resistance. Then it finally reached the lunar bedrock. It would have made a different sound at that point, if sound had been possible. But of course it wasn't.

The drilling slowed down at this point as the drill encountered the top of what everyone hoped was the magma crest they were looking for.

Things proceeded routinely for several hours until suddenly an alarm went off on the robot control panel. Jan came running and looked at the instrument panel.

"Verdammt nochmal!" he intoned with frustration. Jake was there too and felt Jan's concern.

"What's happening?" Jake asked.

"Looks like the main motor bearing is overheating," Jan replied.

"How big an issue is that?" Jake asked, trying to keep the concern out of his voice.

"Oh, it's reparable but I'll have to suit up to go out and fix it." Jan sounded aggravated but not stressed, so Jake took that as positive news.

Jake watched as Jan, fully suited up, walked out across the lunar surface toward the drill bit. Jan was in radio communication with the rover, so Jake could hear the sound of Jan's breathing, could hear Jan musing to himself about how these new drill rigs just didn't hold up anymore. Jake smiled when he heard that. Jan reached the rig and turned back to the rover as if he was about to say something.

Suddenly, a klaxon alarm went off in the rover, and a mechanical voice very loud reverberated through the craft. "Incoming object ! Incoming object! Take cover! Incoming Object! Jake had never actually heard the asteroid detection and warning system go off. It sounded like the voice of doom.

Jake grabbed the radio microphone. "Jan, drop what your doing and return immediately to the rover. This is an emergency! Run!" Jake saw Jan turn and begin to run toward the rover. He hoped they weren't too late. The rover wasn't perfect protection from a strike but the reinforced roof would at least give them some protection. Of course if an incoming meteor was large enough, nothing would stop it.

Chapter Four

Janice leaned back in her chair and took a moment to appreciate the bright sunlight streaming through her office window. She was just back a week from her Yucatán adventure. It felt good to get back into her academic life. Fall classes would be starting soon and she looked forward to teaching again. This year she would be teaching Global Seismology and Applied Geophysics. She enjoyed doing both of these courses. In particular, the Applied Geophysics was a popular course, given its focus on real world topics.

Palo Alto was its usual lush green shade. Early in the century, California had been a dried out almost desert environment that had suffered greatly from brush fires and lack of moisture. Like just about everything else, that had changed dramatically with cheap fusion energy. Desalination plants had been built up and down the California coast, making water widely available for commercial agriculture and all the other applications where water was crucial.

Janice also felt anticipation about resuming her research activities. This year she'd gotten approval to add two more graduate assistants so she anticipated finally being able to make real progress in her key research focus. She had developed a theory that certain seismic profiles of fault lines could be used to more accurately predict timing of major earthquakes and hoped soon to flesh out the theory in more detail. California was still waiting for the "Big One", so her research certainly generated lots of interest in California and all of the "Ring of Fire" countries that had suffered greatly from periodic earthquakes and resulting tsunamis.

Life had changed dramatically for many people during the last 50 years. The rise of artificial intelligence and robotics had been as traumatic and society changing as many had predicted. In the early 2040s, job elimination via automation had put so many people out of work that there was a real crisis. Many people could find no employment and the number of homeless persons rose dramatically. However during the same time period, technology advances were reshaping the world. In particular, both economically viable fusion reactors and commercially affordable ambient temperature super conductors appeared on the scene about the same time, and the result was cheap energy that could be transmitted over long distance low energy electrical grids. The net effect was to finally make it feasible for the complete elimination of petroleum and coal based power generation.

This move for elimination of fossil fuel for power generation had reached the status of global emergency when by 2030, a number of major metropolitan areas including New York City and Miami began having significant annual flooding events that technology investments simply couldn't keep up with.

Spurred on by these events, politicians, under enormous pressure from the public, finally found the will to act. By 2035 petroleum powered vehicles were no longer manufactured, and by 2040, the last coal fired power plant was taken out of service. Natural gas and oil for heating of homes was gradually phased out. The transition was driven by powerful economic factors, since electricity was now available at a fraction of their cost.

And with that, the climate change affects that had been growing more severe with each passing year began a painfully slow turn in the direction of recovery. Scientists had predicted that turning back the damage done to our environment would take decades, perhaps longer and they were right. Modern society couldn't accept such a time line and so governments all over the planet launched a massive program for sequestration of atmospheric $co2$. Again, the advent of cheap energy had made that possible. By 2065, these efforts had reduced atmospheric levels of $co2$ to levels seen in the mid 20th century, and by the present day, the levels were reduced to levels last seen before the start of the industrial revolution. Some of the effects of climate change like heating of the oceans would still linger on for decades, but the corner had been turned on climate change.

So in the end, the technology advances solved the problem of job elimination. Cheap energy meant the elimination of poverty world wide was finally achievable. Countries around the globe were able to implement worker friendly policies including a guaranteed annual income for every person, full voluntary retirement with pension at age 45, and universal health care for everyone.

War had been effectively taken off the table as a tool for rogue states by the Russian- Ukrainian war of 2022, when the world banned together to stop Russian aggression.

The final big challenge facing the world had been the ever increasing human population of the globe. Both uncontrolled growth and uncontrolled decline had negative effects on resource management while attempts to manage the issue had proved to be a thorny problem. People wanted their freedom to make their own decisions but at the same time wanted societal resources to be there when they wanted them. In the end, a combination carrot and stick approach proved to be the best strategy. The United Nations developed a global strategy for managing population size that was implemented in all member countries. Families were offered significant tax incentives for having up to three children, and significant tax penalties for having more than 3 children. The exact numbers varied by country depending on demographics, but it finally struck the balance needed for sustained growth in a balanced way.

Janice called up her friend and colleague Allison Chavez and they agreed to meet for a quick lunch and catch up on things since they hadn't seen each other in several months. Janice reserved a vehicle on her phone, and five minutes later the robotic car pulled up in front of her office building. She jumped in the back of the vehicle, and saw that the destination for lunch was already displayed on the vehicles control panel. Private ownership of vehicles had been eliminated years ago and then gradually as robotic advancements continued, driving by humans at all was eliminated. It had met with some resistance by a significant percentage of the population who enjoyed the act of driving, but eventually people came around when they took the time to sit back and enjoy the ride. The societal benefits had been substantial in terms of virtually eliminating accidents, ending the need for car insurance, and enhancing traffic flow, since every single robotic vehicle was routed by a master program that ensured traffic jams didn't happen.

Janice thought to double check what time the restaurant opened. She blinked and her Internet browser opened up on the contact lense she was wearing on her right eye. The motion of her eye caused the cursor on the screen to move and when she blinked again, the link she selected opened up. She confirmed that the restaurant would be open and then blinked twice to close the browser.

"Well look at you girl!" Allison cried as they embraced on the terrace of the trendy restaurant Janice had selected. "A few months in the Yucatán sun has done browned you up."

Allison laughed and Janice blushed as heads turned from nearby tables.

"So how have you been, Allison," Janice smiled and waited expectantly, knowing Allison was always up to interesting things.

"I've been just fantastic," Allison gushed. "I just got back from the World Biomedical Engineering exposition in Luzerne last week and am still a little jet lagged. But I was thrilled to have the chance to finally give my paper on the results of the phase 3 clinical trials for the Comprehensive Wellness Portal that Stanford has been taking a lead role on."

Janice was immediately interested. "Wow, I had no idea you were that far along. So the results have been pretty positive?" Janice asked.

Allison smiled. "I think its going to be revolutionary in terms of detection of disease. Just imagine; a device the size of an almond implanted under your armpit that can provide early detection of 50 different kinds of cancer plus 20 major chronic diseases. It's like having your own built in analytical lab," Allison gushed.

"That really sounds amazing," Janice replied. " When are you hoping to go for final approval?"

Allison leaned closer with a mischievous look on her face. "Well, don't mention this to a soul, but I think it could be as early as first quarter next year," she beamed, looking like a school girl who just got invited to prom. Janice studied her for a moment and felt a certain sense of wonder and joy that her long time friend had come so far and was really making waves in her chosen field.

"Well congratulations, Allison! I know this project has been years in the making. It has got to feel pretty gratifying to finally be so near to bringing it to fruition," Janice smiled warmly at her long time friend.

"Thanks Babe. We both knew back in grad school that you and I were movers and shakers."Allison smiled back. "But enough about me. What has the world's leading geophysicist and budding archeologist been up to?" Allison asked.

"Oh my summer on the Mayan dig was pretty exciting. For much of my time there it seemed like it was going to be pretty routine, but near the end of my stay, we really had a major find." Janice proceeded to tell Allison all about finding the major lode of hieroglyphs. "We won't know the full significance of the find until the translation work progresses, but right now it looks pretty amazing." Janice leaned back in her chair. "And of course I'm excited to be back at work on my real profession. Got to dig in and make some real progress on my earthquake seismic profiling paper."

Janice and Allison talked for some time over lunch and parted with the usual promises that they absolutely had to do this more often.

Janice was back in her office, working on the Fall courses when her phone rang. A thrill of anticipation went through her when she saw that it was a call from Jake. Calls to and from the Moon had been pretty routine for years, but nonetheless she still felt a certain wonder that it was even possible.

"Hello! Jake how are you? Everything ok?" She blurted out, totally failing in restraining herself.

"I'm doing fine." Jake replied in that faintly detectable south Texas accent that Janice always found so attractive. "I just got back from another rover trip out to the Van der Waals crater and thought I'd see how you were doing. I tried a couple of times to call you while you were on the dig in Mexico but didn't have any luck reaching you."

Jake paused for a second and then continued. "Still reliving fondly that wonderful dinner we had here. Pretty awesome Earth-rise that night."

Janice smiled warmly at Jake on the phone monitor.

"Yeah, I've thought about that night often. Earth-rise over the lunar mountains definitely makes for some enchanted evening," Janice replied, subtly making reference to one of her mother's favorite songs from years ago. "But tell me how your project is going. Getting close to starting actual mining operations?" Janice asked.

"Well, we are making good progress with the core drilling work. We've just gotten some preliminary assays from core samples, and so far they're definitely showing a pretty robust rare earths profile. If the overall pattern shows these results to be reproducible over a good part of our claim site, then I think we'll be a go for commencing actual mining," Jake replied. "We did have one finding from the satellite gravimeter run that has several of us scratching our heads. At the eastern end of our claim site, the survey showed one subsurface feature about 500 feet down that looks like a straight line, running for maybe about 150 feet. We didn't know what to make of it and passed it on to Consortium headquarters but never really heard much back from them. Seemed they were generally dismissive of it as far as having any significance to our project."

Janice and Jake both just sat for a moment while Janice thought about this revelation. Finally Janice broke the silence. "We both know that nature doesn't typically work in straight lines, so do you have any thoughts about what it might be?" she asked.

"We double checked to see if there might have been some previous mining activity for this area, but nothing showed up. So we can't identify any human activity anywhere around this crater. As I said, the whole thing is kind of a head scratcher," Jake explained.

Janice thought a moment longer and finally said "I've had quite a bit of experience with gravimetric data. Why don't you send me the data and let me take a look at it?"

Jake just looked at her for a second and then replied "I'd like to, but I'm a little concerned that the geophysicist who took your place up here, Dr Bryerton might take offense and feel like I'm bypassing him."

Janice knew he was right and replied "I can get in touch with Thornton myself. We go way back to when we both worked as post docs here at Stanford. With your agreement I can just call him and ask about the finding. He has to have been involved in the initial review."

Jake was nodding his head and then replied. "Yeah, that's definitely the right way to handle it. Go ahead and get in touch with him."

Jake and Janice chatted for another 15 minutes or so. Jake mentioned that he would be returning earthside in another couple of months and looked forward to seeing her again. They both agreed to set a date to get together soon and then signed off.

Janice was busy with her school preparations so it took a couple of days for her to follow up with Dr Bryerton Finally she called him up, double checking first the station day/ night schedule to make sure she wasn't calling him in the middle of a sleep period.

"Hi Thornton, Janice Barnes here. How's the lunar assignment going?"

Thornton leaned close to the monitor with that beaming grin he always seemed to have. "Janice! So nice to hear from you! I've been meaning to call you and complement you on the fine shape you left everything in up here. Made stepping in after your return to Earth really easy."

"Thanks Thornton, I've experienced the trauma of following someone who leaves poorly organized records and swore I'd never do that to someone else, so I'm glad to hear you were pleased with what you found." Janice hesitated for a second and then moved on to the purpose of her call. "I was talking to Jake Mackenzie the other day and he mentioned that the satellite gravimetric run for the Van der Waal crater had some anomalous results. I've never heard of anything like that and was interested in learning more about it. Would it be possible to have you send me the data so I can look at it? Nothing official, just for my own academic interest?"

Thornton's warm smile never wavered and he said "You must have been getting my subliminal messages ! Great to know they even work from a quarter million miles away. I actually had thought about calling you to propose the same thing. I've tried several times to have a discussion with the Grand Poobahs at Consortium Headquarters about this and have gotten no response. I would love to hear what you think of this. It's pretty odd. I'll forward the data right away. Give me a call back after your review."

Janice and Thornton spent a while longer talking about their shared post doc experiences and then signed off.

A couple more days passed until Janice finally had a block of time she could devote to reviewing the results Dr Bryerton had sent her. The digital output of the satellite run showed both aerial views and cross sectional views of the claim area on the Van der Waals crater. The normal output of a gravimetric analysis provides a view that basically strips away the regolith and shows the topography of the subsurface terrain under the regolith. The main focus of a typical gravimetric analysis was to verify that a mountain ridge line or so called magma crest ran under the regolith for some distance at relatively modest depth. At first Janice hadn't really found anything unusual but when she increased the data resolution and studied the cross sectional view, she found a faint section where the normal mountain contours were replaced with what looked like a mountain top that had been cut off with a saw- essentially a straight line. She manipulated the data repeatedly but was unable to tease out any more details. But she had seen enough to decide this was something that needed to be delved into.

She decided to get in touch with Dr Wilson. "After all, his whole career has been focused on finding and analyzing buried man made objects, so his thoughts about the possibility of some object made by intelligent life where none should be might help here," Janice thought to herself.

Tracking him down had been harder than expected. The recent find at the Mayan dig site in Coba had turned Dr Wilson into at least a temporary celebrity and he had been traveling both to hit the talk show circuit and to visit with potential donors who had an interest in further funding for Mayan research.

"Hi Graham, glad I could reach you. Sounds like the recent find has really generated lots of interest !" Janice said when Dr Wilson answered her call.

"Yes, it's been pretty amazing," he responded. "Years go by where it's hard to get people to return your calls and then suddenly I'm flooded with calls. How are you doing? I hope you can find some more time for Coba next year."

"I would like that. This last summer down there was very gratifying. Maybe I can do next summer too," Janice responded.

" So to what do I owe the pleasure of this call?" Dr Wilson asked.

Janice briefed him on what she had seen on the lunar gravimetric analysis and then emailed him the images from the test.

" So this is my first time looking at subsurface topography on the moon ! As you can imagine, it's the one place we archeologists view as not being on our list of potential dig sites." Dr Wilson spoke as he opened up the images Janice had sent. "Well isn't that just something!" He was quiet for a moment and then continued. "I would say that if we encountered that here, we would definitely interpret this as a man made buried object. If you look carefully at the far end of the print, you can even make out what looks like a right angle at the terminus of the horizontal. So on the moon, while we may not be able to call it man made, I think it's pretty strong evidence to conclude that something was put there by intelligent life. Have you been able to totally rule out that this was some construction of an earlier mining or exploratory mission?"

" My contact at the lunar dig where this was taken doesn't think there is any evidence of previous activity, but I think the question hasn't been thoroughly researched. As I said before, Consortium management has totally downplayed this result," Janice responded.

"I can see why," Dr Wilson said. "This could end up delaying their mine building, if some effort is launched to more fully assess this find. If this was on Earth, there are laws almost in every country that would allow you to hold up the mining operation at least briefly to more fully assess the find. But none of those apply to the Moon and besides there's no rational way to ascribe this find to human activity. So it's unclear what can really be done here. The only thing I can think of is for you to perhaps contact the SETI Institute and see if they can shake things up a bit. They've been scanning the heavens for ages and have yet to come up with any evidence of extraterrestrial life. So if they heard that there might be something that had been buried on the Moon by extraterrestrials, they'd probably go bonkers. Maybe they can bring pressure on the Consortium to properly investigate this thing."

Janice took a deep breath and finally responded. "This could turn into a bigger deal than I expected. I'm going to have to think about how best to proceed. I think your suggestion about the SETI institute is a really good one, but I'm a little concerned about fallout if I went that route. So far my involvement in and review of this data is all unofficial."

"So maybe the first step is to go back to Consortium management and give them a chance to do the right thing." Dr Wilson suggested.

"I think you're right. That certainly seems to be the place to start. Thank you for your help. I'll let you know how this turns out. And keep in touch about having me work at Coba again next summer!" Janice signed off and sat staring out the window, trying to decide whether she really wanted to dig further into this lunar mystery.

Until she talked to Dr Wilson, no one had considered or even thought about extraterrestrials. But that would seem to be one of the possible explanations She decided to get back with Dr Bryerton and brief him on the results of her discussion with Dr Wilson. Maybe he could go through official channels and get something done without Jake getting in trouble for soliciting her help.

A short time later, she placed a call to Dr Bryerton and briefed him on her analysis of the gravimetric data and her discussion with Dr. Wilson.

"I hadn't even considered the possibility of an extraterrestrial explanation for this thing," Dr Bryerton said. "I'm sure if I contact Consortium management and raise that possibility, they'll have me loaded on the next shuttle home, probably in restraints, and headed for the funny farm."

"Yes, it's really difficult to know how best to proceed," Janice replied. "I wonder if it might be possible for Jake to put down one of his core drillings right on this spot and see what that finds. This isn't like a dig site on Earth, where archeologists have to carefully peel back layers of civilization. The gravimetric results don't suggest there is anything unusual between the lunar surface and the anomaly, so drilling shouldn't damage anything important."

"I think that's a pretty good suggestion. We can get a better idea what's down there without raising alarms. If it turns out to be some natural phenomena, no one will ever hear about two geophysicists who suffered from group psychosis," Dr Bryerton said and chuckled. "I'll talk to Jake and give him our suggestion."

With that they ended their call and Janice set back to work on the more pressing matters around her Fall curriculum.

A couple of weeks passed where Janice didn't hear anything from Jake or Dr Bryerton. Her classes had started and she was busy setting up her next class that would cover fundamentals of seismic analysis. She hadn't really thought too much about the lunar anomaly until her phone rang and she saw it was another call from Jake.

"Hi Jake," she greeted him. She could see the control panel for the lunar rover behind him, so she knew at once that he was still out on the mission. "How's all that drilling going?"

"Oh it's been pretty uneventful til today. Most of the drill holes are showing rich veins of our target rare earth metals, so I'm predicting that the mining operations are going to be green lighted" Jake answered, looking a little weary.

So Janice took the bait and replied. "So what happened today to liven things up? I hope it wasn't another meteor shower."

Jake smiled and leaned closer to the camera and said "Nothing that exciting but definitely interesting. I got your suggestion about trying a bore hole in the area of that anomaly we discussed. It took a while for us to progress with the drilling to a point near the anomaly, but today we were finally close enough that I could adjust the latest bore site just slightly to put it right over that spot. We did our normal core sample drilling procedure and we we got down to around 500 feet, the drill stopped advancing, the topside drill motor started overheating, and we had to suspend drilling. We pulled up the drill piping and found that the drill bit had been destroyed."

"That's pretty unusual isn't it" Janice asked, feeling almost a twinge of excitement.

"Yeah, for lunar strata the diamond rubidium drill bit is pretty much the standard. I've never seen anything stop one before. Whatever we hit down there has to be pretty hard. So the cause of the anomaly is still as much a mystery as before. No, correction, it's now *more* of a mystery!" Jake replied.

"So any thoughts on how to proceed ? " Janice asked.

"Well I'm afraid at this point, any further investigation will have to involve the Consortium central office. The price tag on that drill bit is around $50,000, so I'm really hesitant to try another. I think I need to get my supervisor involved, Conrad Jamison. Perhaps now with the combination of the strange gravimetric analysis results and this drilling problem, it will generate interest at headquarters for a more thorough investigation." Jake sighed.

Janice could hear the strain in Jake's voice. It was clear that several weeks on mission was taking a toll. "So let me know if I can help somehow." Janice said reassuringly. " I think it's important to follow up on, but I know you have lots of other pressures right now." Janice changed the subject and spent a few minutes in idle conversation before signing off.

She sat back in her chair and gazed out her office window, lost in thought for a couple of minutes. *"It really was something but what?"*

Chapter Five

Jake studied the image of Jamison in the rover monitor. It was clear that the topic of discussion was making his boss uncomfortable.

Jake repeated what he had just said. "I believe we have no choice but to specifically investigate this anomaly. We've already lost one DiaRu drill bit and don't know why. There's something down there showing up in the gravimetric analysis that doesn't fit the profile for lunar geology. Whatever is down there could ultimately have a negative impact on our mining operation." Jake concluded his short diatribe.

"I understand what you're saying," Jamison replied. "Do you have suggestions on specifically how we should proceed?"

"I propose we put a camera down the bore hole where the drill bit was damaged and examine the point where failure occurred. Getting a visual on what stopped the drill would be a good start. Then I'd perform a field gravimetric analysis directly over that spot to get a higher resolution image of the original anomaly seen in the satellite imagery," Jake stopped talking and waited for Jamison to respond.

"I agree with your recommendations but I need to brief Consortium Management before we proceed further. I'm sure they won't like it, but sometimes delays can't be avoided," Jamison said.

Knowing the extreme pressure on Jamison, Jake was impressed with how well he was dealing with this new unknown. "Ok, I'll wait to hear from you. I can continue with a number of bore holes on other parts of the site, so this doesn't have to be a major schedule disruption," Jake replied.

"Ok that sounds good. I'll be in touch soon," Jamison signed off.

Within 24 hours, Jamison had set up a teleconference with the Western Consortium Head of Lunar Mining Operations and briefed him on the anomaly and the initial drilling problem that had been encountered. He reiterated Jake's recommendations, which were accepted with the proviso that everything concerning this anomaly would be subject to top level security measures and that any developments would be reported immediately to the Consortium Mining Operations team.

Jamison got back to Jake and let him know that he could proceed with the camera inspection of the bore hole and performing the field gravimetric analysis.

The camera inspection of the borehole was really a simple task, performed by the same robotic equipment that did the drilling. In this case, the drill bit was simply replaced with a camera plus vacuum lines to clear regolith from the drill hole. Jake was watching the process live, when the camera made it to a depth of 512 feet where the original drill bit had been destroyed. He could see several of the drill bit teeth strewn around the hole and a dust covered angled surface at the bottom. He edged the camera down slightly to get the vacuum lines closer and was able to suction off the last layer of dust. What remained gave Jake goosebumps because he found himself viewing a polished metallic looking surface, that only showed superficial scratches from where the drill bit had struck.

"What on earth is that?" He thought to himself, not pausing to consider how this particular metaphor simply didn't apply.

He ordered the robotic unit to retract the camera and pondered his next step. He decided to deviate slightly from the plan he and Jamison had agreed to. He ordered the robotic unit to refit the drill head with a sampling unit and go back down. The sampling unit would return to the blockage point and extract a nano gram sample of the blockage material using a micro cutting wheel. While whatever it was that had been so hard that it had destroyed a drill bit, he felt confidant that the sampling unit would be able to extract the minute amount of material needed to assay the blockage composition.

After the work was completed, Jake examined the sample cassette returned by the sampling unit. He could see a faint dusting of material and thought that should suffice to get an analysis completed. He decided to utilize one of the rover rocket drone units to get the sample back to the South Base analytical lab immediately. Most of the time their work didn't require that level of urgency, but he felt that urgency now, to get to the bottom of what they were dealing with.

Jake looked at his watch and realized it was near the end of their "daylight" shift. He had a light supper and turned in for the night, already running through his mind the preparations that would be needed for the field gravimetric analysis they would execute over the anomaly.

The next day period found Jake and Morrison suited up and out on the lunar plane with the gravimetric sled. The work would have been easier in lunar sunlight, but unfortunately that wouldn't come for another week. The principal was the same as the satellite flyover they had done previously but the sled could provide more sensitive analysis of this local area, giving a view deeper into the lunar strata. For all the high technology, it still required that the sled be guided over the terrain of interest, much like plowing a field. Morrison and Jake had surveyed the area they were interested in and placed electronic boundary markers at the perimeter. The sled would use these markers to determine its mapping path, moving in ever decreasing concentric circles until the entire site had been covered. Jake had decided to map an area of about a quarter square mile. The data output from the sled would be fed to the rover central command unit, where it would be integrated to form a three dimensional plot of the sub lunar terrain down to a depth of about 2000 feet.

Once they completed the setup, Jake and Morrison headed back to the rover. The sled would plod along on its own until the mapping was completed in about 12 hours.

After desuiting, Jake sat down at the rover command console and saw that he had an incoming message from South Base.

He rang up the South Base analytical lab and was immediately connected to one of the lab techs there.

"Hi, this is Jake Mackensie returning your call" Jake could hear the humming of lab equipment in the background.

"Hi, this is Roger Phillips from the Consortium analytical lab at South Base. My supervisor asked me to call you with the results of that sample you sent over to us by drone."

"Wow, that was fast" Jake responded. "Thanks for the quick turnaround."

"Of course, that's what we're here for ! Anyway, I wanted to let you know what we found. We started off with the standard rare earth panel that we do routinely and it came back negative. So to better characterize what you found, we ran mass spectroscopy. That allows us to determine what's present in an unknown sample. The analysis showed a unique metal profile, unlike anything we've seen before. Elements we would see in stainless steels like iron, chromium and nickel were present, but this also had a significant quantity of tungsten and molybdenum. I did a quick check to see if this composition was typically used in any commercially available alloys and the answer is only in very specialized applications requiring extraordinary stress resistance. That's all we can really tell you at this point. We've never seen anything like it in a lunar core sample." Roger concluded.

"Ok thanks Roger" Jake replied. "I'll receive your written report shortly, I assume."

"Oh of course. It should go out in the next hour ," the young lab tech responded.

Jake felt a little guilty not engaging in a longer discussion with the lab tech, but the emphasis that had been placed on maintaining tight security around this issue made him reticent to discuss a lot of the details around this sample. Of course, he wasn't surprised. He knew from the moment he saw the image on the core sample camera that it wasn't going to be routine.

Jake started searching on-line to see what info was out there on tungsten alloys. It pretty much confirmed what the lab tech had told him. He could see why the drill bit had been destroyed. So what had they found, he wondered to himself.

Jake decided to ring up Janice and see what she thought about this latest data. He checked to see what time it was in California and decided Janice might be available.

"Hi Janice, catching you at a good time?." Jake asked

"It's perfect ! I just finished one of my classes and have 3 hours before my next one. So what's up ?" Janice leaned into the monitor and smiled warmly.

"Well mostly I just wanted to hear your voice, but my excuse for calling is to brief you on the latest about our lunar mystery," Jake smiled back warmly.

"Well you know you never need an excuse to call me. I've been hoping to hear from you," Janice leaned back in her chair. "So give me all the latest!"

Jake gave Janice a brief synopsis of what the bore hole photo survey and lab analysis had shown. "Have you ever seen anything like this that was naturally occurring?" Jake asked.

"No never!" Janice replied without any hesitation. "I think your mystery is still a mystery. You said your local gravimetric run will be done soon?"

"Yeah, we should have the data by end of shift. I have no idea what to expect. Going to be almost a letdown if it turns out to be nothing," Jake replied. "I'll give you another call after I've looked at the data."

"Ok, I'll look forward to it. So how are you doing? You've been on this rover mission quite a while. You must be getting a little worn by now," Janice said with concern in her voice.

"Yeah, I am pretty tired. Seems like dust gets into everything, and the food has started to taste like cardboard. But I'm headed back to South Base in a couple of days and then earthside at the end of the month. Which reminds me- I'm hoping we can get together soon after I get back. Can we try to set a date?" Jake asked.

"You bet. I can't wait to see you in person!" Janice responded.

They both pulled up their calendars and identified a weekend they could spend together and then signed off.

Jake had some time to kill before the sled run would be completed, so he challenged Morrison to a chess game. They had played often, and as a result had gotten pretty used to each other's most frequent moves and stratagems. Jake had decided to shake things up a bit and therefore traded queens with Morrison and gained a bishop up advantage. After that it was just a game of attrition with neither of them making any unforced errors until Morrison finally tipped his king over and said,

"Well that was pretty boring ! Watch out cause next time I'm coming for your queen." Morrison made a karate chop motion toward Jake's neck.

They both laughed, then Jake headed up to the control panel and checked the status of the sled run. He saw that it had about an hour to go. He couldn't really see any results yet. That wouldn't be possible until they downloaded the sled data to the central rover computer.

Jake opened up his personal computer and began working on his thesis paper entitled "Strategies for Rare Earth Deposit Explorations in Lunar Strata". He hadn't worked on it for a while and felt concern that he was falling behind on his efforts to secure his PhD. He felt a little pang of regret knowing that his topic would probably set him permanently on a path toward lunar geology when he still also felt drawn to the more conventional world of earthly geology. He looked up from his work and realized that an hour had passed and the sled run was complete.

He and Morrison suited up and went to recover and stow the sled. Once that was done, Jake cleaned up and returned to the rover control panel and initiated the sled download.

After a few minutes, the download was complete and data processing was initiated. The results of the entire run would be cross correlated to provide 3d images of what the sled had found.

Jake pulled up the first image, this one the "aerial" view of the sled survey area. He looked at the image on the screen and felt the goosebumps that accompany "aha" moments in life. He knew that what up until now they had all described as an anomaly had just blossomed into a full fledged major issue, probably one which would soon be receiving global attention.

The aerial view showed a clearly defined square approximately 100 feet on a side. He quickly scanned through the other views, mainly sectional views of different vertical slices, which showed that the aerial view transformed into irregular rectangles when viewed from that angle The shape could have come from the plains of Giza, but it hadn't. "It came from our very own lunar pyramid buried inexplicably 500 feet down on the Van der Waals crater." Jake murmured to no one in particular as if

61

practicing for a soon to be held press conference.

Jake studied the scans for further detail. The surface of the object appeared solid, but the sectional views suggested that the interior space of the object was hollow, although the density of the object made the resolution inside the object less clear. The exterior of the pyramid appeared smooth. There were no indications of anything that looked to be an entry point. Jake could faintly make out the outline of the borehole where the drill bit had been destroyed and see that it intersected the object near its peak. It was also clear that the bedrock had been cut back to provide space for the pyramid. Over the pyramid appeared to be larger bedrock pieces consistent with mega regolith and a deeper than normal amount of fine regolith. The whole thing looked like the product of some previous major construction project.

Jake sat back from the monitor and considered his next step. Of course, Jamison must be notified immediately. Whimsically Jake thought of opening that conversation with the classic "Houston, we have a problem" line, but realized Jamison might not be in a mood receptive to any levity, considering the major disruption that was about to occur to their mining project.

He also considered ringing up Janice to share this with her, but thought better of it. Shortly, there would be major security around their communications.

He decided the first thing he needed to do was share it with his colleagues. "Phil and Jan, can you please join me in the control bay, I have something I want to show you." Jake transmitted over the rover intercom.

"Sure thing, be right there." Phil Morrison responded right away.

"Jawohl, bin unterwegs" Jan responded.

Once they were all together, Jake started. "So I wanted to let both of you see the results of the sled study we just completed. Here are the aerial and section views from the run"

"Wow, what is that ?" Phil asked incredulously.

"Gott in Himmel wir sind wieder in Egyptian!" Jan also reacted in amazement.

Jake smiled. They had reacted just as he had. "Yes, gentlemen, there's something down there, and I suspect we'll be finding out what it is before long! So a word of caution. You can't discuss this with anyone. Top secret until we get release from Consortium Management. Clear?"

"What do you think it is, Jake?" Phil looked at him quizzically.

"I think the first guess is going to be some alien structure." Jake responded. "Beyond that, I have no idea."

Always the jokester, Morrison suggested. "I think the Chinese have burrowed into the crater and are getting ready to jump our lunar claim."

Jake laughed. "Anyway, remember mum's the word."

Phil and Jan headed back to their quarters, and Jake realized it was time for that call to Jamison back at South Base.

"Hi Conrad, Jake here. I wanted to brief you right away on the results of the sled run. Just got the results a little while ago." Jake tried to keep the nerves from his voice.

"Oh great! Thanks for getting right back to me." Jamison replied "So what did you find?" He wasn't able to hide the tension in his voice.

Jake took a deep breath. "Well we've got some kind of major subsurface structure down there. It looks pyramidal in shape, square base about 100 feet on a side, with a total structure height of about 120 feet, lying at a depth of between 500 and 600 feet." Jake paused for a second and looked at Jamison's face on the screen, giving him a chance to jump in. Jamison didn't say anything for a second, just kind of stood looking thoughtful.

"So do you have any indication what it might be?" Jamison asked finally.

"No clue." Jake responded immediately " It certainly bears no resemblance to any subsurface mine feature I've ever seen. And nothing about it suggests what its function might be."

"Do you think it might be something placed there by extraterrestrials?" Jamison asked

"It's possible, but since the shape really gives no clue as to function, it's really hard to say," Jake replied. "But I suspect if we go to excavate it, we'll be forced to treat it as such."

"Yeah, I think so too. Rigorous isolation techniques and decontamination. Won't be the simplest thing," Jamison said. "So I know you already understand this, but there has to be an absolute lid on any information going out about this. I'm going to have to call up Consortium Management and get agreement about how to proceed."

Jamison leaned closer to the monitor "One last thing'" he said " Please start thinking about how we can segregate the remaining exploration work and initial mine commissioning from any requirement that may arise to actually excavate this pyramid. And please suit up and go out and take a look at the area to see if you see anything."

"Will do, sir. I have the data set from the sled run ready to transmit to you, all encrypted of course," Jake said.

"Ok great, I'll be in touch," Jamison signed off.

Jake decided that he needed to follow up immediately on Jamison's last instruction. He suited up and secured a powerful flashlight since they were in the middle of lunar night. He programmed his handheld GPS with the coordinates they had used for the sled run. He entered the lock, and opened the outer door.

There was the faint rush of escaping gas and then he found himself once more on the lunar plain. He followed the directions and realized he had about a 10 minute walk to reach the site where the sled survey had been performed. As he got near it, he could make out the tracks of where the sled had traversed this area. He had programmed the GPS to lead him to the center of the survey area. After walking another few minutes, he saw he was getting close. He looked around to see if anything jumped out at him. It just looked like another endless expanse of gray regolith. He felt a slight irritation that this whole exercise was probably a waste of time. "Always have to do what the chief wants, he reminded himself.

At that moment, out of the corner of his eye he spotted something that caught his attention. It was just this place on the lunar plane where, just as with the subsurface survey, he saw a straight line where none should be. He walked up to it and leaned over and used his glove to brush the ground. When he did that the straight line became more pronounced and longer. He continued brushing the regolith and suddenly found himself looking at a piece of polished stone.

Something was inscribed on it but he couldn't really make out what it was.

He continued exposing the stone and soon could see that it appeared to be a short section of an obelisk, fractured on both ends.

"Holy shit," he murmured. He didn't see anything else. He tried turning the stone over but it was far too heavy. Finally, he took several photographs and headed back to the rover. Once he got back, he immediately rang up Jamison and told him what he had found and sent him copies of the photos he had taken.

Jamison pondered this new information. "It's really just further confirmation of what the sled survey told us. Do you know someone who might be able to decipher this text? Maybe Dr Barnes and her archeology contacts?"

Jake replied, "I'm not sure if they can help, but I'll give it a try."

"Ok thanks," Jamison responded. "It might be worthwhile to do a little more digging around this obelisk to see if there are additional pieces of it."

"Yes, I agree. We'll get to work on that," Jake said and then they ended their call.

Jamison sat looking at the monitor. He wasn't sure why but he had had this feeling that this anomaly was going to end up being a big deal. Maybe it could still be easily resolved, but the fact remained that some very large object made by man or someone else was now sitting buried right in the middle of their next lunar rare earth mine, and they hadn't the slightest clue what it was. And what was this obelisk? A marker? A warning? He wasn't looking forward to the call to Consortium Management. Mine project administrators were supposed to always have the answers to technical and yes even political issues that confronted a project. So how could he present something like this?

The Head of Western Consortium Lunar Mining Operations , Mike Murley, wasn't smiling. Jamison had delivered their findings to the quarterly lunar projects update meeting that included the head along with his entire staff. Murley was a former semi-pro hockey player, renowned for being tough as nails and short on patience.

"So you have no idea what it is? Is that correct?" Dr Murley asked incredulously.

Jamison could see the heads of Murley's staff assistants wagging in disapproval. It was as bad as he had thought it would be.

"Yes Sir, unfortunately, that is the case. We've already started working on a plan to isolate the anomaly site to minimize to the fullest extent possible the impact on our projected mine operations launch timeline. My field superintendent is going to look further at this obelisk,"Jamison tried to sound confidant.

"So what are your thoughts about what to do with this anomaly itself," Murley asked, not looking pleased.

"Well first, I would share with your counterparts on the Lunar Mining Council what we've found and ask them if anyone knows what it is or had previously installed any such structure," Jamison could feel the sweat rolling down his brow .

"Well isn't that virtually impossible, since we are the first mining claim ever placed in this location," Murley asked with a certain degree of sarcasm in his voice.

"True, it may just be a formality, but I think we need to be able to say that we asked the question," Jamison responded. "Next, I would contact the Lunar Artifacts Commission Office and ask them if there was any lunar artifact that could be in this location. I understand that this is also extraordinarily unlikely. The buried object certainly has no resemblance to any space craft or rocket assembly. But again I believe we must be able to say that we asked. Finally, I would try to enlist both the SETI Institute and Cal Tech's Jet Propulsion Lab to help in both the structuring of the excavation project and the evaluation of what we find," Jamison paused for a second and looked up.

"The SETI Institute! My god are those people still around!" Murley thundered with impatience. "What are they going to do?"

"Yes Sir, they're still around. They've been involved in the search for extraterrestrial life for over 100 years," Jamison asserted.

"And still haven't found any!" Murley raged. "So why would we want these people involved, Jamison?"

"Because we could in fact be looking at our first actual contact with aliens or at least a structure placed on the Moon by aliens," Jamison paused for a second to let that sink in. "By involving SETI and JPL, we adopt a high road strategy that tells the world we're approaching this encounter like responsible corporate citizens. And by so doing, we can, on the one hand, offer our considerable lunar mining expertise to resolve this mystery and on the other hand, do some hard negotiating to get assurances that our mining claim will be honored and in fact expedited. I think this high road approach can allow us to successfully proceed with our mining operation despite this unexpected irregularity. I've prepared a very preliminary estimate of how we could allocate resources to investigate this structure and keep our mining plan intact," Jamison stopped talking and looked around the room.

"So tell me more about why you'd include JPL," Murley asked, his tone a little more civil than before.

"First, these people are the absolute apex when it comes to thing like imaging technology. They may be able to help us anticipate what we're going to find inside the pyramid. Secondly, they have expertise that may help us actually understand what we find. No group on the planet is better qualified. If anyone can look at alien technology and understand it, it's these people."

Gradually as he spoke, people in the room started nodding and Jamison thought maybe he was winning them over.

Murley looked at Jamison for a moment. "I see your point. Do you expect any regulatory or administrative roadblocks?"

"Well, the Lunar Artifacts Commission will probably want some oversight function, but I think we can keep them from slowing things down. The big hurdle will be negotiating with SETI how the dig will be executed. We won't agree to making this a full fledged archeological dig but we'll need their buyin with our approach. JPL may not automatically agree to participate, but I suspect they will. Between the lunar surface and the Pyramid there are no other layers of civilization that need to be protected, so we would propose standard lunar excavation techniques down until the pyramid is reached. Then we would have to institute decontamination procedures and the work from that point on would be similar to an earth archeology site."

"Why should we become involved in excavating the object? We're a mining operation, not archeologists," one of Murley's senior staff asked.

"Good question," Jamison replied. "We certainly have both the equipment and expertise to excavate this pyramid. Once the pyramid is actually uncovered, it may well be the time for archeologists to be involved. But if we pull back from this and choose not to participate, I think there is a high likelihood that we simply lose control of the site. Either the United Nations, the Lunar Artifacts Administration, or some other governmental body may well claim imminent domain and once that happens, our ability to proceed with mining operations may be severely hindered or blocked completely."

Jamison had slowly felt the mood in the room changing. He held his breathe for a second, waiting to see what direction this would go.

"So what do you need from us?" Murley asked.

Jamison quietly exhaled.

"An earth support staff of maybe 10 personnel to handle communication, press briefings, etc, regular update meetings with this team for funding requests and progress reports,"Jamison tried to think of anything else he might need, but was too elated by his success winning this group over to come up with anything else.

"Alright Jamison, we'll make sure you have what you need," Murley concluded

"And Jamison,"

"Yes Sir?"

"Good job!"

"Thank you Sir," Jamison felt like he had just come back from the dead. And in a way he had.

Jamison immediately organized a teleconference with the rover crew plus the rest of his staff at South Base. He briefed everyone on the results of his meeting with the management team.

"So who do you want to get in touch with the Lunar Artifacts Commission and SETI ?", Dr Bryerton asked.

"Well I think I will get in touch with the Lunar Artifacts Commission myself. I feel I need to negotiate with them about their involvement," Jamison answered. "With regard to SETI and JPL, anyone have any suggestions.?"

Jake hesitated for a second and then spoke up. "How about Dr Janice Barnes. She's familiar with our project and she's just down the road from SETI's headquarters in Mountain View. And JPL is also based in California. In addition, Dr Barnes has experience in archeological digs which may prove useful."

"That's not a bad idea. Could you get in touch with her, Jake, to see if she's available to help out? Tell her we'll pay her normal consulting rate for any work she does," Jamison said.

"Yes Sir, I'll let you know right away if she's available," Jake replied

"I just want to conclude the meeting by saying that the company has taken what I believe is a responsible position with regard to this very unusual find. We're going to do our best to help unravel this mystery, while also focusing on the critical need to keep the mining project on track and on schedule. No one should discuss this project, yet, with outside personnel until we've notified and held discussions with the appropriate agencies," Jamison concluded. "That's all for now."

Jake logged out of the teleconference and smiled to himself. His recommendation to involve Janice was a good one, but it also pleased him personally to be able to involve her. He had promised her earlier to let her know what happened with the gravimetric analysis, but subsequently hadn't followed through when the tight security had been imposed by Jamison. He rang her up. "Hello there Professor, Lunar Base One calling."

"You don't have to call me professor. For you Frau Doktor will suffice," Janice retorted. "Oh my Jake Mackensie, where have you been? I thought maybe the anomaly had turned out to be a flying saucer and had abducted you!"

Jake smiled sheepishly. "I'm sorry I didn't get back to you. But I

69

have a lot to tell you now!"

Jake proceeded to bring Janice up to speed on all that had transpired, ending with the request that she coordinate liaison with the SETI Institute and JPL

"Oh my god, Jake ! It's so exciting. Can you send me the gravimetric run images? I'll need something to show the folks at SETI and JPL," Janice gushed.

"Of course," Jake responded. "You're part of the team now."

Janice smiled at that. "One last thought. Have you considered what expertise you'll need once you unearth the pyramid?"

"Well I kind of figured the folks at SETI would have recommendations on that," Jake answered.

"I'm not so sure," Janice offered. "SETI has primarily been focused on sending and receiving interstellar radio signals. I'm not sure they will have spent a lot of time on buried objects that may be alien. I'm wondering if you may need an archeology team to actually open this thing up. They're expert at finding and preserving evidence, which could be critical here."

"It's a good question," Jake responded. "Jamison is contacting representatives of the Lunar Artifacts Commission. I would suggest we get recommendations from both this group and SETI about how they think we should proceed." "Yeah, that makes sense," Janice responded. "So I'll try to make immediate contact with SETI and JPL and get back to you. And thanks for getting me involved with this! It's so exciting!"

Chapter Six

Jamison sat waiting for his phone to ring. He had just seen on line that word had leaked out about the anomaly and people were going nuts. He wasn't sure where the leak had occurred, but they had definitely lost control of the narrative. The rumors and misinformation now racing around the globe included that an alien space craft had been found on the moon, that the bodies of aliens had been recovered, that aliens in sleep pods had been found, that live aliens had been encountered, that interstellar warfare had already broken out on the moon, that the Western Consortium was masterminding a cover up bigger than Area 51, that South Base would soon be offering tours of the space craft landing site, and on and on. Soon government bodies, talk shows, even radio shock jock Fred E. Jay weighed in with pronouncements, false information and things guaranteed to just multiply exponentially the level of misinformation.

As expected, Jamison's phone rang. Incoming call from Dr. Mike Murley. Jamison braced himself for what was coming.

"Goddamit Jamison ! How did you lose control of this thing?" Murley bellowed.

Jamison thought about opening with a "Good morning, Sir" but decided to avoid the implied rebuke.

"We haven't been able to determine where this leaked out, but I'm working with our PR folks earthside. We should have a statement ready to go out within the next hour," Jamison replied.

"So the UN Lunar Exploration Administration is already calling for an investigation! The head of the Lunar Artifacts Commission is claiming jurisdiction. The Chinese have suggested that mining claims in the area should be put on hold until this is resolved. The CEO of the Western Consortium has been on the phone chewing my ass out. So I need an explanation!" Murley finally took a breath.

"We were just in the process of notifying all the relevant public and private agencies. The timing of this leak couldn't have been worse. Our PR folks have recommended that the announcement about the find be made by someone in senior management, perhaps either yourself, or the CEO. I think we can calm this down quickly if we act soon," Jamison paused and waited.

"I hope so. I'd like to avoid more ass chewings. Tell the PR team to send me what they propose right away. We also need to contact these damn regulatory groups that have weighed in and brief them so they stop making uninformed pronouncements," Murley said, seemingly starting to calm down.

" Absolutely sir, this morning I'm reaching out personally to the UN, the Lunar Artifacts group, the head of the Lunar Governing Council and the head of the Chinese Lunar Mining Operations to brief them and maybe get them to stop with the knee jerk reactions," Jamison replied.

"Alright, if I'm satisfied with the statement from PR, we'll go with it. I'll be back in touch with you if I'm not," Murley signed off as brusquely as he had started the call.

Jamison sincerely hoped that was his last ass chewing for a while.

Jamison made a series of calls to the list of relevant agencies and felt he was able to calm most of them down. It certainly helped to be at South Base, at least for the calls earthside. Calls from the Moon tended to get people's attention. The administrator of the Lunar Artifacts Commission seemed to be overplaying his hand on this, suggesting that his agency should be in charge of the excavation project. Jamison suggested that technically the Lunar Artifacts Act only applied to man made objects deposited on the moon from national space programs and for that reason, his company's offer to allow Lunar Artifacts to send a representative to participate in the project was in fact "generous."

Jamison got a notice from the PR team that Mike Murley was making a statement at a press conference in 30 minutes. Jamison completed a few more things on his priority list and then dialed into the press conference. Mike Murley of course did a masterful job. He gave a clear account of what had actually been found, what the plan was going forward, and promised to keep the media fully informed as the project progressed. He then masterfully handled questions from the press corp sometimes with elegance, sometimes with withering glares in response to really stupid questions. In the end, Jamison appreciated having a boss who at critical moments could get the job done.

Meanwhile, Dr Barnes was just sitting down with representatives from the SETI Institute and the Jet Propulsion Lab.

SETI stands for "Search for Extraterrestrial Intelligence". Since the start of the 20th century, interest in extraterrestrials had grown and a number of increasingly complex strategies for seeking contact with extraterrestrials or detecting communications from them had been devised. Transmissions of both radio and optical signals across the cosmos were performed. Large array radio telescopes were configured to listen for communications across a broad spectrum of frequencies. At times there had been both public and private funding for these efforts, but after a time the public funding pretty much dried up. In the 1980's, the nonprofit SETI Institute was formed, and since that time, it had remained the key mover for seeking contact or evidence of alien life. While many believed that it was virtually a certainty that the universe was teeming with life, the efforts of scientists and SETI had never yielded one concrete example of alien contact. In addition, there were times when some questioned whether seeking such contact was even a good idea. Would aliens be the benevolent socially advanced society that must surely come with a technologically advanced race, or would we end up with a "War of the Worlds" scenario?

Despite the lack of any contact, the SETI Institute had managed to stay afloat through ongoing public outreach and informational programs for the public. Much to their credit after almost 100 years, they remained the first place people turn when any questions of alien life or contact arise.

CalTech's Jet Propulsion Lab had been at the center of unmanned space probes for over 50 years, taking a lead role in probes that photographed and sampled every planet in the solar system and a good number of other

73

objects including planetary moons and asteroids. They had assembled and maintained world class instrumentation and space craft experts whose work was almost legendary.

"Dr Barnes, thank you for joining us today. I'm Dr Lucas Danforth, Head of the SETI Institute We're excited about your project proposal, but I have to tell you, we've had real misgivings about getting involved with this lunar find, after watching the media circus of the last 24 hours."

"I understand completely," Janice replied. "Western Consortium top brass has just completed a press conference intended to deal with all this misinformation. I think a good way to start our meeting would be to watch a replay of it."

Dr Danforth agreed and they pulled it up on a monitor. Janice thought Dr Murley did a masterful job and felt confidant that the SETI group would be more inclined now to get involved.

Dr Danforth began the meeting again. "That was a great suggestion, Dr Barnes. It certainly dealt with a lot of the misinformation out there, and will let us focus on the real questions at hand."

Dr Danforth had assembled the key department heads from the institute and each introduced themselves and explained their roles to Janice.

Also present in the meeting was Dr Sandra Gupta from JPL. She introduced herself briefly without any fanfare. She had been project lead on several of JPL's most ambitious projects and Janice was awed to have her participating.

Janice then gave them info on her background, training, and her experience with the lunar geology operations. She indicated that she had been appointed by the mining team to serve as a liaison officer with SETI and JPL.

She then launched into her proposal to the Institute. "As you saw in Dr Murley's press conference, we have a buried object, a pyramid that is presumed to have been placed there by an alien society. We don't know what it is, what's inside it, what purpose it may have, or even when it was placed there. The Western Consortium's mining operations has agreed to take a lead role in efforts to uncover this pyramid, but we need to partner with a group like SETI that can help us determine a scientifically sound and safe methodology for this project. We have the expertise that will allow us to excavate this object, but we don't have any expertise concerning what safeguards and methods need to be followed to assure that any finds are properly preserved and don't pose a risk to the project crew, or in a broader view to mankind."

Dr Danforth spoke first for the group. "SETI had certainly invested considerable effort into thinking about what first contact should look like, and although we've never anticipated exactly the scenario you've presented, we do think we have expertise that can help. For example, one of the things we believe will be critical is pathogen control. Anything found in this pyramid will need to be subjected to rigorous decontamination procedures and personnel space suits worn by the crew will require the same level of decontamination. Also, we can set up monitoring to assess whether there are any communications going into or emanating from the pyramid. We also have a team of linguists who can get involved if there are communications of any kind, written, audible, radio that may require efforts to decode."

"We have several personnel in mind to assign to this project. We will need your help in getting them trained and prequalified for lunar surface work."

"Of course," Janice replied. "We have a standard program developed for anyone who joins the project. It requires a physical exam and about a month of training."

Dr Gupta shyly raised her hand. "I think JPL can help with evaluating the find. We have a broad array of monitoring tools. Also, if we find any kind of alien technology, we can draw on a large team of experts to assess form and function. I believe my administrator intends to offer me for this project. I'm excited but a little apprehensive since I've never actually flown in space." That got a laugh from the assembled group.

The group proceeded to discuss the project in great detail. Everything flowed along smoothly and it appeared that the meeting was almost over when another of the SETI department heads raised her hand.

Dr Danforth looked up and saw the question. "Yes, Dr Simonton, you have a question?"

"Yes, thank you. There's just one thing about this that concerns me. We don''t know what we're going to find, how old it is or really anything. I'm concerned that there's no archeologists represented on this project. We may well encounter objects that are quite old, or in an advanced stage of decay or that are fragile or readily perishable. While I understand that this isn't a project to unearth or preserve a record of human activity, it would seem nonetheless that the same principals apply. I think this skill set needs to be added to the team." Dr Simonton concluded.

The group ended up discussing this point at great length and in the end concluded that Dr Simonton was right. Janice made the group aware of her archeological experience and suggested she could contact Dr Wilson to get a recommendation for a candidate to join the team.

With that, the meeting ended. Janice felt positive about the meeting results and thought she had accomplished what was needed today. The recommendation to add an archeologist wasn't a real surprise and she hoped Jamison wouldn't have an issue with it.

Janice waited until she got back to her office in Palo Alto and then rang up Conrad Jamison, hoping she was catching him during lunar "daylight" hours. He answered immediately.

"I just wanted to brief you on the meeting with the SETI Institute and JPL. Both groups are fully on board to participate and I'm planning to initiate training for the people they have designated. We should probably also start a series of meetings to hammer out an agreed upon project plan. There was only one development beyond what we had previously discussed." Janice proceeded to tell Jamison about the recommendation for an archeologist.

"I'm not surprised either. We just need to manage how that impacts the project. I think Mike Murley is afraid that will mean the entire dig is done using tablespoons. The debate will be over how the regolith that needs to be removed will be processed. I would think we can get agreement to use bulk removal techniques possibly with filtering of removed debris,"Jameson replied.

Janice was glad to hear that Jameson wasn't upset with this development. "So with your permission, I'll get in touch with Dr Graham Wilson, who I worked with down in Mexico to see if he can recommend an archeologist to join our team."

"That's fine. I think the budget we've set up for this can support an additional team. Just try to get someone who understands this dig is in the middle of a commercial mining operation that needs to stay on track," Jameson concluded.

"Understood. I'll be in touch soon," Janice signed off.

Janice sat back in her chair and took a deep breath. She had been so enthralled with the opportunity to be involved with this lunar mystery, that she hadn't fully worked out how she was going to balance this with her teaching schedule, research deadlines and everything else in her busy life. She decided her next step needed to be a discussion with the dean of the Geophysics Dept. She hoped he would be supportive.

The next day Janice tried calling Dr Wilson, and got a voice mail indicating he was on an extended book tour but that he would be checking his messages daily. A couple of hours later, the phone rang and she saw it was Dr Wilson.

"Hi Graham, thanks for getting back to me! How are you? Book tour! Sounds like things have really heated up since the big find at Coba," Janice said warmly.

"So nice to see you Janice," Dr Wilson replied. "Yes, it's been crazy. Talk shows, book signings, symposia everywhere. I hardly have any time left for real archeology. So are you coming back to Coba his summer?"

"I'm not sure. I'd like that, but things are getting pretty hectic on my end too. We'll see how the next few months unfold. I have a more immediate thing I need to discuss with you," Janice said.

She proceeded to describe the need to find an archeologist for the lunar pyramid project and solicit a recommendation from him.

"I'm going to kick myself for doing this, but I would recommend Dr John Higgins. You remember him don't you?" Dr Wilson asked.

"How could I forget him," Janice replied. "His announcement of the major find at Coba last summer was riveting. Do you think he'd be interested?"

"I think there's a good chance. I remember a conversation I had with him shortly after you left. He talked about how envious he was of your having done that lunar assignment. Think of now offering him a project in his field *but on the moon!*" Dr Wilson gushed. "And you can't find a more qualified candidate. He is my pick to take over at Coba when I retire in a couple of years."

"Would you be comfortable with me contacting him and making him an offer?" Janice asked.

"Absolutely, as long as he can be back at Coba within 6 months."

"I think that's doable. Thanks for your help, Graham. I'll be looking for you on that next talk show," Janice said goodby and signed off.

Janice was busy with other things, mainly promises made to the dean after her meeting with him, so you didn't get around to calling John Higgins until the next day. She was a little nervous calling him. He had been an impressive figure on the Coba project, the person who played a key role in the glyph's find that had rocked the world of Mayan archeology, a 30 something PhD, and frankly just a little bit sexy. She punished herself for that thought. "Come on Janice, let's stay professional!"

"Hi Dr Higgins, Dr Janice Barnes here. I'm not sure if you remember me. I was on the Coba dig last summer," Janice started.

" Of course, I remember you," Dr Higgins replied warmly in his deep baritone voice. "The geophysicist who helped us find the glyph trove."

"Oh, you're too kind." Janice replied and blushed slightly. "My contribution was really minor. But kind of you to say."

Dr. Higgins smiled. "So to what do I owe the pleasure of this call"

Janice gave him an overview of the lunar pyramid project, the team that was being assembled and the rationale behind recruiting an archeologist. She mentioned that Dr. Wilson had endorsed the idea of Dr Higgins participation.

"That in a nutshell is why I'm calling." Janice concluded.

"Holy smoke, you've blown me away. I never in my wildest dreams ever thought an opportunity to work on the moon would arise. I have to say it's tempting, but I definitely need time to consider it and how it will impact my other work. So you think 3 months is a doable time frame to complete this?" Dr Higgins asked.

"I do, as soon as regulatory and logistical hurdles are resolved. We're shooting to commence digging in 2 months," Janice replied.

"My other concern is the degree to which archeological standards of excavation and evidence preservation will be adhered to. If we're going to find artifacts, even alien in origin, I want to be able to defend the work we do to the scientific community." Dr Higgins said.

"I totally understand that and concur with you completely. The project manager has instructed me to tell you that all measures followed upon entry to the pyramid will be under your control. His only request is that the preliminary digging be done using conventional mining techniques, with excavated regolith screened for any sign of pertinent artifacts," Janice offered.

"I think I could live with that. As we already discussed, there is no human record of activity that we need to try and preserve. So give me a couple of days to think this over and I'll get back to you," Dr Higgins concluded. "But I don't think it's realistic to just have a single archeologist on the project. For something of this scope, I would think we need minimum of 5 archeologists."

"I'll double check with the project lead, but I think if that's your staffing recommendation, they'll go along with it. I look forward to hearing from you," Janice signed off. After talking with Dr Higgins, she really hoped he would accept. He would bring just the kind of academic credibility that would help reduce regulatory and public resistance that might arise to this project.

Meanwhile, back on the Moon, Jamison had concluded a series of meetings with the different governing bodies who regulated lunar activities. He felt they had gotten all they could out of this negotiation. The Western Consortium was guaranteed that their permit to commence mining operations on the Van der Waals crater would be fast tracked. A plan had been developed to physically separate the pyramid excavation from the remainder of their claim. They would maintain control of both their original claim and the pyramid access point.

In return for assurances that their rare earth mining could proceed unrestricted, they had agreed to manage the pyramid dig and provide the technical and logistical resources necessary to support that work, including assembly and training of a dig project team, construction of a decon and artifact handling facility, construction of a regolith screening building, and construction of temporary underground living quarters for the project team.

The total investment was somewhere north of $50 million dollars, but Jamison had successfully sold Dr Murley on the idea that it was a pittance compared to the mining revenues they expected from the rare earth lodes found in the crater. The only other thing they had been required to promise was that representatives from the Lunar Governing Body Commission and the Lunar Artifacts Agency would have unrestricted access to the pyramid dig and would receive regular progress reports on the project.

After the initial furor that arose about the pyramid, when wild and sometimes wacky rumors had been circulating, the Western Consortium public relations team had done a good job of getting the truth out and quelling public concern. Of course, none of that eliminated the public's fascination with the underlying questions that still remained:Who had buried this pyramid? What was its purpose? How long had it been there? Why was this location on the far side of the moon selected?

These questions continued to lead to a string of theories that still caused some consternation among those susceptible to such things. One held that the pyramid was actually a beacon and that once disturbed, signals would be sent across the cosmos and aliens of malevolent intent would descend on earth. Another was that the pyramid was the burial site for a long lost Egyptian king, who was intent on finding a tomb design and location truly out of reach of grave robbers. Another theory held that the pyramid was actually a gateway to a lunar civilization that dwelled inside the Moon's core. The public relations team did their best to dampen down these kooky theories, but it was understood that this would continue until there were real answers to the public's questions.

Janice checked her email and was excited to see she'd gotten a message from Dr Higgins. When she opened it, it gave her a feeling of satisfaction; Dr Higgins was accepting a place on the project team. It was doubly gratifying because now the team was complete and she could move her focus to getting the team trained and ready to work on the Moon.

She had worked with Jake and Jamison to develop an overall project plan and now she just needed to start executing her part of it. Naturally, Jamison was listed as the overall Project Lead. Jake was the Operations Lead, who would be in overall charge of day to day activities with regard to the dig site. Everyone working on the lunar dig site reported to Jake and he was in overall control of anything that happened there. She was happy for him getting what was really an important job on this project. She felt a lot of confidence in his ability to execute this role well. She was listed as the Technical Lead meaning she was responsible for assuring manpower and logistics for the project were procured and available when needed. Dr. Higgins was listed as the Academic Lead, meaning he was responsible for managing the techniques used for finding, securing and evaluating any artifacts recovered by the project. James Stefano, who had many years experience managing both earthside and lunar mining facilities was the Facilities Manager. She along with Stefano and Dr Higgins reported to Jake. Jamison as overall lead would receive regular project updates but only would be involved in day to day activities to the extent that he felt compelled to make changes or course corrections.

Jake had recently returned to Earth to coordinate final project preparations and today he and Janice were meeting for lunch prior to a planned meeting with the entire earthside staff.

"Janice! How are you," Jake gave Janice a warm hug and a kiss.

"I'm great, Jake," she replied, enjoying just for a brief moment being wrapped in his arms again.

"So this has been a real roller coaster ride! I never expected that our next chance to be together would find us so embroiled in a major project that we had no time to pursue our own relationship," Jake said in a heartfelt way that Janice found very endearing.

"I know Jake, but I'm excited for the opportunity it gives both of us. I think we just need to focus on the task at hand with the understanding that we both think our relationship is important and that once this is over, we'll come back to it and refocus on "Us"." Janice looked in his eyes and he nodded in understanding. "So at least for the next few months you're my boss and you don't need to give me any special consideration. I expect you to demand and me to deliver top notch performance."

Jake almost looked a little misty eyed. "You're just the best, Janice. This is the one aspect of this project I've been worrying over and now I feel like it's going to be okay. When this is done I want us to figure out a way to spend some serious time together." "We'll make it happen," Janice said and then they kissed one more time.

After lunch, they both headed over to the auditorium where the team was assembling.

Jake stepped up to the podium and looked around the room. "Ok everyone, it's time to get this meeting started. First, welcome to all of you. I know for many of you it's been a busy few weeks with training and flight certification. I imagine for some of you who haven't been in space before, you may be feeling a little nervous about what's coming, but I want you to know you're going to be surrounded by an experienced crew who will be there when you need help. The purpose of today's meeting is to go over our timeline and respond to any questions or concerns you may have. Now I'd like Dr Barnes to lay out the schedule coming up."

"Thank you, Mr Mackenzie. So we're scheduled to have everyone arrive at South Base on or before April 15th. Accommodations are booked for everyone at the South Base Hilton. For those of you who haven't been there before, it's quite the experience. We'll be there for several days so please plan to take advantage of some of the fun activities. All expenses are of course covered by the project." A faint "all right!" could be heard in the room followed by laughter.

Janice continued "Once we're all assembled we'll have several days practicing in space suits and the construction and archeology teams will go over operating procedures. When we feel the teams are ready, we'll be heading out to the Van der Waals crater. We have 6 rovers assigned to the project and each of you will be assigned to one. We will spend a day or so on rover procedures including foreseeable emergencies and evacuation. We will have medical staff with us on the project. Dr Casey please raise your hand." Dr Casey, an experienced MD with extensive experience on the Moon, stood up and smiled at the assembled group.

Janice smiled at Dr Casey and continued "Once at the project site, we plan for most of the work to be completed within 30 days subject to some variability based on unknowns about exactly what we're going to find. We place the outermost time frame at 45 days and if for some reason, we're still not done, we'll begin rotating back earthside anyone who requests it. That's just my quick overview. Now I'd like Jim Stefano to come up and talk a little about our facilities for the project. Jim."

"Thanks, Dr Barnes. Well, it's nice to see all your smiling faces. I want you to know we have been busy and I think we've put together a pretty good project facility. Here is a slide showing the layout. In the center is the underground housing facility with suit decon stations, entry and egress locks, and suit removal stations on either end. The underground construction assures that you won't get excessive radiation exposure.

"Adjoining that is the archeology bay which has artifact decontamination bays with the same arrangements for entry and suit handling. The one thing you will all soon be expert at is donning and removing space suits. I wish I could tell you that it's not cumbersome but..," Jim just smiled. "The last building on the right houses the digging equipment and maintenance facility, plus regolith processing equipment. No desuiting facilities there. The archeology building and housing unit are joined by underground passageways, so movement between buildings can occur without suiting up. The command rover will be tied into the buildings, too.

"The final structure you see is the emergency shelter. This is there for the extremely rare possibility of an incoming meteor storm. I know you were hoping that was the skyway bar and grill, but sorry no such luck," Jim concluded his remarks. The attendees chuckled nervously.

Jake came back to the podium. "That's all I intended to cover today. But I also wanted this to be an opportunity for you to ask any questions you might have."

One of the staff archeologists raised her hand "Where is an artifact storage facility."

Jake turned to Dr Higgins and asked " Could you take that question for me? "

"Of course" Dr Higgins went to the podium. "Our plan right now is to use one of the rovers as a temporary artifact storage room. We'll have it set up with inert gas chambers and storage cabinetry. We also have a facility back at South Base we can utilize if the volume of materials warrants it." The questioner nodded, seemingly satisfied with the answer.

Another hand was raised. "Why doesn't the emergency building have locks and desuiting stations."

Jake came back to the podium. "Excellent question. The emergency shelter is only used if you're suited and the meteor alarm goes off. If you're not suited up, you will just shelter in place. The housing unit is considered a safe location because of its underground design, and the archeology building is reinforced to be strike resistant. Keep in mind, also, that meteor strike risk is very very low."

Jake continued. "That reminds me about one other topic, radiation dosimetry.

Your personal dosimeters are required to be worn 24/7 and failure to do so can result in an early trip home. Safety on this project is a top priority and dosimetry is an important personal safety measure."

After that, there were no more questions and Jake wrapped up the meeting. "I'd like to thank each of you who has agreed to participate in this project. I know for some of you, you're really stepping out of your comfort zone. I think this project may well end up having major and historical significance as our first bonafide contact with an alien culture. So I for one am excited about what we may find and I hope all of you share that excitement with me! See you soon on the Moon!"

Chapter Seven

The project was called "First Encounter." Always depend on public relations types to look for a dramatic flair, Jake thought to himself. Today was the final project team leadership meeting at South Base. All project team members were present, some enjoying themselves more than others. With final sign off at this meeting, the project team would be ready to head out to the crater.

Jamison spoke first. "Before we begin, I have a little surprise."

Everyone looked at each other, not knowing what to expect.

Jamison continued. "Our beloved US government has decided late in our planning process to throw us a curve. Seems someone high up decided that our little project has national security implications. They have slapped a "top secret" classification on us and have required that everyone on the project pass a top secret clearance review. That has already been completed. All of you in the room passed. Unfortunately one team member each from archeology and the technical team didn't and they have already been notified and are heading home. Additionally, a military security detail is going to accompany us. The final impact on us is that all communications from the project will be encrypted and subject to pre-release by the military staff. That pretty much sums up what I know so far. Any questions?"

Dr Higgins raised his hand. "Are we going to replace the people who were sent back?"

"We'll do our best, but at least initially you'll have to get by without them," Jamison replied.

Jake spoke up. "So do we expect this to have any substantial impacts on our daily activities?"

Jamison gave a slight smile and said, " I don't know but let's bring in someone that does." Marjorie please bring in Major Atkins.

"Good afternoon ladies and gentlemen, my name is Major Charles Atkins, US Space Force, assigned to the 49th Tactical Wing stationed here at South Base." Major Atkins paused for a second and looked around the room. "I know the addition of my detail to your project will have come as a surprise, but I want to reassure you that my team is ready to go and has already been briefed on what's expected of them for this mission."

Jake broke the silence. "So Major, could you give us a brief overview of how you see your men participating on our project."

"I'd be glad to Mr Mackenzie . I understand that you're the project operations lead, so I would envision you and I working closely together. I expect the main function of my team, which consists of a squad of 30 paratroopers, will primarily be perimeter security. We'll establish a zone around the project and prevent any unauthorized entry. With regard to that part of our work, you'll hardly know we're there. The other part will be to screen and release all communications from the project. We've already worked with the project communications personnel to put those controls in place. Finally I would request that I be included in project staff meetings to keep me abreast of project developments. I know all of this comes late in the game, but you should know that a lot of cable traffic has been picked up worldwide suggesting some of the bad guys out there are very interested in this project. One final piece of this. In the end, no one knows what this thing is. We don't know what's going to happen. An alien encounter, while seemingly unlikely, could occur. And of course an encounter could be friendly or otherwise. So I hope I've answered any questions you might have. I'm certainly willing to take more questions now."

James Stefano spoke next, "We hadn't really designed things like our housing area to accommodate this number of people. Will you need facility support from us?"

"Great question Mr Stefano!" Major Atkins responded. "We will be totally self sufficient. We'll be bringing 4 military grade rovers to the project, one of which is outfitted as a dining vehicle. We're packing provisions for 6 weeks, so I think we won't need to utilize you project facilities."

No one came up with other questions. They had certainly been surprised by this, but the Major had done a good job of addressing their initial concerns.

Major Atkins sat down and Jamison walked to the front of the room. "Okay, folks, let's get this meeting going. Per our agenda, each team lead will review their readiness report. Jake will you run this part of the meeting?"

Jake nodded and pulled up the agenda on the monitor "Dr Barnes, do you want to start for the Technical Team?"

Each team lead in turn reported on personnel readiness, any outstanding issues and problems still requiring resolution. In general, it seemed like they were at a good point with really only a few minor sticking points.

Jake spoke again. "So let's go over our initial plan of attack at the pyramid. I know all of you are familiar with this, but I think going over it will make sure we're all on the same page. On arrival, we'll spend the first 48 hours in equipment set up and calibration and verifying that all required infrastructure is in place and functioning properly. Prior to commencement of any excavation, the technical team will set up the broad spectrum monitoring equipment and check for any signs of electronic activity to or from the pyramid. The archeology team will do a ground penetrating radar run in the area of the obelisk remnant looking for the rest of it. Anything they find, will be excavated with robotic equipment and by hand to the extent deemed necessary by the archeologists. The obelisk parts will be laid out adjacent to the archeology building for further study.

"The initial phase of the pyramid excavation will involve sinking a shaft at the pyramid peak. The shaft will be dug by robotic equipment. We intend to screen this initial material being removed during the shaft excavation, checking for any objects or artifacts, and also monitoring radiation levels during the dig. The accumulated regolith will be deposited using our robotic ore carriers at the spot designated on the map as "project waste area" When we reach a depth within about 10 feet of the pyramid peak , the automated JPL unit will be sent down to remove the remaining rock and powder, with constant observation top side by archeology. Once the peak of the pyramid is exposed, we'll do a camera survey and see what we've got. After the robotic equipment digs and reinforces the shaft, we'll install a man lift to allow personnel to reach the pyramid peak Once the peak is exposed we'll send personnel down and look for any sign of a hatch in the area of the exposed peak.

"We'll verify that the composition is the same tungsten alloy found in the earlier core sample. Once this work is completed, assuming no hatchway is obvious, we'll be setting up high energy ground penetrating X-ray radar which should give us the highest resolution pictures yet of the pyramid. We've had to select this approach because nothing else will allow us to see through this titanium alloy. It produces certain exposure concerns meaning the entire pyramid area will be cleared prior to commencing the imaging run.

Once the imaging is complete, we'll go over the results in detail to see if it reveals anything that looks like an opening."

James Stefano raised his hand. "Why don't we cut a hole in the exposed structure to get access. Seems like that would avoid a lot of additional work."

Jake replied immediately."We considered that, but, for one, this alloy will be very difficult to cut through. More importantly, we don't know what's inside. We're concerned we could trigger an explosion. We also are concerned that it could result in introduction of a vacuum into the pyramid which could damage or destroy what's inside."

"Finding a designed entry point into the pyramid is really critical," Jake continued. "If the X-ray penetrating radar study doesn't point us in that direction, then our backup plan is to sink a shaft down the side of the pyramid looking for any irregularities. Hopefully it won't come to that. Once we find an entry point, we'll gradually start to unbutton it, checking for outflow of any gases. If we detect anything coming out, we'll sample it and button up the pyramid until an analysis is completed. The analysis will determine our next steps. If there is an atmosphere inside we need to maintain, then we'll construct an airlock at the opening that prevents the pyramid contents from escaping."

"At this point we'll be ready to initiate entry. We'll first send a camera inside to get an initial visual. Then we'll proceed to investigate. I'm not going to go over the entry protocol again, but as you know, Dr Higgins' team will take the lead here."

Major Atkins spoke up. " We haven't had a chance to discuss this yet, but I'd like to request that one or two of my troopers be present for the initial entry."

Jake nodded and replied. "Ok, duly noted. Does anyone have any other questions at this point."

There were none and the team leads were instructed to let their people know that departure for the crater would be 0800 the following morning.

Jake and Janice passed in the hallway. Jake smiled and said " Dinner tonight at our favorite restaurant?"

"Of course," Janice replied.

Their second dinner at Over the Moon was again enchanting but also electric with the prospect of the adventure to come.

Bright and early, the caravan prepared to depart. It made for quite a sight, with 6 project rovers plus the 4 military rovers. It reminded Jake of settlers setting off from Kansas City on the Oregon Trail. There was lots of activity, project members coming and going, technicians loading supplies, paratroopers loading their gear into the big oversized military vehicles. A group departure like this was virtually unknown from South Base, so there were lots of gawkers. Besides, their mission had gotten a lot of press world wide, so many showed up just to be able to say they had seen the launch of the "First Encounter" mission.

Jake requested each rover lead to verify readiness, and when all had responded, he instructed his rover driver to head for the airlock. Thankfully, the lock could accommodate multiple vehicles, so it only took 20 minutes or so to get all 10 vehicles out on the lunar plain. They were traveling in full sunlight, so they were able to make good time over the rocky regolith.

They had one delay arise, when one of the military rovers broke down in the rough terrain of the Schroedinger crater. Major Atkins' troops responded quickly and soon had the vehicle rolling again. Once past that crater, they traveled through the Valle Planck which was a valley that headed right at the Van der Waals crater. The whole journey took more than 20 hours, so the driving crews had to be rotated several times.

The miles slowly rolled by and finally Jake could spot the low crater's edge marking the southern boundary of the Van der Waals crater. He radioed all the rover units to let everyone know they were about an hour out.

Once they arrived, Jake was impressed with how the landscape had changed. A large fence had been installed circling the entire pyramid site. Several low buildings were visible within the perimeter and Jake could spot the survey markers that had been installed to delineate the pyramid perimeter.

Jake instructed each project rover to have their people begin suiting up. The drill of donning suits and then subsequently the procedure for reentry into a pressurized environment would be the biggest challenge that many of those new to the Moon would face. Good to get them doing it right away. Jake could still remember his first time, how awkward he felt, and the slight feeling of claustrophobia that came each time he pulled on the helmet. And the suit procedures weren't just awkward. A mistake could be fatal. Sudden depressurization or failure of the air supply could cause unconsciousness and death. So now was a good time to get everyone comfortable.

Jake had instructed his team leads to keep close tabs on everyone during this initial excursion. He saw that several team members had already exited their rovers and were engaging in a little lunar "play", experiencing the light on your feet feeling of 1/6th gravity. Soon there were a whole gaggle of penguins flapping their arms and experiencing the wonder of standing in a space suit on the Moon. Jake told the team leads to take everyone for a short walk around. He didn't intend to have them enter and inspect the housing and scientific areas yet. He would be satisfied if everyone simply made it out and then made it back into the rovers without any drama. As that thought flashed in his head, almost on cue, a cry came through his headset. He turned quickly, ready to respond , and saw that one of the JPL team members had lost their balance and was finding out first hand how hard it was to stand back up. Several of his colleagues gathered around him and pulled him back up.

Jake smiled and thought to himself "Please lord let that be the worst we experience."

Everyone did reenter the rovers successfully. It took a while as everyone had to get used to cleaning off their suits, desuiting and stowing the equipment. For this initial day or two at the site, the crews would stay on the rovers.

Jake, still suited up, went with Jim Stefano to inspect the housing quarters, the scientific building and the equipment building. Everything was in pristine condition. Jake turned to Jim and said. "You've done a helluva job here, Jim. I know what this place looked like two months ago and you've really transformed it."

Jim blushed slightly and replied in his south Texas drawl. "Nothing that couldn't have been done by anyone whose smart, good looking and equipped with a mega budget!"

Jake laughed. They finished their tour. Jake felt good about the project's readiness to proceed.

The tech team had surveyed the dig point the night before for any radiation and found none. The SETI personnel had been monitoring a broad spectrum of radio waves for any indication of activity and also found none.

Bright and early Dr Higgins and his team were out and initiated the ground penetrating radar scan around the obelisk fragment. After just a short time, Dr Higgins called Jake over his suit radio. "I think we've found it. Looks like four or five main pieces all quite near the surface. We'll go ahead and start uncovering them."

Jake called back. "Roger that". He saw that Dr Higgins and his team were readying a couple of the robotic digging units the team had obtained. These allowed the scientists to move lunar soil with minimal effort, but a high degree of control, so that they could easily stop at any point and examine any finds and do the final removal by hand. This had been important because digging by hand in a space suit could be pretty exhausting.

Within a couple of hours, Jake saw that several of the obelisk pieces were exposed. He decided to put on a suit and go down and take a look.

He walked up to Dr Higgins who was just giving one of his folks some instructions. "So anything reveal itself right away?"

Dr Higgins turned to him. The sunlight created a bright reflection on his helmet. "Looks like the entire obelisk is somewhere around 20 feet long. The base is still in the ground and is probably about 6 feet long. It appears a meteor strike may have taken it down. Looks like a section of the obelisk is missing, probably pulverized by the strike. There is the same inscription on all 4 sides, not any characters or language that is any way familiar. There is one symbol at the top that looks familiar but I just can't place it."

Jake looked down and could see the figure Dr Higgins was referring toJake looked at the figure. He felt a thrill at the thought that he was looking at the first inscription anyone had ever seen crafted by an alien hand. "Wow, that's really something!"he exclaimed.

"Yeah, I know what you're feeling. First contact with any culture is a moving experience." Dr Higgins said quietly. "We're going to load the obelisk sections on the robotic carrier and move them all to the space beside the archeology building. I'd like to scour the area one last time and look for any of the missing pieces. Once that's done, I think you can proceed with digging that first shaft."

"Ok, I'm going to get Jim going with the excavation robots." Jake replied.

Within a short time, Jim had the heavy digging equipment ready to go. It was the same equipment that was used for their mine work. Jake always enjoyed watching it. Modern robotics had really made big advances over the last 50 years. The shaft digger was a four tracked vehicle. It operated off of large solar powered batteries. At the edge of their planned work area was a large solar panel array and a group of equipment batteries. The digger would periodically stop work, and a battery truck would take a fully charged battery and deliver it to the digger and swap out the used battery. Uninterrupted power and a limitless power supply. All of this continued seamlessly without any human intervention.

The digger had already been programmed with the exact coordinates required to place it directly over the peak of the pyramid. Jim Stefano stopped at this point and checked with Jake for permission to proceed. Jake gave that permission, and was pleased to see the digger begin churning up the regolith, the rotary auger head moving in a rectangular motion which corresponded to the shaft diameter that had been programmed. The sequence was a repeating cycle of churning up the lunar soil to break it up, followed by insertion of an auger into the middle and capturing the loosened material and conveying it to the waiting robotic ore hauler. This would repeat until the level in the shaft had dropped by a couple of feet and then the rotary auger would be lowered down and repeat the process. At intervals of around 10 feet, the rotary auger head would swing up and out of the way, and the framing machine would be lowered into the shaft and would install steel bracing and heavy duty screening which would provide structural integrity to the shaft. Then the whole cycle would start over.

Once it got started, not much was visible from the surface. This was time tested technology and Jake had confidence it would work well. The only difference here was that once the shaft got within about 2 feet of the pyramid peak, project personnel would actually be going down in the shaft. During normal mining operations, it was never required to send a person down the shaft, but this project made that a necessity. For that reason, after the shaft was completed, a man lift would then be installed that allowed personnel to travel to the bottom. The man lift was an open design that allowed personnel to simply step on a platform, grab a hand hold, attach a safety harness and then be lowered down slowly. Once on the bottom, they simply boarded the same platform now headed up. The whole system was monitored from the control rover and any misstep or issue would cause the whole thing to be stopped virtually instantly. The man lift also served to convey hand removed soil out of the shaft.

This man lift design was not standard. Engineers for the Western

Consortium working with Dr Higgins had come up with this design. As Jim Stefano liked to joke "Ain't been a lot of archeology on the Moon!" They hadn't really had a chance to field test it, so Jake was determined to be extra cautious in its initial use.

The ore haulers in use were programmed to deliver their contents to a large industrial screening unit, where anything found could be removed and studied by the archeology team.

Jake went back to the control rover and reached out to Janice to see how things were progressing in her area. "Hi Janice, just wanted to see how it was going," Jake smiled.

"Oh thanks Jake, I think we're doing well. The radio monitoring by SETI personnel is up and operating, with no signals detected. The JPL team has the imaging equipment ready to go. As soon as you give us the word, we can proceed. We did some initial radiation monitoring near the obelisk remnants this morning, no issues found. We're also ready to put radiation monitors down shaft #1 as soon as you complete initial construction. Last thing- everyone's dosimetry badges are within daily dose limits." It all had spilled out of Janice and now she took a deep breath.

"Is everyone dealing with life in a can on the Moon ok.? Once in a while, the whole thing can make some people freak out just a little bit. " Jake asked.

"Everyone seems fine so far." She replied. "I haven't seen much of our military escort, so I'm not sure how they're doing, but I guess they're all old hands on the moon."

"I'll have to check in with them, too,"Jake said. "Ok, I'm going to run. Thanks for the update. It all sounds good!"

Jake gave Jim Stefano a call. "How are we progressing in getting everyone moved into the living quarters? I'd like to get everyone out of the rovers." "Well, everyone should be moved within the next couple of hours," Jim reported.

"That's great ! Everything else going ok?" Jake asked.

"Haven't run across any major glitches,". Jim replied.

"Ok Jim, thanks for the update."

Jake rang up Major Atkins. "Good morning, Major. I just wanted to check in and see if everything's ok with you and your men"

"Thanks for the call, Mr Mackenzie. We've set up a perimeter out about half a kilometer and established a 24 hour watch schedule. We have radar set up, so no one can approach your location without us detecting it. Everything's been quiet, although we have picked up a Chinese vehicle on the perimeter of the Western Consortiums claim area. "

"Yeah they've been there for several months. It's pretty typical that once one of the lunar mining companies stake a claim, others are out trying to figure out if an adjacent claim might be lucrative," Jake explained. "Ok Major, thanks for the update." Jake signed off.

Lunar "evening" was approaching so Jake decided to stop in the living quarters. When he got there, he saw that most folks were just finishing eating.

Jim Stefano stood up and announced in a loud voice. "Ok it's movie time"

Jake laughed and joined the others while Jim started the film. It was "Interstellar" starring Matthew McConaughey, Ann Hathaway and Jessica Chastain. There was a groan from some of the group.

"Couldn't we have something that's not so freakin dated?"

But they all enjoyed the diversion. Some focused on the scenes of Earth while others took pleasure in knowing that their risk of being sucked into a black hole was quite low. Jake marveled at Jim Stefano and how he had this way of making life on a place like this a little more bearable.

The next couple of days were taken up with the shaft work plus the archeology team working on reassembling the obelisk. They confirmed that a section of it had not been found.

On the morning of Day 4, Jim rang up Jake and reported. "The shaft excavation and framing installation is all done. We're ready to put in the man lift.

That afternoon, Jake headed to the excavation area. Jim Stefano had scheduled a training session for Dr Higgins and his team in use of the newly installed man lift. Jake wanted to also get the training.

"So you can stop and start the man lift with this control . Strap this to your suit. When you're ready to step on, hit the power button, everything stops. Step on, attach the safety harness to this clip, hit the power switch again and you'll start descending. Not fast, around 2 feet per second . When you are approaching the bottom, a foot or so above the bottom, hit power again and unhook the harness and step off. That's it. You're there. Once you're ready to come up, just go to the other side and attach the harness and hit power again. When you reach the top, hit power, detach your harness and step off. Last safeguard- cameras and lighting have been installed down the entire shaft. Anything unplanned happens, you're being monitored constantly. My man will instantly stop the lift himself."

Jake said "It sounds like a good design. I feel comfortable doing this. Dr Higgins do you have any questions."

Dr Higgins said " I'm also impressed. Seems pretty foolproof. My only question is why the necessity to attach and detach the safety harness. With 1/6th gravity, isn't a fall no big deal?"

Jake and Jim looked at each other and smiled. Jim proceeded to give Dr Higgins the "no terminal velocity on the Moon" lecture and ended with "….so at the bottom of a two hundred foot shaft, you'll be moving faster then a prairie fire with a tail wind."

All three of them laughed.

"So I'm ready to give it a try," Jake said

Jake followed Jim's instructions and stepped onto the lift and attached his harness. Jim radioed his operator to stand by and then Jake hit the power button. Jake felt the slight jolt as the lift motor started up and soon he was slowly descending through the newly dug shaft. He was impressed with the job the robotic equipment had done. The shaft was smooth and gave a feeling of sturdiness. He was so enthralled with checking it all out, that he suddenly realized he was close to the bottom. He hit power, unharnessed and stepped onto the shaft floor. It didn't look any different then the rest of the shaft. He reminded himself that just 10 feet below him was the top of the pyramid. The JPL unit was sitting there, the LED display showing all green.

Jake spoke into his radio "Worked like a charm, Jim."

Jim replied immediately "Well, just remember it's the return trip that counts the most."

Jake smiled and started back up. On top, he saw Dr Gupta had arrived. "So Dr Gupta, Dr Higgins, are we ready to proceed with the final removal of debris from the shaft?"

Both replied immediately in the affirmative.

Shortly, the object of many months preparation and much speculation would be exposed for the first time to human eyes.

Chapter Eight

D
r. Gupta took the remote control wand for the "lunar automated archeologist" and hit the power button. A monitor set up near the shaft entry allowed them to watch the unit begin working at the bottom of the shaft. Dr Gupta turned to Jim Stefano and said. "Please start up the man lift." The digger began painstakingly scooping regolith from the shaft and placing it on the man lift steps Soon thereafter, regolith began showing up at the top of the shaft, where it was dumped onto a conveyor table manned by one of Dr. Higgins team. He would look for any sign of artifacts and then the regolith would be dropped off the conveyor table into the robotic ore carrier for transport to the waste dump area. Dr Higgins had worked closely with JPL on this design. It was really the first time such an automated system to look for artifacts had been devised. It was made necessary by the moon's harsh environment and the limitations of working in a space suit. Jake watched the operation for a while, and at least to his untrained eye, it all seemed to work perfectly.

This was expected to go on for several hours. There would be a stop point, where both the digger and the man lift would be removed to allow the robotic shaft machine to cut out and frame the last section of shaft exposed by the digging equipment. This would bring them to within about two feet of the pyramid top. At this point, Dr Higgins and one of his team would go down the shaft and clear the final bit of rock and then photograph the initial exposure of the pyramid.

Jake prepared to head back to the command rover. "Dr Higgins, please let me know when you're ready to go down and complete the final digging."

"Roger that, Mr Mackenzie!" Dr Higgins responded.

Later that day, Jake got the call from Dr Higgins. He suited up immediately and headed to the shaft. "So are you both ready to head down?" Jake asked.

Dr Higgins replied "Yes, the shaft is clear down to our target depth, the final shaft clearance and framing is in place, and the digging equipment has been removed. We have our own digging equipment for removing the last bit of rock and debris, a camera to get some initial pictures of the pyramid, and sampling equipment to verify the pyramid composition."

"Ok, you may proceed. Double check your oxygen tank levels before you start. We'll be watching the two of you make history!" Jake said and patted Dr Higgins on the back.

One by one, Dr Higgins and his associate stepped on the man lift and slowly disappeared from view. Jake was able to watch the cameras installed in the shaft on the topside monitor and knew that most of the other project team members were watching the same in the living quarters. The team of archeologists reached the bottom a couple of minutes later. Nothing noteworthy to see yet. Just a shaft that terminated with a floor of gray regolith. Both men took out short spades and began placing shovelfuls of the rock on the man lift. They did this for maybe 20 minutes. Dr Higgins stooped to take the next shovelful and hit something hard. He would have almost sworn that he heard a metallic clang, but of course that wasn't possible. Dr Higgins got down on his knees and began pushing by hand the last bits of rock and powder out of the way. Suddenly, without fanfare or a flourish of trumpets, there it was. The pyramid top was simply a semicircular ball maybe eighteen inches in diameter. Dr Higgins noted that the top had appeared virtually dead center in the shaft, an unbelievable testament to the navigation and survey work that had been done. He stood up and clicked several pictures, then went back on his knees and resumed clearing away rock and sand. The pyramid was obviously metallic. It had a brownish silver hue that made him suspect this would mirror the same composition found in the core sample. By the time they were done, they had exposed about 3 feet of the pyramid. They took some additional pictures and finally decided they were ready to head back up.

They knew that others had been watching their activity, but they had no clue as to the cheering and whistling going on up in the project buildings. When they got back to the surface, Jake greeted them warmly and when they desuited and reentered the living quarters they got a greeting normally reserved for rock stars. For everyone this moment marked the point when it all became real. They all *believed* the pyramid was there, but until this moment not a single human being had ever *seen* it.

The next day, planning proceeded with the next step, sending an X-ray radar unit down into the shaft to get the best image yet of the pyramid and hopefully locate an entry route. Jake was meeting with Janice and Dr Gupta to review the plan. "So Jim Stefano will have the X-ray unit lowered into the shaft by tomorrow. What's involved in the final setup for the equipment?" Jake asked.

Dr Gupta began "I and my JPL colleague will go down the shaft and set up the instrument stand so the X-ray beam is properly aimed down through the pyramid body. We'll then head back up and make sure that the whole dig area is evacuated. This high power X-ray puts out quite a bit of radiation, so we need to keep everyone away while we doing the imaging. The imaging itself only takes a few minutes and the results will be sent to our receiver in the technical center. Then we just have to extract the unit. We should leave it down there until we're sure no more imaging runs are needed."

"So how long do you think you'll need?" Jake asked.

"We can probably be done by Tuesday, about 2 days," Dr Gupta answered.

Dr Barnes spoke up. "And we've done a risk analysis and concluded that radiation risk to personnel in project buildings will be negligible. We're going to have monitors set up around the pyramid perimeter to measure released radiation."

"Ok good " Jake replied. "That was the next thing I was going to ask." Jake was keeping his fingers crossed that this last analysis would show a way into the pyramid. They simply didn't have the resources or the time to excavate the entire thing.

100

Janice enjoyed attending meetings with Jake.. The project had been keeping them going in opposite directions. It was nice to see him in action. She thought that almost without exception he had gained a reputation with the team as a capable project leader, one who tried to look out for the best interests of the entire group.

She had been very busy with lots of different support activities. Because the project involved so many unknowns, they were trying to be ready for and anticipate a myriad of possibilities. Distinguished linguists in ancient languages were standing by if an unknown language was encountered. Infectious disease experts were retained to respond to both questions about infection control measures and help respond if some infectious agent was encountered. She had assisted the archeologists in coordinating with South Base to set up artifact storage containers including maintaining items under vacuum, not a normal requirement. She was coordinating with the earthside PR team to prepare the press releases that would occur as finds took place.

Finally she was monitoring team members to assess morale and mental health.

She had a lot on her plate, and she loved every minute of it. This was a grand adventure and she almost wondered how she would cope when it was time to return to the academic world.

Dr Gupta and her JPL team were suited up and had moved the X-ray imaging camera to a point beside the shaft. Jake had suited up to observe the activities and be there if help was needed or problems arose. Jim Stefano was also present and oversaw the lowering of the camera down the shaft. The camera was larger and bulkier than Jake had expected, but the process of lowering it to the pyramid peak went smoothly nonetheless. Once it had been deposited at the bottom, the lowering winch was removed, and the man lift was reinstalled. Jake reviewed the man lift usage with the JPL team and then they proceeded to take the man lift to the bottom.

Jake watched their activities on the top side camera. Dr Gupta and her colleagues proceeded to position the X-ray imaging equipment directly over the pyramid peak using adjustable extension legs. They spent some time adjusting and rechecking its placement. They all understood that getting this right on the first try was important, since the logistics of the process were so cumbersome. Finally, Dr Gupta reported that the equipment was ready and the JPL team started back to the surface on the man lift.

Once topside, all of the personnel in the area including Jake and the JPL team evacuated the area. The X-ray camera would need to use a high energy radiation beam to get the required penetrating power, so everyone was removed to a distance of almost 1000 feet for safety. Dr Gupta remotely actuated the camera, and verified that it had functioned properly.

Once Dr Gupta and her team had extracted the imaging and reviewed them, they scheduled a meeting of the team leads to review the results.

"So the imaging results are pretty clear. Seems like the X-ray technology gave us the penetrating power necessary to get through the structure." Dr Gupta started into her summary. "I guess I was surprised when the results came back and it was..... well less than I expected."

"Less? Dr Higgins asked. Dr Gupta still hadn't pulled up the survey images.

Finally she did and they all saw what she was referring to.

"Wow!" Jake exclaimed. "It just looks empty."

"It does, doesn't it," Dr Gupta replied.

"We can see some kind of structure in the center at the bottom, and a couple of other things also on the bottom, but the structure appears to be just the pyramid shell and nothing else." Dr. Gupta added.

"Disappointing," Jake said aloud what they all were thinking. "Almost like the tombs of Egypt where grave robbers usually got there first"

Dr Gupta interrupted Jake's lament "But there is some very good news also." No one spoke, they just waited.

"There is what looks like an entrance hatch or doorway on the eastern face at the base." She took a pointer and showed what she had seen on the monitor. Dr.Higgins spoke up. "Yes, I see it also. It does look like an entryway."

Jake spoke next. "Well, that is very good news indeed. Really critical to the project. So we can move forward with sinking a second shaft adjacent to this entry point." Jake tried to sound positive, but definitely felt a little deflated by the pyramid image. If they had organized this multimillion dollar project to find the first ever recorded alien object and all they found was an empty shell....

Word soon leaked out among the project team members about what had been found, and the feeling of deflation spread among the entire group.

That night, in the housing unit, after evening meal had been served and most personnel were done eating, Jake felt compelled to speak about the find.

"I know that word has spread about what we've seen on the pyramid imaging and that it has kind of deflated folks. I just want to encourage everyone to not be disappointed. Whatever we find inside the pyramid, it will still be historic. We need to bring our best science to this endeavor and not lose sight of that," Jake said with conviction.

"I want to second that," Dr Higgins said. "Great archeology has rarely been glamorous. It's been done by painstaking attention to detail and not overlooking the smallest thing. When we open the pyramid, we'll be walking into a space last occupied by a culture from a far off planet. We need to stay focused and stay positive."

There was a smattering of applause among project team members. Jake hoped this would lift spirits at least a little.

Work commenced next day on the second shaft that would be sunk to what they hoped was the pyramid entry point. The technique was exactly the same as the first shaft, but about 100 feet deeper. First requirement was to perform surveying to translate the pyramid image into an exact location to commence the dig. Jim Stefano and his crew completed that in a couple of hours and reported back to Jake that they were ready to set up the robotic digging equipment.

"We're good to go," Jim reported. "I was concerned that we might have to do drilling and breaking through lunar bedrock, but the X-ray scan actually shows that the bedrock has been cut well back from the pyramid base, so just like the first shaft, we'll just be going through regolith and reasonably small loose rock."

"Does the added depth introduce any additional technical issues." Jake asked.

"No, this same shaft design has been used in our mines down to a depth of a mile or more," Jim replied.

"How long do you anticipate the digging will take," Jake said.

"We're probably looking at a week." Jim replied.

"Ok, go ahead and proceed," Jake smiled and headed back to the control rover.

Jake decided this digging period would give him an opportunity to complete some of the administrative chores required of a project lead.

First thing was to get in touch with Jamison and give him an update on the project. He wondered how Jamison would respond to an empty pyramid.

Jake gave Jamison his report and sent him a copy of the imaging report.

Jamison's first comment was "I think this is really good news. Finding an entry point means we can open this thing up and potentially start thinking about finishing this project."

Jake expressed a little of the disappointment he felt.

Jamison smiled and said "Truth be told, I don't give a rat's ass about pyramid archeology. If our alien friends chose to build this massive structure and then not put anything in it, that's not our problem. In some ways it's a positive. We can open it up, confirm it's empty and then close down this project and get back to our real jobs."

"So you're not concerned that all the money that's gone into this project will be seen as a colossal waste." Jake asked.

"Not at all!" Jamison replied. "We'll be seen as good corporate citizens who were fully prepared to do the right thing, but just came up with a dry well as they used to say in the oil drilling business."

Jake signed off. He knew that Jamison's attitude was correct. But Jake had really gotten into the historic nature of this work and had wanted the project to yield something remarkable.

Jake reviewed some of the reports that the project team had begun generating. The archeology team had done some initial examination of the obelisk and reported that there was some kind of text on it, but it was obscured by a build up of deposits which probably would require acid treatment to remove. They recommended sending the entire set of obelisk fragments to the lab at South Base, which was better equipped to handle the cleaning process. Jake approved the request and forwarded it to Jim Stefano's team.

Jake also looked over various reports on everything from site radiation surveys, readiness testing for the meteor defense system, site oxygen inventory levels, rover maintenance logs and equipment readiness reports. Everything he saw confirmed that his team leads were on top of things and made his review almost unnecessary. He would follow up with Jim about getting that incoming meteor drill completed.

Janice had prepared a preliminary draft press release that would tell the world about the obelisk find. It would include the first pictures released by the project of an actual find. Jake saw that Major Atkins had signed off. Jake did the same and forwarded it on. It would be subject to multiple additional reviews starting with Jamison, including the PR folks and ending with Mike Murley. "Welcome to corporate life," Jake thought to himself.

Meanwhile, a quarter million miles away somewhere on the Russian steppe, Dmitri turned to Olav. "So, my vodka saturated friend, have you been following the "aliens on the moon" story?"

"If you're referring to the little green men who appear at the very bottom of every Stolichnaya bottle, I try to mostly ignore them." Olav replied, slurring his words.

"No you imbecile! They are digging for real aliens on the Moon," Dmitri chastised Olav.

"And why are you interrupting a perfectly good afternoon buzz to tell me that?" Olav looked disinterested and half asleep.

"Because an object shown to be of alien origin will be valuable beyond anything we've ever seen," Dmitri replied. He stopped talking once a loud snore came from Olav.

He sat back and looked at the sky thinking about the possibilities.

Several days passed with Jim Stefano reporting daily good progress on the second shaft excavation. Jim reported this morning that they were within 20 feet of the bottom. Jake and most of the project team stopped what they were doing to watch the final digging activities on top side monitors. At about 15 feet to go, there was excitement as the vertical side of the pyramid came into view. After another 5 feet of digging, the regular surface of the pyramid wall was broken by a 3 inch protrusion that was about 48 inches wide. Continued digging a few inches further down caused Jim Stefano let out a sharp whistle.

"If that's not a door hinge, then I just fell off the turnip truck." Jim added.

Gradually the door emerged. I think they were all surprised. "Looks awfully anthropomorphic," one archeologist commented.

And indeed, when the digging was done there it was- a door. Four feet wide and 12 feet tall.

This latest find electrified the project team. After months of work, they would soon be entering the pyramid.

Jake and his team leads met in the control rover. "So Dr Higgins does it surprise you to find a conventional door?"

"Not really. Unless you're in zero gravity, a door like configuration would accommodate a wide variety of life forms. The dimensions of the door may provide some clues. It suggests that the aliens weren't too different from us in size. The door also features what looks like a conventional hand operated latching mechanism suggesting that the aliens had something akin to hands.

So no, I'm not really surprised. After all, a pyramid structure is also a conventional geometric form."

"So let's talk about our entry procedure." Jake began. "We'll send down a 2 man archeology team, who will crack open the door and immediately test the atmosphere. The doorway should be closed immediately while the sample is analyzed. If the pyramid is simply under vacuum then no further concern is warranted. If there is an atmosphere then we'll have to evaluate the impact. Once we've passed this hurdle then the next step is to insert the mobile camera into the pyramid. The camera will screen the immediate area of the door and if nothing concerning is detected, then the team will proceed with entry. Prior to entry the team should verify adequacy of suit oxygen supplies . Suit helmet cameras should used during the entire entry and any failure of one or both cameras should result in the team immediately exiting the pyramid. A standby team will be stationed at the shaft entrance in the event that a rescue of one or both team members should prove necessary. Also two of Major Atkins troopers will be stationed at the shaft entrance per his request. I think that's it. Are there any questions?"

Dr Higgins raised his hand. "I think that covers it. I'm planning for Bob Flaherty from my team to accompany me for this first entry."

Everyone was anxious to move forward, so shortly thereafter the two men suited up and made their way to the second shaft entrance. After getting the go-ahead from Jake, the two archeologists stepped onto the man lift and disappeared from view. This time Jake opted to observe from the control rover. The monitor picked up successive motion sensor activated cameras as the 2 men descended. Finally they were standing on the bottom, the large doorway looming in the background. They took a few moments to get themselves oriented, then Dr Higgins tried the door latch and found it couldn't be moved. He took out a mallet they had brought for this eventuality and he carefully started tapping on the latch. Nothing happened and so he started putting a little more force into it.

Jake realized he had been holding his breath "Give it one good shot doc!" He muttered under his breath.

Just about the point when Jake was convinced it wouldn't open, the latch moved ever so slightly. Then a little more and finally on the last blow, not only did the latch move, but the door released ever so slightly.

"I think it's free," Dr Higgins said. First Dr Higgins broke open a small smoke tube and verified that there was no outrush of pyramid atmosphere or inrush of lunar vacuum occurring. He took out the atmospheric sampler connected to a portable gas chromatograph and inserted it through the door opening for the prescribed 10 seconds. They had to wait approximately 5 minutes. Dr Higgins looked at the readout and reported "The pyramid is just under vacuum, no atmosphere found. Now with that hurdle was completed, Dr Higgins positioned the small mobile camera they had brought down and switched it on. Immediately the topside pictures were replaced with a live picture from the handheld unit. "I think we're ready."

Dr Higgins opened the door slightly and reached the camera inside. It was mounted on four small wheels and included a small lighting unit.

Everyone on the entire project team was holding their breath at this point. The first images came back from the little camera. The entire group saw the light shining off into the void and picked up exactly......nothing. It looked just like what the X-ray images had shown- a big empty space.

Dr Higgins said "The camera doesn't show any threats or issues- I'd like to proceed with entry." Jake thought about being more cautious but in the end he was anxious too.

"You may proceed Dr Higgins," Jake replied.

Dr Higgins and Flaherty entered the pyramid. Jake couldn't see them for a moment since the handheld camera was still transmitting.

Suddenly, Jake heard Dr Higgins voice. " We have a problem. Oh my god man, what's going on."

Jake called to the control room operator "Switch back to their helmet cams."

The tech did so and immediately there was a jumble of images. Flaherty looked like he was falling down and Dr Higgins seemed to be trying to hold him up.

Suddenly, Flaherty's voice came through. "I can't breath. I think my oxygen's running out."

As soon as Jake heard that, he called out "Rescue team one down the shaft immediately with supplementary oxygen. Dr Higgins exit the pyramid!" Within 2 minutes, the rescue team were at the shaft bottom .

Flaherty was lying on his side, a look of fear in his eyes. The feelings of claustrophobia that a spacesuit can evoke are amplified a hundred fold when one starts to feel like they're not getting enough air.

They immediately hooked up the supplementary oxygen to Flaherty's suit. He hadn't lost consciousness but was breathing rapidly. Soon the rescue team had him calmed down and one of them headed up with Flaherty, keeping a close eye on him.

Dr Higgins and the other rescuer also started back up. Jake had immediately started suiting up as the incident unfolded. He asked Jim Stefano to also suit up and come with him. When they got to the shaft entrance, all four men had made it up. Jake asked Jim to interview Flaherty and the 2 rescuers while he would talk to Dr Higgins.

Jake approached Dr Higgins and first said "Are you ok?"

Higgins nodded "Just a little shaken up"

"So what happened." Jake asked. " It seemed like as soon as you entered the pyramid, things started to go wrong."

"That's right. I was in the lead and I looked back and Flaherty was breathing hard and wobbling and started to fall. I caught him and immediately pulled him out the door." Dr Higgins said.

"So was there any indication that something inside caused this?" Jake asked.

"I don't know," Dr Higgins replied honestly.

"Did you see anything in there," Jake followed up.

"Absolutely nothing," Dr Higgins replied, the disappointment in his voice clear.

"Ok, thanks for your report. Let's cancel the entry for today until we can sort this out."

Jake turned and walked over to the other men. He immediately asked Flaherty how he was and got a response indicating he was feeling fine. He thanks the rescuers for their prompt and well executed response.

Finally, he turned to Jim Stefano and discretely asked him if he was able to piece together what happened.

"Yeah, I think so." Jim replied. "Maybe we can head back over to the command rover and I can tell you what I found out."

They sat down in the rover and Jim began. "I'm virtually certain that this has nothing to do with the pyramid or what's inside it. I've seen this happen before even with space suit experienced men. I think Flaherty must have inadvertently turned off his CO_2 scrubber. That isn't life threatening. After a while the air will start to feel a little stuffy. A natural reaction is increased respiration rate. Increased respiration would also be a natural reaction to the adrenaline rush Flaherty must have been feeling, standing there getting ready to enter this alien vessel. God knows my adrenaline was flowing and I was just watching from the command rover. Increased respiration leads to hyperventilating and that leads to unsteady gait and possibly falling. The first rescuer on the scene immediately checked the CO_2 absorber switch, found it was closed, and reopened it. They then checked Flaherty's suit status and verified that he had plenty of oxygen. So that's almost certainly what happened . Once he got back into the shaft and calmed down, he was fine."

"So what follow up would you recommend?" Jake asked.

Jim began "Retrain everyone about checking CO_2 absorber status frequently. Also, I think we should not do anymore entries without at least one lunar work experienced crew member present. I think if my staff had been down below, they could have headed this off."

"Finally, I wouldn't send Flaherty down again until the pyramid has been fully explored and the entries into it have become more routine. I think we can do that and not have him feel publicly humiliated. I feel for him. I can still remember my first times in a suit."

"Thanks Jim, I knew you could get to the bottom of this. I'm going to put something out to the entire team indicating the nature of what happened. I think we need to dispel any notion that something in the pyramid caused this."

"Absolutely, I couldn't agree more," Jim responded.

The incident had been observed by virtually the entire project team and a couple of ludicrous rumors were nipped in the bud by Jake's communication.

Jake also talked privately with Dr. Higgins and reassured him that they had determined the cause of the incident. They agreed that Dr Higgins, another archeologist and one of Jim Stefano's men would retry the entry the next day.

That night in the housing area, Jim Stefano with his uncanny ability to tweak morale at just the right moment came up with another movie. It was another very old movie, this one a cult classic- Mars Attacks! with Jack Nicholson and Pierce Brosnan among many others. By the end, the project team members were in stitches. Just the comic relief everyone needed.

The next morning, the new team assembled at the shaft to the pyramid. Once again there was a 2 man rescue team up top. All 3 men were equipped with powerful flashlights. It had been agreed that both the atmosphere testing and the mobile camera step would not be done this time. Jake was again on hand and gave Dr Higgins the thumbs up to proceed. One by one the three men entered the shaft. Within a couple of minutes they were at the bottom. The technician in the command rover confirmed that all three helmet remote cameras were working. Without further ado, Dr Higgins opened the door and walked in. The other two men followed.

Shortly thereafter an "oh my god" was heard on the radio. A second later a second "oh my god" was heard, this time a different voice.

Finally, the voice of Dr. Higgins came through " You don't need to worry any longer about the pyramid being empty."So far observers in the control rover hadn't been able to see much. A lot of darting flashlight beams but not much else. Finally, Dr Higgins took his helmet cam, pointed it skyward and shined his flashlight on the wall. What everyone saw was stunning . The tungsten alloy walls of the pyramid were covered from floor to peak with thousands of symbols. It appeared that laser engraving had been done. There were images, drawings of objects, characters that could be an alphabet in some alien language. Dr Higgins knew that the entire project team would be watching this live, so he slowly moved down the wall with camera and flashlight pointed up to give everyone a view of what they were seeing.

In the middle of the pyramid, was an uncovered enclosure about 25 feet tall. This occupied the entire center portion of the floor. Dr Higgins had initially been preoccupied with the magnificent displays on the walls. Now he finally took a walk around this partition and found there was an opening on the side farthest from the pyramid entry door. When he walked in, he was overwhelmed by the sight that greeted him. There were 2 large beautiful three dimensional laser etched glass statues, maybe 10 feet tall.

The aliens who for months had been this abstract concept were now standing in front of him. They looked remarkably humanoid but there were subtle differences. They had eyes larger than ours and ears that were also larger and pointed on the ends. He guessed that he was looking at a male and female, in all their naked glory. The female had a pouch in front and no breasts or nipples. The male was slightly larger. Both had legs that more resembled an ostrich than a man's. Both had hair on their heads similar to our own. And both were smiling, a warm smile that seemed to say "We're not so different." Dr Higgins had made sure to slowly and carefully scan these figures. He imagined folks on the team were going nuts- and they were!

Finally , Dr Higgins looked at the raised platform situated between the two alien figures. The placement at the absolute center of the entire structure suggested whatever these thing were, they were highly important to the builders of the pyramid.

Dr Higgins looked at his watch and realized he had been here over an hour. Probably needed to head up for now. He knew he would be spending lots of time down here, so it was ok to leave now. But of course he had to force himself.

Chapter Nine

They weren't prepared for what came next. It took a few days to gather momentum. Initially, the project team members all had opportunity's to enter and see the pyramid contents. But these were professionals, who entered respectfully and studied the images in hushed tones. They speculated on the meanings of the symbology, the anatomical differences revealed by the statues and so on. But meanwhile, Janice worked with the Public Relations team to compose and put out an accurate, calm description of the find. The final review had top brass like Mike Murley advocating for something more over the top, but in the end accurate and calm prevailed. But it didn't matter.

Within 24 hours of the release, the world collectively lost its mind. Images of the 2 alien statues were on the front page of every electronic newspaper in the world. The inscriptions on the inside of the temple were analyzed and interpreted by a broad array of highly unqualified would be linguists, even though the press release only showed a minute fraction of what was actually there. Jake, Janice, Jim Stefano and Dr Higgins almost overnight achieved international acclaim , with countless requests for interviews, magazine profiles and marriage requests. Jake's square jawed rugged profile was all over the media and he became the next Indiana Jones, although most people had long since forgotten who that was.

Jamison immediately established a communications blackout for the team, requiring that any contact with anyone on the team first be screened and approved. That also gave Mike Murley the perfect excuse to go center stage and bask in the glory. After a while most media outlets grew tired of his droning on about what a good corporate citizen the Western Consortium was and what had inspired him to have the vision to make this project a reality.

Jamison just watched it all with amusement. Having the big boss endlessly pontificate meant he was happy and a happy boss had less inclination to dish out the occasional ass chewing, so Jamison was happy too. This could have been a real fiasco, but "It looks like it's going to turn out ok," he thought to himself.

Of course, there were also those with a negative slant. Some observed that the aliens bore some resemblance to ostriches. Others were able to tie the whole thing to doomsday in some indecipherable way. Those who believed aliens would someday conquer us were convinced that the pyramid was a signal beacon, calling the invaders to start their conquest. In that regard, the monitoring that SETI had been doing was helpful to debunk that rumor. There were even those convinced that the whole thing was just a charade and would soon be announced as the next Disney theme park.

There was considerable pressure on Jamison and the team to provide someone from the team for interviews. They discussed this in detail and finally settled on Janice. With the opening of the pyramid, at least some of the functions of her technical team were completed. With her stunning good looks, solid academic credentials and calm presentation style, everyone on the leadership team was convinced she would be a great spokesperson. Janice initially wasn't sure, but Jake pointed out that as their spokesperson, she would be in position to stay fully informed about project developments. That argument won her over, and soon she was packing up and getting ready to leave for South Base and then the return to earth.

On her last night at the project, she and Jake met in the project dining area.

Dinner was over and most team members were relaxing in their quarters. "So, I guess this is it, at least for a while." Janice said

"I guess so," Jake replied with just a hint of sadness. "Seems like life just keeps coming up with reasons for us to be in different places."

"Well, it won't be much longer, Jake Mackenzie!"

"How can you be so sure?" Jake asked.

Janice looked around for a second, seeing that no one was nearby and then softly whispered. "Because I love you Jake! And I'm convinced nothing can keep us apart. The last few months have been sweet torture. So close yet unable to kiss or hold each other."

She took his hand and pressed it.

Jake exhaled and also spoke in a low voice. "I love you too my darling. Have known it for a long time. We'll be together soon. I'll call you often."

They both sat for a few moments smiling with shared love and trying to enjoy this last moment they would see each other for a while.

After the initial pyramid entry, most team members were given an opportunity to enter and see it for themselves.

An elaborate network of powerful theatre grade lighting was shipped from Earth and installed in the pyramid and connected on the surface with a powerful solar array and battery station. With that arrangement, the magnificent laser etchings were brought to life. The entire set of wall etchings was photographed in 3D detail, and discussions were under way regarding how best to process all this data.

On the day after his initial entry, Dr Higgins returned. He had had hardly any opportunity to view the dramatic etchings covering the walls. He was surprised how many symbols there were. He recognized something that looked like a star. There were things that looked like gears and levers. There were humanoid figures. And interspersed with objects were characters, apparently some alien language. There was so much. It was overwhelming. He was sure the linguistics experts would be able to make headway on this.

He also realized that in his haste to exit after the first entry, he hadn't really focused in on what the center platform actually contained. He continued to think that the placement suggested that whatever was there was of high importance. When he returned to the central enclosure, he saw now that there was a large circular gleaming metal sculpture suspended on a long cable from above. It was about 4 feet in diameter, precisely placed equidistant from the two etched glass sculptures. Dr Higgins took a picture of this sculpture.

After that, he proceeded to study the objects on the raised platform underneath the sculpture. In the center was a third etched laser image in glass, about 3 feet in diameter . It appeared to be a two dimensional representation of a globe, with a large landmass depicted in the center. That might suggest that the aliens also came from an aquatic planet, he thought to himself. On either sides of the globe were 4 perfectly clear discs, each about 3 inches in diameter. Each disc was mounted on end in what appeared to be a glass holder. That was all there was. They could well be some data storage media, but it didn't really resemble anything in current use. Dr Higgins decided to place these artifacts off limits until a team of experts could examine it.

Within a couple of days, Jake convened a team lead meeting to discuss initial conclusions and next steps.

"So I'd like to start by asking the question: What conclusions and hypothesis can we draw right now concerning the alien race that constructed the pyramid, and why they built it."

Dr Higgins spoke first. "Well, one first observation is that it seems to have been built to last an incredibly long time. The burial on the Moon suggests an effort to protect it from meteor and asteroid strikes. The decision not to build on Earth seems curious and worth exploring. The use of laser etching and keeping the pyramid in lunar vacuum means these writings could probably survive millions of years. If the discs stored at the center of the pyramid turn out in fact to be data storage devices then it would seem they have some story to tell. They weren't trying to hide the pyramid. The obelisk should be seen as a hand raised saying "Hey we're over here." Maybe burying it in the Moon was their way of assuring that it would only be found by a technologically advanced society."

"With regard to the aliens themselves, they seem incredibly humanoid but with clear differences. That's about all I've been able to come up with so far," Dr Higgins stopped talking.

"Do we have any clues how long it's been here?" Jake asked.

Dr Higgins spoke up again. "We've taken a sample from the pyramid wall, just a few milligrams, and are running a uranium thorium lead analysis. The ratios of the various isotopes will give us an indication of its age. We'll have results in about a week."

"What about carbon dating?" Jim Stefano asked.

"That really only has application for things that were once living." Dr Higgins replied.

"So I guess the bottom line is that we really don't know much yet. So where do we go from here?" Jake asked.

Dr Higgins began, "Decoding the inscriptions is key. We have released a full set of high resolution photographs of the pyramid wall etchings to 10 universities worldwide that have ancient language programs. I think we will let them all study the data for a while and then see what any of them have been able to determine."

"The other critical piece are the discs found on the center platform. I've talked to several data experts who have agreed they look a lot like the fused quartz storage devices similar to what we've developed over the last 30 years. They describe it as the go to method if you want to preserve data for a million years. Laser etching in 5 dimensions can make highly concentrated almost indestructible data. "

"Like how concentrated?" Dr Gupta asked.

"Maybe 10 terabytes of data per disc." Dr Higgins answered.

"Is that a lot?" Jim Stefano asked.

"Maybe like 3 libraries of Congress per disc," Dr Higgins said.

They all just sat stunned for a moment

"Wow!"

"So how do we proceed with this part?" Jake asked.

Dr Higgins continued. " We don't know how to read these discs and we don't want to make any mistakes. If we do this right, a whole world of data may open up to us. And if we do it wrong…..". He didn't need to finish the sentence.

The meeting concluded, and Dr Higgins decided to suit up and spend some more time examining the obelisk fragments before they were shipped off to South Base. In the whirlwind of activity they had been left lying adjacent to the archeology building.

He had been thinking about the project and where they went from here. In some ways, he was disappointed the way things had unfolded. True, what they found was drawing worldwide acclaim, but there wasn't any more real archeology to do here. The wall etchings had all been recorded, the processing of the discs would be in the hands of others, so it really seemed like the field work here could be shut down and the archeology team could return to Earth. He was disappointed that they hadn't found real artifacts of the aliens. He also felt like he was missing something. He looked across the lunar plane and suddenly it hit him. He turned and tried to run, which ended up looking like the lunar version of hopscotch. He desuited and hurried to the command rover.

Jake was sitting in the control bay.

"Do you have a minute, Jake?" Dr Higgins asked

"Of course, what's up?" Jake smiled and invited him to sit down.

Dr Higgins took him through his thought process and concluded with; "but then it suddenly hit me. Beyond where we had positioned our waste mound of regolith coming out of the excavations there is another mound I never really paid any attention to. But now it's clear- I'm convinced this is the mound of lunar rock removed by the aliens in building the pyramid. As such, there may be other artifacts, things that may further our understanding of this race. Rather than shut down the archeology team, I'd like permission to spend a few more weeks and sink an exploratory cut through the mound to see what we find."

"It makes sense to me," Jake responded. "I'll need to check with

Jamison but since the project was already slated to run another month, I would think we could do what you're asking. We don't want to shut down the field work prematurely."

Jake rang up Jamison for their regular meeting. He gave Jamison an update on all aspects of the project. He briefed him on Dr Higgins proposal to excavate the mound. He also brought up the topic of starting to shut down project operations and got a surprise from Jamison.

"Believe it or not, but our big boss got so full of himself the other day during an interview with Forbes Magazine, that he made the statement that the pyramid should be preserved and open to the public. It probably would have just faded away, but the head of the Lunar Artifacts Commission must have read the article and the next day he's in the New York Times talking about what a great idea it was, and how the commission was totally on board and yadda yadda yadda. So of course, Mike Murley can't back down now, so you can expect a visit from the Lunar Artifacts Commissioner next week to see the pyramid and talk about turning it into a place the public can visit. I'll have to come along too. I'm sure it's going to be a real dog and pony show."

Jamison continued, "So, I think the SETI and JPL teams can be sent home.

I'm fine with the archeology team staying one more month but that's all. Jim Stefano and his facilities team need to be retained, possibly for several months. I think you need to continue as operations lead at least until this last dig is complete. And I have one more piece of news for you. You've gotten a lot of attention from this project. Murley is convinced you can do no wrong. And frankly I've been impressed too. So after you complete the project, we would like to offer you 6 months of paid leave after which you would assume my position."

This was totally unexpected and Jake had trouble holding down his excitement . "But where are you going?" he asked Jamison.

"I'm getting kicked upstairs," Jamison replied. "Earthside . I can't wait. My wife is thrilled. I've spent way too much time on the Moon. So think it over. Big raise. Major benefits boost. We can talk more about the details later," Jamison signed off.

Jake sat in the control bay and stared at the monitors without really seeing them. Things had been moving so fast lately it was hard to keep up. A few months ago he was just a lunar geologist and now he was being offered what was a big promotion. He had to sort it all out. If he took this job, did that mean that his relationship with Janice would just continue to languish? What about his PhD. Hard to imagine trying to do Jamison's job and completing his thesis.

But no time to rest right now. The project still demanded his full attention. Dr Higgins wanted to meet to discuss the quartz discs.

Dr Higgins began " I've had detailed discussions with a group of professors from the University of Southampton who have been leading researchers in highly compressed data storage on fused quartz. We've come up with a plan to have one of the professors brought up on the lunar shuttle. We would be required to transport the disks to South Base. We have the appropriate instrumentation there for this researcher to be able to examine the discs. It's not a certainty, but he might be able to learn enough to figure out how to read the disks."

"Can we do that safely?" Jake asked.

Dr Higgins continued "I think we can. We would construct a padded temperature controlled vacuum chamber in which to transport the discs, so they would remain in the same atmosphere that they're currently in. I think with that precaution, we can be sure they don't degrade in any way."

"We've talked about how these discs may be the single most important thing found on the project, so we don't want to take any excessive risks. Could we send half of them and keep the other half?" Jake asked.

"Well if we do that, it may delay getting the data contained on them out to researchers. The professor coming up may try to build an actual reader and if he succeeds then all of the discs could be read," Dr Higgins said.

"OK, it's your call," Jake replied.

That night, Jake called Janice. "My darling."

"Jake!" The excitement in her voice sent a thrill through him.

"So how is the star of stage, screen and television." He asked.

"Oh Jake, it's just been a whirlwind. People just can't get enough. I'm on three late night talk shows this week, plus testifying at a congressional hearing next week and filming a promo with the SETI Institute. I guess their private funding has skyrocketed. After that I'm trying to get back to Palo Alto. If I don't reach some kind of agreement, my classes next semester may get cancelled. And week after next, I'm actually going to meet the President. Just a foto op I think." Janice finally took a breath.

"And how are you Jake?" All of his developments spilled out in much the same way Janice went right to the issue confronting Jake "But if you take Jamison's position you'll put your PhD in jeopardy and you'll be on the Moon even more."

"I know, I know." He replied. "But 6 months just hanging out with you could be heavenly."

"Yes, that would be nice," Janice said softly.

Josh Friedman was sitting at his desk in the Oriental Institute in Chicago. He was a PhD whose thesis was on decoding ancient Sumarian language. Long ago he had studied under the great Michael Civil, renowned in his day as the premier expert in the Sumarian language. But Michael was long dead now and Josh was near retirement. He had been one of a number of people who had received photographs of the pyramid etchings and he just couldn't put them down. He was convinced that the pyramid walls constituted one big dictionary with many examples of recognizable symbols and something that resembled text. But so far any recognizable pattern had eluded him. People who don't study languages didn't understand all the myriad of ways ideas could be strung together in a language. Left to right, right to left, top to bottom, symbols in a box. Languages that have simple morphology tend to have more complicated syntax and periphrastic structures. Polysynthetic languages like many American Indian languages are difficult because they have very complex morphology. English and Chinese are difficult because they have complex syntax and many lexical phrases.

He continued looking for some recognizable pattern. Finally, he decided to take a step back and think about what others have come up with as a method to communicate with extraterrestrials. He reviewed the following citation:

Lincos (an abbreviation of the Latin phrase *lingua cosmica*) is a constructed language first described in 1960 by Dr. Hans Freudenthal in his book *Lincos: Design of a Language for Cosmic Intercourse, Part 1*. It is a language designed to be understandable by any possible intelligent extraterrestrial life form, for use in interstellar radio transmissions.[1] Freudenthal considered that such a language should be easily understood by beings not acquainted with any Earthling syntax or language. Lincos was designed to be capable of encapsulating "the whole bulk of our knowledge"(Wikipedia) Josh thought to himself "Lincos was a language developed with the expectation that it would have to be transmitted on a radio telescope. The language starts out teaching numbers, then mathematical functions and then jumps into concepts of time which could be tied to signal pulses.The third section is perhaps the most complex, and attempts to convey the concepts and language necessary to describe behavior and conversation between individuals. So let's see if they've tried to teach us their language."

After a number of misstarts, Josh finally found a pattern in the wall etchings that appeared to be conveying basic numbers. Rows of dots next to single characters he decided to interpret as a translation of the aliens numerical characters. Josh felt a surge of excitement. Maybe, just maybe, the aliens had left us their own version of Lincos. In another section, the characters that appeared to be numbers appeared in rows that could be mathematical expressions. He had to try different translations of the numerical operators until he had an equation that worked. "OK, now let's try plugging that in over here." He said to no one in particular. "Oh my god, it worked!" Now Josh had identified the alien symbols for + and - and =. Another line opened up the operators for < and >.

Having their first few numbers was a start, but he needed more. Did the aliens use base 10 or something else? He had encountered what he thought might be larger numbers but the pattern didn't make sense. He was sitting looking at the picture of the alien statues online, when he had an idea. He clicked on the picture and expanded it and started counting. "First the hands: One, two, three, four. Now the feet one, two, three, four". He went back to the etching photos. Base 8. He tried reworking his numbers in base 8 and it worked. Now he felt confident he could identify numbers at least into the hundreds.

Ok, he thought to himself "what would they try to teach us next?"

122

Suddenly, it hit him. "Chemistry!"

The periodic table was a universal truth. He pulled an old well worn copy of the periodic table. So how could they tell us about chemistry. Josh found several papers that had explored the idea of chemistry as a "lingus universalis."One proposal focused on transmitting the emission spectra of certain key elements including hydrogen, helium, carbon, oxygen, magnesium. These would alert an alien observer that we were discussing chemistry. Josh had probably never looked at an elemental emission spectra in his whole life, but after a short while, he thought he understood. "So did you guys leave us any spectra?" Josh felt a little foolish . It seemed a little preposterous.

He combed through the photos of the etchings. He was about to move on when "Holy shit" he exclaimed. That definitely looked like a spectra. He took out the spectra he had printed out and one by one held them up beside the photo. "That's definitely magnesium!" He started looking for more. These spectra had not captured his attention before this. Now in quick succession he found carbon and hydrogen. There were several others that he couldn't identify. That forced a couple hour delay while he printed out emission spectra for some 40 odd elements. Soon he had identified spectra for calcium, zinc and lead. Which meant he now knew what the alien names for these elements were. Armed with these names and atomic numbers, Josh soon found the entire periodic table listed in the pyramid etchings, each element identified by its atomic number. Joshes head was reeling. "Oh my god, what are you going to teach me next?"

Josh struggled here. Were the aliens a carbon based life form and might move on to organic chemistry? Maybe physics? Well, certainly states of matter were something that any species would recognize. That one had him searching images for almost an hour. Suddenly he was sure this was it. A container shape with an irregular object on bottom, a line across the middle and alien text near the irregular object and under and over the line across the middle. Josh felt a rush of adrenaline "So now you've taught me what you call a solid, a liquid and a gas ! Ok guys, we're on a roll ! What's next ?"

He continued to study the photos, hoping for some other inspiration. Finally, he noticed a circle that had a formula inside. He recognized the elements described here. The formula basically showed 2 hydrogen atoms combining to form 2 helium atoms combining to form 2 beryllium atoms.

Josh wasn't much of a chemist but he looked it up and discovered it was the basic reaction that the sun and every star used via nuclear fusion to create light and heat. So now they've communicated their formula for fusion. Running from the circle was a line that led to a smaller circle along with a number along the vector and another number at the small circle.

Josh thought about continuing, but he knew that what he had already found was enough. With this info in the hands of the global team of linguists maybe with the help of a few chemists and physicists they would have what was needed to come close to a full translation.

He sat down and slowly documented his steps, with images from the vault and some discussion of his process. This wasn't going to be a peer reviewed paper, so niceties were cast aside in the interest of speed and clarity. He worked late into the night and finally sent off his findings to the linguistic working group.

When he woke up late morning, he checked his email and was almost surprised at the large number of responses. The Asian team members had seen it and began analyzing it right away. The European members, 6 hours ahead had also dived into it. There were lots of congratulations and Josh felt gratified that he had made a contribution.

Over the next few days, the global team made great strides. They confirmed that the etchings delved in a big way into organic chemistry, suggesting the aliens were also a carbon based life form. Physics content gave us the alien vocabulary for time and distance and even the speed of light. A variety of chemical reactions provided the translators with a rich dictionary of chemistry nomenclature.

Most interestingly was when a couple of electrical engineers were consulted, it appeared that the etchings contained specific instructions for construction of a laser high speed reader. That section was going to require some detailed analysis, but it provided hope that the key to actually reading the fused quartz discs was almost in their grasp.

Just as the lunar team hadn't really anticipated the global response, Josh was overwhelmed with press contacts, interview requests, and, yes, even a couple marriage proposals. He turned down virtually everything. He just wanted to get back to those Sumarian texts he had been working on.

Dr Higgins had also received Josh's email. He was gratified to see the progress that was being made. When he later saw the comments of the 2 electrical engineers, he immediately forwarded it to the professors at Southampton University. He wanted to be sure they were kept abreast of anything that might facilitate designing a disc reader. He called them later that day to verify that Professor Bartlett was on track to make the lunar shuttle next week. The thought that they might soon be reading the discs filled him with anticipation. So much of archeology focused on drawing big conclusions from the most scanty of information. The idea that soon they might be swimming in *"terabytes of data"* left him almost giddy.

Chapter Ten

Jake was as busy as ever. Now that things were slowing down some with the dig, he had to turn back to the mining operation and make sure things kept moving along. After completing the entire core sampling study, the results that came back indicated a rich vein of both lanthanides and scandium. A mining site plan was worked out and construction begun on an ore processing facility. The ore removed from the mines would be pulverized , then subjected to a froth floatation process, then treated with hydrochloric acid and then roasted in a kiln. The process was similar to processing on earth, just done in closed processes. Jim Stefano was heavily involved in this construction phase, so between continuing to oversee the pyramid facilities and this project, he had a lot on his plate, too. Work had begun sinking the first mine shafts and there was a constant bustle of activity.

The SETI and JPL team members had left after Jake organized a proper send off for them. He surprised them all with one week passes to South Base resort facilities as an appreciation of their work. Everyone who had worked on the project felt proud of their discovery and looked forward to ongoing revelations coming out of the project.

Early one morning, Dr Higgins burst into the control rover where Jake was at work.

"Jake, I just got the results of the uranium thorium lead test I ran a couple of weeks ago on the pyramid!" Dr Higgins said, obviously a little wound up. Jake enjoyed the fact that he and Jim had developed a friendship and no longer used titles.

"So what did you find out," Jake asked.

"I'm a little stunned by the results. The test says that the pyramid is 300 million years old." "What? No way! Is that possible?" Jake couldn't believe it.

"Well, you remember I said it looked like the pyramid was designed to last a long time. I've checked the data and talked to the analyst. I think it's most likely correct. The ratios of the various decay products are consistent."

"So it just heightens the mystery about why it was left here in the first place," Jake said.

"It does," Jim agreed.

Work continued on Earth to fully translate the "dictionary" that the aliens had left on the pyramid walls.

A team of engineers had developed what they believed was a working laser reader that they hoped would be able to read the fused quartz discs. The prototype was being sent on the next lunar shuttle and would arrive at the same time as Professor Bartlett from Southampton University. If his examination of both the discs and the reader design suggested a high chance of success, then he would proceed with reading the discs.

The linguistics working group had met at least twice and refined their translation of the dictionary. They all agreed that if the data discs could be read, they expected to be able to achieve at least a 75 or 80 percent translation rate, and that would just improve with time. There was much speculation about what the discs might reveal. The alien technology that had built the pyramid was on a par with modern earth technology but not demonstrably superior, except of course for what appeared to be a more advanced space program.

The age of the pyramid was a hard data point to assimilate. To think that it had been waiting on the moon since before the age of dinosaurs was impressive and depressing all at the same time. People had somehow had this vision that they might one day meet this race whose glass etched smiling ambassadors had become known around the world but now it seemed more likely that these alien visitors had long since passed on to extinction. Certainly the fact that they hadn't been back in 300 million years argued strongly for this view.

Dr Higgins and his archeology team had been busy, trying to do their best in these last 30 days to run a trench through what they now affectionately called the slag pile. Ground penetrating radar hadn't revealed anything, but Dr Higgins wasn't surprised by that. This was after all just a waste pile.

They found impressions of rock cutouts showing where the aliens had cut back the lunar bedrock. There were small fragments of the tungsten alloy found, bits of debris as the pyramid was assembled. Some very small bits of what might have been the cutting tools used on the pyramid were found. Dr Higgins sent these off for analysis since there was much interest in how the aliens shaped and cut this super hard alloy. There was much excitement one afternoon when they found a grommet, made from some copper alloy. Initially it was feared that it had come off of someone's space suit, but in the end is was deemed a genuine artifact, maybe a piece off the suit of an ancient astronaut. That was all they found. Dr Higgins felt gratified that they had done this work. First, it felt like real archeology and secondly, he felt they had now gleaned all that was here and he could shut down the project with no regrets.

Jake wasn't looking forward to the next several days. The dog and pony show was about to begin. There was added stress when it was revealed that Mike Murley himself was coming. After blurting out the "pyramid as public space" idea, he had bought in 100% and wanted to be sure that no one forgot whose idea it was. Starting tomorrow, Murley, James Monroe, the head of the Lunar Artifacts Commission, and Jamison would be here along with assistants and press representatives.

Jake was concerned first and foremost about safety. He needed to get these folks in and out without a scratch. Secondly, he hoped the planning wouldn't get too elaborate. He was trying to wind down the pyramid project, and a sudden requirement to change or upgrade facilities could through a wrench in his plans. He and Jim Stefano reviewed the visit plans.

"Murley, Monroe and Jamison will be staying in the large individual suites?" Jake asked

"Affirmative," Jim answered.

"Space suits cleaned and size appropriate are ready for all delegation members?"

"Affirmative."

"You have crew members ready to accompany each delegation member down the man lift?"

"Affirmative."

"The pyramid lighting system backup power source has been tested?"
"Yes sir."

"Each of your men will be carrying hand torches as backup?"

"Affirmative."

"Backup Oxygen cylinders will be placed at the bottom of the entry shaft?" "Yes sir."

"The cook is preparing a gourmet steak dinner for the entire delegation?"

" Yes sir, with fresh strawberries and whipped cream."

Jake turned to Jim and laughed "You are just the best. Thanks for putting up with my hysterical manager grilling."

"Hey Chief, if it makes you feel better, that's a good thing."

"I won't even dare to ask how you pulled off the strawberries thing."

" Good idea, Jake!"

The next morning, Jake got a radio transmission that the delegation rover was about 10 minutes out. He checked a couple of final items, then went to wait at the housing facility. The rover pulled up and the hydraulic air lock device moved slowly forward and mated with the rover hatchway. A burst of air pressure confirmed air tight seal, and the rover hatchway was opened. They had rushed to install this new feature so their visitors wouldn't be compelled to immediately don space suits.

Jake greeted his visitors, greeting each by name. "Welcome to the First Encounter Project. It's a pleasure to meet you in person, Dr Murley."

"Welcome. Dr. Monroe I've read often about your work with the

Lunar Artifacts Commission."

"Hello Carl. Good to see you again."

The visitors all came in along with their aides.

Jake had made arrangements for liquid refreshments. Members of the archeology team had been invited. Everyone mingled and the event seemed to be going smoothly.

At dinner, Jake tapped on his glass a few times and stood up. "I just want to take a moment to welcome our distinguished guests."

The room had been buzzing, but after a short time everyone quieted down and looked at him expectantly

"Dr. Monroe, I had the personal pleasure of visiting Tranquility Base last year. I think the work of the Commission is vital to preserving the legacy of our space program and I'm honored that you're here to see the results of our project. Dr Murley, thank you for joining us here. It was your vision that made this project a reality and it is an honor to be able to show you the results of that vision. Mr Jamison, I don't need to introduce you to our find. As project leader you've been here every step of the way. I'd also like to take a second to talk about the team that made this all possible. Many of them have already headed back to Earth, but I'd like Dr. Higgins, the head of our archeology team, and Jim Stefano, in charge of facilities, to stand."

Both men stood up, looking a little hesitant.

"Both of these men played absolutely key roles on the project and I'd like to ask that you give them a hand."

The archeology team and the facilities personnel both hooted and clapped in appreciation and both men smiled and sat back down.

"I'd also like to thank Major Atkins for the security detail provided by the US Space Force. Having his troopers guarding our site perimeter was very reassuring."

Major Atkins rose and acknowledged the applause.

"Tomorrow at 0900 we'll get started with the site tour. Just a reminder that safety is our top priority here, so the visitor groups will be broken down into two person teams, each accompanied by one of the facilities personnel. Now our facilities personnel will escort you to your quarters."

Jake was about 90% sure that the evening wouldn't end just yet. High level execs like Dr Murley couldn't let a chance go by to show they were in charge.

Dr Murley tapped on his glass a few times and then stood up. "Thank you, Mr Mackenzie, the arrangements are very satisfactory and Dr Monroe and I are looking forward to tomorrow. As an old mining guy, first on Earth and now the Moon, I never expected at some point in my career to oversee the first contact in recorded history with an alien race. But that's what has happened. Dr Monroe and I are agreed that this event needs to be treated in a manner befitting its importance. Therefore, it is my great pleasure to announce that the Western Consortium is surrendering the mineral rights to the pyramid site and recommending that this property be annexed by the Lunar Artifacts Commission and established as a public trust, where members of the worldwide public will be able to visit and see this remarkable find. Furthermore, the Western Consortium is making a first donation of $50 million dollars to be used for the development of this site. Dr Monroe, I yield the floor to you."

As soon as it became clear that the evening was turning into a major news event, the press representatives started making frantic notes; they knew this was going to light up the global news networks.

Next Dr Monroe stood up. "Thank you Dr Murley. On behalf of the Lunar Artifacts Commission, I want to thank the Western Consortium for this historic gift. I believe some day this site will become a prominent part of our global heritage, on a par with Tranquility Base and even the US national parks. Per our discussions, we are looking at establishing a lunar hotel here, with a dome enclosure and facilities to eventually accommodate 5,000 visitors per year. Thank you."

Dr Monroe sat down and there was sustained applause from the room. Project team members felt pride that they had been a part of this and that they had the opportunity to be present for the big announcement.

Jake was a little stunned. He sought out Jamison and sat down next to him.

"You're going to do fine in management Jake. It's clear you've grasped the key point already,"Jamison smiled.

"Really? What is it?"

"Always stroke the big boss first," Jamison laughed.

"Well I'm a little shocked by the announcement! What happens to our mining operation?"

"All worked out." Jamison replied. "We surrender mining rights to this little parcel where the pyramid is located, but in return we're getting expedited mining approval for the rest of our claim. Access to this future lunar artifacts site will be carved out of the eastern end of our claim and our mining activity is for the most part unaffected. Never underestimate Mike Murley. He can appear generous in a situation like this, but he never loses sight of his business priorities."

The next morning, the tours for their VIP visitors occurred without a hitch.

Jake could envision this as a place that many people would come to see. The sight of the illuminated etched glass statues of the aliens and the magnificent etchings covering every wall would be an unforgettable experience.

Drs. Murley and Monroe chattered away while they were in the pyramid. It sounded like the planning for this new facility was already taking shape. The housing units currently here would be replaced by the new hotel and dome. The current crude shafts would be replaced by real elevators and a breathable atmosphere would be introduced into the pyramid, so visitors could come here and see it without the hindrance of a space suit.

Jake made a note to talk to Dr Higgins about how they could assess whether introduction of an atmosphere in the pyramid could potentially damage any of the contents.

Later that day, Jake got a call from Janice.

"Hello, my darling! How are you?" Janice spoke warmly.

"I'm terrific, except for missing you constantly!" Jake replied.

" I just wanted you to know that Mike Murley's announcement has gone off like a bomb down here. Things had started to quiet down here and now this has the pyramid back on the front pages. I'm working with our pr folks to draft a concept drawing that will depict what the Pyramid Hotel will look like. I think I'm probably going to end up doing another round on the talk shows."

"So are you going to end up so famous that some movie star courts you and wins your hand?" Jake smiled and winked.

"Not likely since I'm already hooked up with one of the most famous people on the planet. I think you have no idea, since you've been sheltered from all the media hype. When you get back to Earth, I seriously doubt you'll be able to go to a restaurant without being swarmed by swooning females and amateur archeologists," Janice smiled back.

Jake chatted with Janice a few more minutes and then signed off. Janice was right of course. He had been sheltered and he had no idea. He'd never thought about being famous before and he wasn't sure he liked the sound of it.

Later that day, Jake bid a fond farewell to his visitors. He was relieved that the visit was over and had gone well.

Meanwhile at South Base, Dr Theodore Bartlett had arrived. He was a professor of electrical engineering at Southampton University and one of the acknowledged experts in the field of super dense 5 dimensional laser etching. He was part of a research team trying to develop the technology that would provide long term stable data storage. In their work with fused quartz crystals, they believed they had something that could provide stable data storage for perhaps thousands of years. People had bemoaned the fact that the age of digitalization had produced a seemingly endless stream of rapidly obsolete technology. Historians asked whether any of the history and technology of our modern society could ever be preserved in a really long term way.

Dr Bartlett thought to himself, "And won't it be almost ironic if the first proof of concept turns out to have been produced by an alien society?"

He was excited with the progress that had come out of the engineering group working to decode the technical messages contained in the pyramid etchings. It appeared they had found a waveform, that conformed with the pulse of a

CO_2 laser. If they could tune the laser to conform to the 5 dimensional data array he expected to find, they could be on the verge of unlocking a treasure trove unlike anything ever experienced by man.

Dr Bartlett hadn't been on the moon before. He had expected it to be more difficult and he was pleasantly surprised with the South Base amenities.

He visited the South Base analytical lab facility of the Western Consortium and was pleased to see that they had procured the laser setup he had sent them specs for. He communicated with Dr Higgins to let him know he was ready to receive the alien discs. He had reviewed in detail the handling procedures that would be followed. He felt confidant in their chances of success.

Back at the project site, Jake and Dr Higgins were meeting with Major Atkins about transporting the discs to South Base.

"So I've confirmed Prof Bartlett has arrived at South Base. He has reviewed the laser reader setup he requested and is satisfied with the result. He indicates he is ready to receive the discs." Dr Higgins reported.

Major Atkins spoke next. "As we've discussed, we're planning to assign one of our military rovers along with two of my troopers to transport the discs back to South Base. Dr Higgins has one of his archeologists who will accompany them and make sure the storage conditions are properly maintained."

" Yes, I'm planning on sending Flaherty. After the incident with his spacesuit in the shaft, he's seemed to remain a little skittish about space suit work, I think deploying him back to Earth now is probably a good idea." Dr Higgins said.

Jake brought the meeting to an end. "Ok, we've been over this a lot. I think we're good to go. Go ahead and schedule the departure for tomorrow morning." But of course, morning was a term that suggested sunlight rising over the horizon, but at this point they were in the middle of the two week lunar night.

The next morning, Jake was watching from the control rover as the 2 small vacuum boxes were loaded onto the military rover. Dr Higgins and Major Atkins were out in their suits supervising. It only took a few minutes. Bob Flaherty was there, looking fine and not seeming to have any suit issues. Major Atkins troopers gave a salute, sealed up the hatch, and in a couple of minutes their rover had disappeared into the lunar night with the powerful headlights fading from sight.

Jake had a meeting scheduled with Dr Higgins and Jim Stefano to go over the issues associated with turning over the project to an engineering company whose charge would be to transform this scientific endeavor into a public facility.

Dr Higgins started. "I believe the question of what will occur if an atmosphere is introduced into the pyramid is significant. Oxidation could darken the etchings. We don't know enough about the composition of the statues to know how they'll react. I think someone has to agree to fund a study to find out how the pyramid will respond. I also think that the slag mound where we've been digging for artifacts should be protected for any future archeological inquiries that could occur.

Jake responded "Those are both excellent points . I'm putting together a communication to Dr Murley and I'll be sure to stress both of these points." Jim Stefano spoke next. "I'm not sure there has been adequate consideration of what it's going to be like having a theme park next to an operating mining facility. While I'll grant you that the ore refinement processes are closed systems, there are still going to be ore waste settling ponds and tailing piles. Not sure if the Kumbayah moment for pyramid visitors will be ruined by industrial blight on the horizon."

Jake laughed. "I think if I could capture your phraseology, management would get the picture. Another excellent point."

"I also have a question about whether there are adequate reserves of lunar water to support a dome atmosphere. The location of South Base and a key to its success was the fact that it's located next to the largest H_2O reserves on the entire Moon. Electrolysis of the water produces oxygen for breathing and hydrogen for fuel. I'm not convinced we can find enough water and I don't think transporting it from South Base is viable either.

"Ok, thanks to both of you. Great points I will pass on"

Jake returned to his sleeping quarters and spent some time going over paperwork. Despite being protected from the broader media by a blackout, he still found himself receiving a lot of inquiries. Magazine article requests, interview questions, and so on.

He closed his eyes and drifted off for a moment.

When he opened his eyes, Jim Stefano was standing in front of him, looking very serious and not his usual sardonic self.

"Jake, we have a problem."

"The rover to South Base is overdue."

Jake was instantly awake. "Have you checked their position?"

"Yes, they are sitting about five hours out from South Base, in the area of some of that rough terrain around the Schroedinger crater. They stopped moving two hours ago. They aren't responding to any signals. We don't know what has happened." Jim Stefano reported.

"What should we do," Jake asked.

"South Base emergency crews can get there faster than we can. I recommend we call them in."

" Ok, please go ahead," Jake said. "I think we should mobilize a rover and head there regardless."

"I agree," Jim Stefano said.

Within 20 minutes , they had mobilized a rover. Dr Higgins insisted on coming also. Major Atkins joined them since the mission had been under the control of his men.

They had about a 15 hour ride at top speed to get to the vehicle's last known position.   Jim Stefano confirmed that South Base emergency crews were responding.

Jake felt a feeling of dread that he couldn't shake off. Having a vehicle go completely silent was virtually unknown. The rovers had primary and backup communication channels. One way or another the crew should have been able to reach them.

When they had been traveling for about 5 hours, Jim Stefano got a call. As Jake watched him, he could see the color leave his face. He didn't say anything until he finally ended with. "Ok thank you, we'll be there in about 10 hours."

Jim turned, "The emergency crew arrived. There were three fatalities, no survivors. The South Base police have been summoned."

"Oh my god!" Jake said. "What happened?"

"It appears all three crew members were murdered," Jim said quietly. "No other details at this time."

No one knew what to say. Crime on the Moon was so unusual that one hardly ever thought about it. Just surviving on the Moon presented so many daily challenges, that crime was just not a viable option.

So all they could do was wait to see what on earth had happened.

Far off before they ever arrived, they could see the flashing lights of the emergency vehicles. There was almost an expectation to hear a wailing siren, but of course there was none.

Finally they arrived. In front of them they could see the backside of the military rover and the emergency vehicles. They all suited up and went out. They first encountered the emergency response battalion chief.

"It looks like your men were ambushed. Both of the troopers were taken out immediately by high powered rifle shots through the rover windshield. The third man just died from sudden vacuum exposure when the front windshield was blown out. The door to the rover was open and there are tracks leading from it to another vehicle. That's all we have at this point." the battalion commander concluded. "We've never seen anything like it."

The three men walked around to the front of the rover and were immediately confronted with this horrific crime scene. Both troopers were still buckled in. It looked like they never had any chance to respond or protect themselves.

Jake had already decided that he knew what was coming next, and he was right. They walked around to the open hatchway where they could see the footprints of the intruders. Jake and the others took care not to enter what was now officially a crime scene. The space where the 2 vacuum boxes had been sitting was now empty. The entire collection of alien discs had been taken. They carefully entered the rover and found the body of Flaherty. Jake wasn't sure why but he felt a particular pang of guilt for having sent this poor man to his death. His last act had been to once again struggle with a space suit.

They were asked by the battalion chief to wait. The South Base police department was responding and arrived within 20 minutes or so. The police inspector interviewed each of them. He couldn't prevent himself from a startled look when he was told what had been taken. Everyone knew about the discs and now he found himself embroiled in the crime of the century.

Jake was really at a loss as to what he should do. Should they try to get the police lieutenant to keep a lid on this news? Jake decided there was no way to stop the news getting out. He immediately contacted Jamison and told him what had happened. Jamison was stunned. He immediately got in touch with Western Consortium senior management and notified them.

Jake left it to Major Atkins to notify next of kin for the troopers. Dr Higgins insisted on calling Flaherty's family. Jake was present during the call and he could see that Dr Higgins was having a difficult time maintaining his composure. So was Jake. Nothing about this project had ever centered on good vs evil or life vs death. Sure, people's safety was always a concern but that was something within their power to manage.

After the police inspector finished with them, the three men started the long ride back to the pyramid. No one really talked much. All were too affected by the events to know what to say.

Chapter Eleven

Once they arrived back at the dig site, Jake immediately summoned all of the project personnel and briefed them on what had happened. No one could believe it.

One of the archeologists raised a hand "So every single one of the quartz discs has been lost, is that correct?"

"I'm afraid so," Jake replied. "We just didn't anticipate that this could happen."

Jake returned to his office. He saw that he had received a call from a Lieutenant Blake. Jake dialed him up immediately.

"Thanks for returning my call, Mr Mackenzie . I'm special agent Blake with the FBI. I'm based in our office at South Base. We'd like to come out and see you to get more details on this crime."

"Of course," Jake replied. "We can provide you with sleeping accommodations here if necessary. How many of you will be coming?"

"Thank you, that would be most helpful. It would just be myself and special agent Rasmussen. We plan on leaving right away, so I guess we can be there in about 20 hours" Agent Blake said.

"Is there anything I need to prep for your visit?" Jake asked.

"Yes, we'll want to look at the personnel records for everyone on the project and interview anyone who was involved in preparing the quartz discs for shipment to South Base," Agent Blake responded.

"Ok, we'll start putting that together," Jake responded.

Jake signed off and sat staring at the monitor. It never occurred to him that anyone on the project might have played a role in this. But clearly the FBI inquiry wasn't ruling that out.

As he sat there, another call came in. He saw it was Dr Murley. He dreaded taking this call.

"Murley here. So how the hell did this happen, Jake? Where was our Space Force security?"

Jake tried to respond calmly and deliberately. "We just didn't anticipate the threat. I reviewed the transportation plan with our military liaison and signed off on it. So I take full responsibility. "

"Didn't anyone consider not sending all the discs at one time. Seems like a pretty basic precaution," Murley continued.

"Yes sir, we did consider it and decided to send them all to expedite the disc reading work. As I said, we failed to recognize the threat level," Jake said quietly.

"Well heads are going to roll over this. I just need to decide whose," Murley signed off abruptly.

Jake pulled up online news sources. As expected, the theft was now a worldwide sensation. There was lots of speculation about who had done it and what their motives were. Some assumed a ransom demand was imminent. Others guessed that the thieves would seek to pedal the discs on the black market. One editorial comment opined that the thieves had been premature in taking them, since no one knew what the discs contained. He phrased it as "May just be alien home movies."

Jake learned a few details that he hadn't seen before. The South Base police reported they had tracked a rover from the crime scene to a point several hundred miles to the north. Units sent there found the unit abandoned with no real clues found. The rover had been taken from one of the South Base rental agencies. There were signs of another vehicle leaving that scene, but no electronic record, indicating the criminals had disabled the transponder for the getaway vehicle. Satellite surveillance had not shown any visible signs of the vehicle. One satellite's infrared trace briefly showed a hot spot, but on subsequent passes of the satellite, that

140

had disappeared. Authorities had launched greatly tightened inspections on all vessels headed earthside, but finding the discs in this way was on a par with finding the proverbial haystack needle.

Dr Higgins called Dr Bartlett at South Base and broke the news to him. They considered having him remain on the moon a while, but after discussion decided he should just head back to Earth. Both scientists couldn't hide their bitter disappointment in losing the artifacts of the century.

Meanwhile, somewhere on the steppes of Kazakhstan, Dmitri was holding a fused quartz disc up to the light. "I don't really see anything. What if they just contain nichego takogo" he said to no one in particular.

Ivan replied, "Well, if they are empty, then we're going to be on the hook for 500,000 rubles to pay off the lunar crew."

Dmitri and Ivan were ex FSB agents. They had been players in the Russian security apparatus up until 2050, when the UN in conjunction with NATO, invaded Russia and established a military government. After almost 130 years of Russia being the aggressor, the rogue nation, the endless supplier of bad guys, the world had had enough. Democratic reforms including the rule of law were established and slowly and systematically the Russian people were shown what democracy actually felt like. While the oligarchs resisted this all with great tenacity, they were overmatched and one by one found their way into prison or legal enterprises.

This became known as the golden age of Russia. A people known for the arts, for intellectual prowess, for chess grandmasters, for a world leading space program found themselves without an oppressor. No tsar, no communist party boss, no new Vladimir Putin.

The people flourished in this new environment, and over a 20 year period their economy exploded. A strong middle class developed in Russia and taught a whole generation that hard work brought rewards and that stealing wasn't necessary. The occupation forces gradually withdrew, and in 2060, Russia was once again a free and independent country, on the road to world leadership and a full and welcomed member in the brotherhood of nations.

Dmitri and Ivan were remnants of this earlier time and had never been able to adjust to the new reality. In their world, success came from doing bad things for people with money, or extorting protection money from legitimate businesses or roughing up those who fought for individual liberty.

It had gotten significantly more difficult to ply their trade once Russia began systematically rooting out corruption. In a world of seemingly bottomless reservoirs of data, hiding crime became more difficult. Cash became fully traceable with every legitimate transaction including the serial numbers of the cash. People still tried to launder money, but as soon as the first legitimate transaction occurred with any cash, it became visible and traceable.

Thanks mainly to the Chinese, facial recognition software had advanced continuously to the point that virtually anyone who showed their face in public would be found.

Databases of criminals had been fully integrated globally, so committing a crime and then jetting off to a remote corner of the globe just didn't work anymore.

But bad guys are resourceful too. Dmitri had become convinced that the pyramid find was a potential gold mine, and he immediately began thinking about how to cash in. He understood that law enforcement around the globe would be pursuing them relentlessly and so he planned carefully. He had told the crew on the moon that staged the abduction not to hurt anyone but "В тихом омуте черти водятся". Too bad about the soldiers and archeologist.

So how to cash in and get away?

He set up a projector screen and donned a rubber mask, one he believed in English speaking countries was known as "Bozo the clown"

He practiced his speech several times using the voice masking software, which he believed totally canceled out his Russian accent. Finally he was satisfied and turned on the video camera.

"My fellow citizens, I am sending this to you to let you know that I have come into possession of certain little things I think you may wants." He held up one of the fused quartz discs. "My little friend here has several other friends and I am here to help get these little friends back to their mommy. But I have to warn you that my friend (camera pans to Ivan, also masked, holding a hammer) doesn't like my little friends and wants to smash them to tiny pieces. So I will send you soon what you should do for getting your little friends back."

Dmitri spoke no English and had put together what sounded to him like a well composed ransom demand using his Russian English dictionary but of course it just sounded like a demand from a five year old.

He stopped the camera and then uploaded the video to his computer. He then emailed the video to an address in Buenos Aires. There it would automatically be forwarded three more times, making it virtually untraceable. Dmitri wasn't good at English, but he excelled at subterfuge. The final step would be to send the email to Jacob Mackenzie. He had read about the young geologist leading the pyramid project, and already had decided that Jake should play the role of Dmitri when the movie came out.

Of course, Dmitri had no way of knowing that emailing Jake directly wasn't possible. The pr team member responsible for deciding which emails actually went to Jake at first thought the video was a joke. But he finally decided to forward it on to Jake with a cc to Agent Blake at the lunar FBI office.

Meanwhile Agent Blake had arrived with his colleague at the dig site. Initially Jake met with them alone. He was dismayed to sense that the agents regarded everyone at the dig including himself as possible aiders or abettors in the crime. He hadn't even considered that possibility but the agents made clear that they were going to take a close look at everyone.

"I'm sorry, but I had never even considered the notion that one of my people might be involved in this. Is there something that points in that direction?" Jake asked.

"Just the precision with which the attack was carried off. The attackers knew right where to wait in ambush and they knew that the cargo was in transit. It seems like they were tipped off." Agent Blake responded.

"There were a number of people at South Base who knew the goods were coming. So I'm not saying you're wrong to look here, but a tip off could also have come from one of those folks." Jake commented.

As Jake was talking, he saw that an email had arrived for him. He didn't recognize the sender and clicked on it.

As soon as he saw the clown mask, he told the two agents "You have to see this. I think maybe I've been contacted."All three of them watched the video several times.

"Did that look like one of the fused quartz discs? " Agent Blake asked.

"I think it did, but let me get Dr Higgins in here. He's worked more closely with the discs."

Dr Higgins watched the video and immediately confirmed that it looked like it was legitimate.

He noticed one feature on the video that none of them had noted. "Yeah that's definitely one of the discs."

Agents Blake's and Rasmussen decided to forego any more interviews for the moment so they could get the FBI forensics team looking at the email.

"Please call us immediately if another email comes in." Agent Blake said as they were leaving.

"Of course." Jake replied.

After they left, Dr Higgins came back in.

" Oh my god, did you see that guy handling the discs. No vacuum, no gloves, I hope they're not already destroyed." Dr Higgins looked miserable.

Jake commiserated for a few minutes and then Dr Higgins left.

As he was starting to assemble the data requested by the FBI, his phone rang. Jake saw it was Janice.

"My love, are you ok?" She asked at once.

"I'm pretty blue." Jake replied. "This is one of those times when being in charge doesn't seem so great."

"When I heard the news I was frantic. First reports just told us there were fatalities but I had no way of knowing whether you were ok." Janice said tearfully.

"When are you headed back to Earth, Jake? I need to see you soon."

"I'm not sure Janice. Right now all my plans are kind of up in the air," He said, wishing he had a better answer. "After the conversation I had with Mike Murley today, I could be headed home way sooner than expected."

" You don't think they blame you for this, do you? Janice asked beseechingly.

"I think I could have better anticipated this risk," he said quietly.

They talked for a few more minutes, then signed off.

Dmitri thought about his next move. Now he needed to formulate his demand. He was sure that someone would pay a lot to get the discs back, but the kicker was always how to give them what they wanted, get what you wanted, and not find yourself looking down the wrong end of a Kalashnikov.

He decided it was time for his second video

He suited up again and started the video camera. After getting flack from several of his colleagues, he improved the quality of his second ransom note.

"So here is another of my little friends. If you want to see many of your friends again, you need to deliver 5,000 pounds of gold bullion in a truck marked with the UN logo to Balkhash in central Kazakstan in exactly 1 week from today. For that you will receive exactly 4 discs. The other 4 discs will stay with me as insurance. If you accept my terms, place an ad in the New York Times personal ads within 3 days which reads "Looking for good looking rich playboy". Any funny business and you know what happens."

The second video was sent off to Jake and was soon being studied by the FBI.

The video created much consternation. The ransom amount was in excess of $100,000,000.

The place they wanted it delivered was in the middle of a vast dry desert beside Lake Balkhash.

So who would pay, how would they get the gold there without being robbed , had the discs been damaged or destroyed by the abductors and were they willing to do all this for only half the discs?

A special secret session of the UN General Assembly was held. Drs Higgins and Bartlett presented all that was known about the discs, how they resembled current high density laser etched storage devices, and how their placement in the pyramid spoke to their importance.

In the end, the UN appropriated the funds, the ad appeared in the New York Times, and Seal Team VI was assigned the task of delivering the gold.

The logistics of meeting the extortion demands were nearly overwhelming. The demand for gold bullion meant that one of the large national gold reserves would have to be tapped. Initially no country stepped forward to offer their reserves. Finally the US President agreed to release gold reserves from Fort Knox, with the proviso that the UN would guarantee payment to replenish the gold.

But that was just the start. Then the gold had to be moved to Kazakhstan safely. Once again the US President came through and authorized a C130 transport to fly the gold from Kentucky to Almaty. A special operations team was mobilized and flown to Almaty to accompany the gold ransom to its final destination.

Slightly less then one week later a procession of military vehicles led by one heavily loaded UN vehicle wended its way across the Kazakh desert. The success in pulling this all together had been a huge accomplishment. Drs Higgins and Bartlett were both present. They were there to ensure that what was received was the real deal. Dr Bartlett had packed a portable refracting microscope to allow him to look at the discs.

Once the caravan was within approximately 5 miles of Balkhash, the military vehicles circled up and stopped. The special operations team had instructions to go into Balkhash only if some hostilities broke out.

The UN vehicle continued carrying just the two doctors and the driver. The driver was a navy seal, ready to respond with force if the deal started going south. Once the truck entered the town, there were some moments of uncertainty about where to go. Finally, a man off on the right side of the road waved at them. They weren't sure if this was the right person, but as they got closer to the man, his Bozo the clown mask was unmistakable. He jumped on the running board of the truck and signaled them to keep going.

They entered what looked like a town square and shortly found themselves surrounded by a number of Kazakhs all heavily armed. The man on the running board signaled them to stop. From a low building across the square two men emerged. They both appeared to be Russians. They approached the truck.

The one in heavily accented English said "I am the good looking playboy you advertised in the New York newspaper.

Dr Higgins spoke first "We are here for the discs. We must see them before we pay." He wasn't sure anyone understood him. Finally one of the men walked around the back of the truck, lifted up the covering tarp, then nodded to the man in front. The man in front held up one disc and handed it to Dr Higgins. The two doctors spent a few minutes examining the disc. Dr Bartlett studied the disc under his microscope. They both agreed it looked like the real thing. Dr Higgins made a sign with three fingers, trying to ask for the remaining discs. As they were speaking a small beat up looking pickup truck pulled up beside them. The first man signaled for the three men to get into the pickup truck. Dr Higgins held up three fingers again, the man nodded, handed him the three discs, and Dr Higgins gave the navy seal a prearranged signal that they were satisfied and the transaction could go forward. The pickup truck driver drove the three of them back the way they had come in.

Shortly, the 2 doctors and the navy seal rejoined the special operations team and they began their return trip with their precious cargo. Within a few hours the caravan had arrived at Almaty and the 2 doctors were conveyed by military transport planes to London.

Dr Higgins accompanied Dr Bartlett to Southampton University, southwest of London where Dr Bartlett had erected the 5 dimensional laser reader per what they believed was a correct translation of the instructions on the pyramid wall.

Dr Bartlett had the laser reader hooked up to a large monitor. To Dr Higgins, it seemed like Dr Bartlett spent an eternity turning knobs, checking alignments, all the while whistling maddeningly to himself. Dr Higgins was extremely nervous. He and Dr Bartlett would probably never be allowed to set foot in another University if this $100 million dollar gamble didn't pay off.

Dr Higgins got distracted for a moment. When he looked back, he gasped. There scrolling across the screen were what appeared to be an endless list of file directories, all written in that alien text which Dr Higgins had come to know well. Dr Bartlett gasped as well. They danced around, they hugged, then felt embarrassed, then danced around some more. The flood gates were open and the data that the world was about to receive was unlike anything man had ever seen.

Dr Bartlett started opening individual files. They revealed mountains of text. There were other files that looked like they could be videos but they would have to do considerable programming to learn how to read those.

After the initial exuberance, Dr Bartlett established a main frame connection and initiated a full down load of the disc. It just kept going and going. Finally after two hours it stopped.

Dr Bartlett exclaimed "Oh my god, that one disc contained 12 terabytes of data. Incredibly dense storage media."

By this time, it was 2:00am and both of them were exhausted. Dr Higgins suddenly realized that he had slept about 4 hours in the last 72 hours. He had to go to sleep but he had to make one last call.

"Jake, we got it. It's all there. It's incredible," Dr Higgins almost cried.

"Thanks Jim! But get some sleep!" Jake smiled.

The next day within hours, the world learned of the brave doctors and their mission to rescue the discs. At first the UN tried to deny the ransom amount but eventually it came out. There was a lot of criticism dished out for negotiating with criminals and the incredible size of the ransom. But there was also incredible excitement. Drs. Bartlett and Higgins issued a joint press release and they struggled to sound academically objective when they both believed the find was unparalleled in human history. The thieves were credited with a canny approach that made it difficult to apprehend them and one writer noted that the area where the gold had been delivered was a large ore processing area, so the gold had probably already been melted down and transformed into some more transactional

148

shape.

But of course with huge data discoveries come huge translation burdens. The original 17 academic locations that had worked on translating the pyramid wall etchings were now given access to the first disc download. The data was loaded to a central server that all of the participants could access. The reaction of several of these institutions was the same "oh my god, we've got to add staff." The disc presented a monumental challenge, and they all knew that data from three more discs was on the way.

They also had the added issue that they weren't sure where they were in the book. Is this first disc, the beginning , middle or end? No one knew.

Researchers from Purdue University had taken their initial translation of the pyramid etchings and established an electronic dictionary.

Using an automated process, they applied their dictionary to the first 1000 files from the disc. They estimated that with their dictionary they got about a 45% translation rate on the files examined. One of their researchers started opening files and seeing what they could read.

"In the year 1175, in the time of the great famine, the _____ peoples were united to _____ the _____ and resist the ____ of Pharon.

And another file The Rhojani united their peoples to resist the ____. The times were difficult but _____ Multiple researchers all agreed relatively quickly that the disc seemed to contain a lot of historical references. The term Rhojani occurred often to the point that some researchers began to refer to the alien race as the Rhojani.

Within a few days Dr Bartlett had downloaded the remainder of the discs, a staggering 50 + terabytes of data and distributed the files to the central server. Several of the locations responded with complaints of being totally overwhelmed at the magnitude of the data provided.

Finally linguists launched a machine learning program that would determine word meanings from pattern and frequency analysis and then dynamically apply those meanings to update the translation record. Within weeks, the translation percentage had risen to 60 % and would go even higher as the machine learning program made further progress.

Researchers were particularly interested in one segment of this historical record. They located what appeared to be a record of the contemporary society and started to learn insights about their degree of technological advancement. The Rhojani had first experimented with atmospheric flight in their 8th century, although century didn't quite apply since it appeared that they marked time in cycles of 64 years. It told our scientists that Rhojani also inhabited a planet with an atmosphere. Within a "century", the Rhojani began experimenting with rocket travel, and reported on manned voyages to their moon.

This same section of the historical record gave exciting incites into the daily lives of Rhojanians. The typical family contained 5 members, two parents and three children. Consistent with the female statue in the pyramid, mothers carried their young in a pouch. The stature of the Rhojani became a point of interest. Were the statues life size or not? That question remained unresolved for some time. The Rhojani were apparently vegetarians. Records detailed their agriculture, but made no mention of the domestication of animals. Random facts from various parts of the downloaded record continued to emerge, until finally a working group of historians and scientists met and agreed to organize a systematic analysis of the data.

After completing their excavations in the slag pile, the archeology team was heading back to earth. Dr Higgins was there, coordinating the shut down of archeology. He had become something of a rock star himself after his role in rescuing the discs and being present with Dr Bartlett when the first successful downloads occurred. He was getting ready to head back to Coba and resume work on the Mayan glyphs. Jake hosted a going away party for the archeologists and gifted them with a week stay at South Base, as he had done with the earlier departures.

Jake and Dr Higgins had a final meeting before Dr Higgins departure.

"It has been a pleasure to work with you," Jake started.

"And the same for me, Jake," Dr Higgins replied. "I just wish it had ended differently...."

"Yeah, me too." Jake said. They shook hands and then Dr Higgins boarded the rover and departed. Jake watched the line of rovers head off across the lunar plain, feeling a little sense of loss.

The FBI investigation at the project had gone on for a time but in the end never revealed any evidence that a project team member had been involved in the theft, as Jake had never doubted. Now the focus had moved on to Kazakhstan and the efforts to identify the criminals who took the discs.

The fact that the first 4 discs had provided a mountain of data about this alien civilization did not lessen the interest in the scientific community in recovering the other 4 discs. No one knew what they contained but everyone was sure it would be as breathtaking as the first four had been.

The blackmailers had made good on their escape. Within days, the gold bars delivered to Balkhash had been melted down and reduced to a course granular consistency. The gold became a sensation on the black market, sold at a bargain price, and soon appearing in jewelry items worldwide.

But of course the authorities had immensely powerful technology they could call on. During the exchange in Balkhash, powerful satellite cameras had been trained on the UN truck. After the exchange, the cameras stayed on the truck and photographed several figures who approached the vehicle well after the Drs. had been taken back to the military convoy. They noted one in particular, who looked in the back of the truck and then proceeded to do a poorly executed Hopak, ending up falling on his ass but clearly exuberant.

That single act of sheer joy helped international police decide that Russians should be at the top of their list of suspects.

The satellite surveillance team spying on the scene brought to bear an orbiting co2 laser and shone it sequentially on each figure standing around the truck. The beam was invisible, so none of the men on the ground was aware of it, but within 500 milliseconds, the beam recorded a cardiac signature of each person. In addition, each person's face was recorded, although the chances of getting facial recognition at this high "angle of attack" were low. The cardiac signature was almost as good as fingerprints. It was top secret technology that was employed only very selectively.

The UN truck was followed by the satellite camera and as expected only traveled a few miles to a copper smelter. There the truck was unloaded. Once it had been emptied, the truck was taken out in the desert and burned. Several times the satellite had been able to pick up the previously identified cardiac signatures as men entered and left the smelter.

At this point, the dilemma facing police was determining who had the discs. Their logic was that whoever had the gold also probably had the discs. They also believed that whoever the gold belonged to would be very inclined to keep close tabs on it. After a couple of days monitoring the smelter, an old beat up looking truck was brought to the smelter. Several of the confirmed cardiac signatures were reconfirmed milling around the truck and there was clearly a loading process going on.

Surveillance agents decided this was the big move where the bullion, now in small granules would be moved to a place for safe keeping. They were watching the next day as the old truck slowly wended its way north. After a full day, the truck pulled into Ust Kamenogorsk , a moderate sized town still in Kazakhstan. The truck was refueled and then back on the road. Within a couple of hours, the truck entered the Alta Krai province of Russia and passed through Rubtsovsk and later Barnaul. The truck continued driving late into the night, but of course satellite tracking of it continued unabated. Finally at 4:00 am. the truck reached the city of Abakan in the Republic of Khakassia. It drove through the city and then entered a heavily forested area. At this point, the satellite trackers lost them. They monitored for some time around the perimeter of the forest and never detected the truck re-emerging, so they felt some confidence that somewhere in the forest had been the destination for the gold truck.

The surveillance team reported their findings up the chain of command, with a recommendation to launch a recovery / apprehension mission focused on Abakan.

Chapter Twelve

The recommendation of the surveillance team was not acted upon. The whole world was aware that there were 4 more discs still out there. Everyone had an opinion. The academics argued that the discs were absolutely priceless and there was a real possibility that they would open up heretofore undreamed of technologies. They believed that the world should pay whatever it cost to safely retrieve the discs. The main opposing argument was that the disc thieves were also murderers and needed to pay for the slaughter of innocent people on the Moon. And of course both arguments were compelling. Hawkish types in the military wanted to go in with guns blazing but others pointed to the utter irreplaceability of the discs. The result was inaction. The UN posted a reward notice of $10,000,000 for anyone who actions resulted in the capture of the Russians.

Seal Team VI developed multiple scenarios for a lightning strike on the Russian compound, but none was approved to go forward.

Meanwhile, the working group laboring to come up with a systematic summarization of the first four discs had put together a directory of what had been found. It appeared that the first several discs were probably among the missing. They had agreed on what they believed was the fourth disc. It summarized the history of the Rhojani for a period of approximately 500 years. Translators were stunned to find no mention of war during this entire 500 year period. The documents described ravages by disease and periods of famine, but no where was there a mention of strife among the Rhojani. This disc appeared to entirely involve a recitation of history. When the disc ended, it seemed to be about 200 years before the time when the discs were actually produced. They had also identified the fifth disc. It began right where disc four ended and it covered the final 200 years up to their "present day"

As with disc four, there was no mention of warfare and some of the linguists working on the text began to wonder if it was just an intentional omission. The disc seemed to be written from the perspective of an omniscient observer. Events in different countries were described. When the documents weren't talking about natural disasters, they tended to focus on celebrations and important milestones. Occasionally they would highlight some technological achievement. Some of the linguists just found it all stunning, when contrasted with descriptions of our own history which teemed with warfare, national and local rivalries, double dealing, backstabbing and sudden death. The final portion of disc five contained descriptions of their political systems and social structures.

Various national governments mirrored our own parliamentary and democratic institutions. There was even one country that had what very much sounded like a communist form of government. Certain Rhojani were clearly revered in the writings but they were never military leaders, always statesmen or philanthropists or scientists and their accomplishments were always about betterment of the people.

With regard to negative events, there appeared to be a lot of meteor impacts which played havoc with their day to day lives. Scientists concluded that the alien planet was more active than Earth with regard to meteor strikes.

There were numerous embedded objects in the files, but so far they had been unable to read them. Dr Bartlett along with a team of engineers were working hard to decode these file formats.

Disc Six summarized the sciences of the Rohani. Sections on inorganic chemistry, organic chemistry, physical chemistry, thermodynamics, classical physics, nuclear physics, biology, architecture, metallurgy, astronomy, electrical, chemical and mechanical engineering laid out in great detail the development of science in their culture. At this early stage, the translations weren't ready for distribution to the broader scientific community, but early looks by subject matter experts suggested there were going to be lots of discoveries once that occurred.

154

Disc Seven was a treasure trove. This disc was all about the Rhojani technology and it featured thousands of pages of specifications on everything from shoes to booster rockets. The Rhojani appeared to have been every bit our equal from a technology standpoint and there were huge expectations about what this disc would yield.

Disc Eight was among the missing, and based upon the way the series of discs seemed to be building to a crescendo, there was much speculation about what Disc Eight might cover.

Dr Higgins found it very satisfying to be back doing his chosen work, once again studying Mayan ruins in Coba. He had to get all of his colleagues to settle down a bit. They kept wanting to hear about the Moon and about Kazakhstan. He humored them for a while and then finally announced to all within earshot one day that he was done talking about these things. That seemed to work, and after a while he had settled back down into the academic life of an archeologist.

During his absence, the team and Dr Wilson had continued to work on the treasure trove of Mayan glyphs that Coba had yielded. The translations were progressing nicely. He attended a session where one of the junior staff members was giving his most recent translation.

"And this one discusses the gift from the Earth Mother that was passed down through the generations. It makes reference to a symbol that isn't in our glyph dictionary. Not sure if anyone has seen this before."

The young scientist put a picture on the overhead projector.

. Dr Higgins had been looking at his phone, not paying full attention. When he looked up, he stared at the screen for a moment.

"Is this some kind of a joke?" He said angrily.

"I'm not sure what you mean sir." The young staff member stammered.

For a moment the room started to spin for Dr Higgins. Then the magnitude of what this meant hit him full on.

'Oh my god." Dr Higgins ran out of the tent and back to his quarters.

He immediately dialed Jake on the Moon, not bothering to check that Jake was probably asleep.

"Jake, you're not going to believe this! We've had it wrong all along. The Rhojani aren't aliens. They're from Earth, our Earth, Earth of 300 million years ago." Dr Higgins went on to explain how deep in a Mayan ruin, the same symbol had appeared that they first saw suspended over the discs in the pyramid.

Jake had been asleep, but was soon wide awake, infected by Dr Higgins excitement.

They talked for some time. They both agreed that this was going to be news that rocketed around the globe. It wasn't totally clear how people would react. Were they certain about this interpretation?

Just then it hit Dr Higgins like a lightning bolt. "Jake, the confirmation is right in front of us. I'm willing to bet that the globe we found in the pyramid presents an image consistent with what geophysicists have projected for the Supercontinent Pangea. Because we always thought of the Rhojani as aliens we never critically examined the pyramid globe."

Rather than run with this theory, Dr Higgins first did some research, looking up the pictures of the globe in the pyramid. He then pulled up projections of what Pangea was thought to look like. The match was stunning. He was certain now that he was right.

Before he did anything else, he searched out the young staff member and explained to him why he had reacted the way he did. And he made the young man feel good when he pointed out that his presentation had been the catalyst for this discovery.

Next, he invited all of his former pyramid project staffers to a teleconference to discuss this finding. He felt they had a right to be the first to know. When he went over it with them, all seemed rapidly convinced. One question came up "So how could there be absolutely no trace of this earlier society in Earth's archeological record."

"Well, one thought I have is that we have been so invested in the idea that we are the first and only specie to ever attain our current level of technological development, that we simply haven't looked for them in the right way. Plus think about the time span put another way- 300,000 millennia."

They were all stunned by this new revelation. Dr Higgins felt this new development needed to get out. Since it was related to the pyramid project, he thought he should give Janice and the Western Consortium PR team the first chance at releasing this. He called Janice and filled her in. She was as stunned as everyone else She thanked Dr Higgins for the call and then got with the team. As first they balked at going forward with it, but Janice pointed out that it would be coming out with them or without them, so they got on board and prepared a press release.

The reaction around the world was interesting. It didn't really change much about the way people regarded the Rhojani. People had always. known that they were a different species but thought of them in terms of some far off planet. What changed for people was how they thought about Earth. The idea that man wasn't the first advanced civilization on Earth rocked everyone's world. It made some wonder if there were even more.

Once the news came out, the translation teams started to look for any clues in the Rhojani discs that would further confirm this new and startling theory. A group of astronomers noted that Disc Five contained some star charts. No one had spent much time on them, but with this new theory, they began computer simulations rolling back the positions of stars by 300 million years and looking for matches. Archeologists had pointed out that the dating technology had a several % error range. So astronomers kept moving back the clock until they got a match. Seems the night sky in the Rhojani star charts pointed to a night 312,347,628 years ago. And for that date, the match was perfect.

Armed with this number, geophysicists charted the movement of continents and confirmed that the two dimensional globe in the pyramid bore a striking resemblance to their predicted layout of Pangea

Meanwhile, young Dema looked again at the online reward notice. He had lived with his mother in Abakan for 5 years now, every since his father died in a vodka fueled rage at the local.Бар. His mother struggled to provide for them. She earned money cleaning houses, but it was hardly enough to get by. He looked at the notice again. Was it really dollars? He did the calculation again. So in rubles that would be 652,000,000 . He thought to himself what he would do with that amount of money. He looked at the phone number on the notice. Was that a Moscow number? He was terrified but he knew something, something that might be worth 652,000,000 rubles. He dialed the number. A voice answered in Russian "pyramid disc hot line, my name is Sasha, what do you wish to report?"

Dema hesitated for a second, then said "Four men came to Abakan last week. I think they're from Kazakhstan. I think they're the men you're looking for. My mom was hired by them to clean their house and when they went to pay her, they offered her a little bag of gold powder. My mother of course refused, believing they were just trying to cheat her."

"Ok thank you for your call, please record this incident number. You will need to present this number should you try and make a claim for the reward."

Dema carefully wrote down the number and stashed it in his pocket. He hung up and wondered if anything would ever happen.

Sasha recorded the call and promptly forgot about it. Such boring work she thought to herself.

The report she filed was immediately given top secret status and was communicated to the disc recovery task force. Anything with Abakan in it was treated this way, but the security officer who read this one recognized it could be a game changer. He passed it up the chain.

The team decided this was what they had been looking for. Within an hour Dema was contacted by a member of the Russian security service and he provided them with the location of the compound where his mother had been hired. They were excited that the location was in fact in the forest in which the truck had disappeared.

A clandestine team disguised as a logging crew was sent to the forest and within a short time had found the compound and set up surveillance. The compound was a Soviet era ramshackle farm house, a barn in an advanced state of decay and a few animal pens where chickens and sheep were being kept.

The surveillance confirmed that three of the cardiac signatures detected in Kazakstan were in fact present in the compound. The surveillance team reported back their results. They noted the compound residents gave no signs of preparing to leave. The conclusion was that this was their final destination. The clandestine team was ordered to pull back to avoid any risk of detection.

The decision was made at this point to simply wait. They expected that the Russians would now be plotting how to cash in with the other four discs. Their assessment was correct and within a couple of weeks Jake received another email reporting that the other discs could also be purchased. This time Dmitri had increased the price to 7,000 pounds of gold bullion and specified that it also be delivered in one week again to Balkhash.

The security forces handling the response knew that the Russians would realize they were vulnerable once the final discs were turned over, so they expected some twist to be introduced and they were correct. The email to Jake said that the Russians had a group of 50 hostages who would be murdered if security forces tried to capture them after the exchange.

Once again the whole process was repeated. The one week deadline again proved challenging to compete and some resistance had started to build among UN member countries to giving in once more to the extortion. But the contents of the first set of discs had been so compelling, that in the end it was agreed to go forward. The leaders of the G9 were given a secret briefing in which the intel about the compound in Abakan was shared.

The gold was assembled and transported under incredible security to Ramstein Air Base in Germany. From there, it was flown by military transport to Almaty, where the gold convoy was again assembled. Drs Higgins and Bartlett again were asked to participate. The instructions were to proceed exactly as they had the first time.

In the meantime, word got out that the Russians had made good on their hostage threat. A group of American embassy personnel enroute to Nur-Sultan to visit the Baiterek tower had been ambushed and taken prisoner.

Dr Higgins found it almost surreal that they were repeating this whole thing over again. Off across the barren landscape, he could make out the outline of Balkhash, shimmering in the haze. The oppressive heat had everyone in the convoy drenched in sweat and the stress of what they were about to do made him sweat even more. The first time he did this he had naively had this feeling that nothing could go wrong, but this time inexplicably he felt a deep sense of foreboding.

The UN convoy arrived on the outskirts of Balkhash and the security team went over the plan again with the two doctors.

"We don't expect any funny business from the Russians. In view of their hostage threat, we're certain they feel pretty safe," the head of the security team emphasized with the two doctors. "We'd like you this time to inquire about the safety of the hostages and also ask when they will be released. You probably won't get a straight answer, but any info you can glean will be helpful. In the end, if you're satisfied these last four discs are the real thing, go ahead with the transaction. We have a high altitude drone in position that will be watching you throughout the exchange. If the Russians try anything like taking the gold without handing over the discs, Dr Higgins please just raise your hand once over your head. If that happens, the security team will be there within 2 minutes. If that happens, things could get pretty dicey, so I'm asking both of you to wear body armor during the exchange."

Dr Higgins and Dr Bartlett looked at each other with mutual expressions that confirmed the stress both of them were feeling. "So can you affirm for us that you have no plans to come in with guns blazing if the transaction proceeds normally?" Dr Bartlett asked the security team head.

"I can affirm that doctor. We have a plan, but none of it will be executed now. We intend to hand over the gold and let the Russians get away," the security team head replied.

At the appointed hour, Dr Bartlett and Higgins once again got into the UN truck and the driver started it up. The truck was sitting low, almost over its load limit with the huge cargo of gold bars. The driver was the same navy seal that had driven them the first time. He gave them a curt greeting, and put the truck in gear.

The drive into Balkhash only took a few minutes. Out the right side, they were traveling close to Lake Balkhash, its deep copper blue waters shimmering with the intense afternoon sun. Once in the city, they were again signaled by a person on the side of the road. They pulled over and the man jumped on the running board and pointed for them to proceed ahead.

They arrived at the same exchange point as before, and there was Dmitri waiting for them.

"Hello Gentlemen, so nice to do business with you again!" He signaled one of his men to open up the rear of the truck. Dmitri walked around back and looked in.

"Ah , the color of money!" He proceeded to check the gold bars at several points and was satisfied that load was the demanded gold.

"And here are your discs." He pulled four discs out and handed them to Dr Bartlett. Dr Bartlett took out his microscope and proceeded to examine the discs. He was able to confirm that the signs of high density laser etching were apparent.

"I believe the discs are the real article," he told Dr Higgins.

Dr Higgins turned to Dmitri. "So what about the hostages? Are they safe? When will you release them?"

Not far in front of their UN truck, a tractor trailer was sitting. Dmitri signaled one of his men, and they swung open the rear doors of the truck. Inside were a large number of men and women , all looking terrified and suffering from heat exhaustion.

Dmitri spoke "They're all fine. They will come with us and we'll let them go when we know you're not following."

Dr Higgins felt this almost irrational desire at this point to raise his hand. It was difficult to see all of these Americans being terrorized. He wondered what was going to happen to them.

"Before we finalize our deal, I insist that you let us give the hostages

161

food and water!"

Both the UN truck driver and Dr Bartlett looked at Dr Higgins. This hadn't been part of the plan.

Dmitri looked irritated but decided he might as well go along, since he had no real idea how he was going to keep the hostages alive during the long drive across the Kazakh desert.

"Ok but one false move and your discs are lost." He reached out and took them back from Dr Bartlett.

Dr Higgins called the convoy lead and asked him to send a truck up with food and water. The truck arrived a few minutes later. Dr Higgins took the lead in opening the tractor trailer and proceeded to pass out food parcels and water. He asked several of the hostages if they had been harmed and try to offer many of them words of reassurance. They indicated they hadn't been harmed but had had no food or water for some time.

Once that was done, the supply truck turned around and headed back to their convoy.

"So, can we proceed now?" Dmitri asked impatiently.

Dr Higgins responded. "Yes, I think we're ready now"

Dmitri handed the discs over and one of his men got behind the wheel of the UN truck. A battered looking pickup truck pulled up and Dmitri signaled for the UN group to get in. The two doctors and their driver were conveyed back to the UN convoy without incident.

"So what happens now?" Dr Higgins asked the security team head.

"So we get the two of you back to civilization and we monitor the extortionists until an opportunity comes to rescue the hostages and nab them."

Once again the Russians were followed via satellite as they left Balkhash. This time they didn't stop at a smelter to break down the gold ingots. They immediately took a route that looked like they were headed back to Abakan, this time with the tractor trailer containing hostages accompanying them.

The FBI had taken a lead role in the effort to capture the extortionists and get back the gold. They monitored the UN truck constantly. They wanted to do their best to protect the hostages if the Russians gave any signs of harming them, but so far there was no sign of such intentions. The FBI had a high altitude drone in position, equipped with non explosive missiles that could take out a single individual without causing mass casualties. Should the Russians show any signs of harming hostages, they would be taken out before they even knew there was a threat.

The FBI had flown in a team of agents who were waiting at Dmitri's compound in Abakan. They had stormed the compound in the middle of the night and found just a couple of people who they took into custody. They believed they had acted swiftly enough that no one in the compound had been able to call out. They searched the compound and with little difficulty found a huge cache of gold pellets, obviously product from the earlier disc transaction. The find reassured them that the Russians were heading back to the compound.

As the Russians neared the Russian border, Dmitri started to feel pretty good about their chances. He knew that the Americans would be in a frenzy to recover their embassy personnel. He decided that a diversionary tactic would help them successfully elude any pursuers. He waited until the two vehicle convoy entered a densely wooded section of highway and then pulled over. The tractor trailer driver opened the back of the hostage truck and then climbed into the UN truck with the other Russians. They left the trailer with the hostages there and sped off.

The FBI team monitoring their movement had lost visual contact with the convoy. When they saw the UN truck re-emerge from the forest, with no sign of the hostage vehicle, they feared the worst and immediately scrambled a helicopter squadron of navy seals, who were on the ground at the spot where the trailer disappeared within 15 minutes.

The FBI team lived through some anxious moments but let out a spontaneous cheer when the calm reassuring voice of a navy seal came over the radio reporting "All embassy personnel are safe, no signs of any casualties."

But of course Dmitri and Ivan desperate diversionary tactic was for naught. They were no match for the technology arrayed against them.. Not suspecting a trap, the Russians drove into their compound. Without warning, a huge spotlight shone down on their vehicle, small arms fire seemed to be coming from all directions and a megaphone called for them in Russian to come out and lay on the ground,. They knew they were lost and meekly crawled out of the car and threw themselves down.

The FBI handcuffed the Russians and began interrogating them individually.

Dmitri recognized his excessively bad bargaining position, and immediately gave up the identity of the lunar crew who murdered the three men. Within hours, 3 men were apprehended on the Moon. Additionally, he identified 2 men who had kidnapped the embassy personnel.

And with that, the whole thing was over. The 4 remaining discs were sent by charter jet to Southampton where Prof Bartlett examined the discs and pronounced them intact and undamaged.

Jake heard about it shortly after the story came out. He was glad it was over, and relieved that the bad guys had all been caught.

Shortly thereafter, he saw that a call was coming in from Mike Murley. "Well here it comes" he thought to himself.

"Hello Jake" Mike Murley started. "I just want you to know, I've changed my mind. No heads are rolling and you're still my man once Jamison retires" he immediately signed off.

"Wow, " Jake thought to himself. "How much good news can I get in one day?"

Dema had listened to the news and knew that the discs had been recovered and that men had been arrested. He dialed up the hotline number again and once again reached the bored Sasha.

"I'm calling to claim my reward" Dema said.

"Ok fine, what's your claim number."

Dema read it off to her and she entered it into the system. She wasn't prepared for what came next.

Bells and whistles and instructions to keep the caller on the line. Soon Dema would learn that he wasn't getting 652,000,000 rubles.

The exchange rate had drifted in his favor. He was getting 654,000,000 rubles.

Jake realized that the time had come to put in for that 6 months leave he had been promised. Things at the dig were winding down, mining operations were ramping up slowly, all major crises seemed to have abated, and the woman he loved was waiting for him.

He decided to let Janice know what he was thinking.

"Hello my darling," he said "I have a surprise for you."

"Ohh, Jake, you know I love surprises."

"I've put in for my 6 months leave. I'm approved to start in 2 weeks."

"Oh Jake, oh my god, I can't believe it. I can't wait."

They spent the rest of the call talking about all the places they were going to go and the things they were going to do.

The next two weeks seemed to take forever.

Jake was at the South Base spaceport, buckled into his seat, awaiting takeoff. He couldn't believe his luck. He had gotten the last seat for a shuttle headed directly to San Francisco. That meant no need for a jet shuttle once he landed on Earth.

The flight attendant came by and gave him a smile. He smiled back. This last stint on the Moon had seemed to last a long time. He was ready for blue skies, In-n-Out Burger and of course Janice. They had talked over a range of options for things they might do with this chance to be together and surprised each other when they both thought the idea of camping sounded fantastic.

Janice reserved a campsite at Sequoia National Forest, along with an Uber and a complete camping setup. They would be picked up the next morning at Janice's apartment and be dropped off for a fantastic week getting back in touch with nature. She was headed to the spaceport. She hadn't told Jake she would be there. It was a surprise.

Jake ambled off the lunar shuttle. He was surprised how heavy he felt. He had lived several months in 1/6th gravity and now he found each step required an effort. In keeping with current recommendations he had exercised almost daily on the Moon and done a good amount of weight training, but right at this moment he felt like he hadn't done enough. Those feelings were forgotten in an instant when he looked up and saw Janice smiling at him outside of customs. He hurried through and wrapped her in his arms. They hugged and kissed for several minutes, then finally stopped and took a breath.

"Wow, you look lovely!" Jake smiled at Janice. He noticed a different hairstyle and an attractive tan that was new. She was dressed in grey designer slacks and a lilac silk blouse.

"Well, this job I've been doing comes with a few perks like free hairstyling and a wardrobe, so I've been able to up my game a little," Janice laughed. "Would you prefer to have the dowdy university professor back?"

"I want you however you come packaged. And the university professor was never dowdy!"Jake replied

They kissed again and then went out to the curb and picked up their Uber.

"I scheduled the Uber camper to pick us up tomorrow morning at 9am. I thought maybe we could go out tonight and have a nice welcome home dinner," Janice told Jake.

"That sounds terrific," Jake responded. "Maybe a place where I might see a real sunset again!"

"Somehow, I just knew that might be a priority. I already made us a reservation at a great seafood restaurant in Pacifica that boasts a great sunset, sometimes even comes with a green flash," Janice beamed at Jake. "I just can't believe you're finally here. All that time on the Moon where we were together but not together. Just torture."

"I've dreamed of this moment for months," Jake smiled.

Before dinner, Jake got to experience something Janice had tried to warn him about. The entire wait staff and kitchen crew filed out and asked if they could have a picture with Jake and Janice. Janice had been right about Jake being famous, but didn't fully appreciate that she was famous, too. Jake responded warmly to the group and posed with them until they were all satisfied.

Jake and Janice enjoyed a wonderful dinner at the Half Moon Bay restaurant. Jake hadn't had fresh fish in months, and also really enjoyed the Caesar salad paired with an exquisite dry Riesling. Janice tried some red snapper and also thought the Riesling was wonderful. They basked in the knowledge that they had no where they had to be or go. They could simply luxuriate in being together. They ended up being a little naughty and went for the second bottle of Reisling. They laughed, and relived memories on the Moon, and caught up on the status of different people they had worked with. The evening flew by, and finally they asked the waiter to call their Uber. Two minutes later it arrived and they were headed back to Janice's apartment.

Jake's suitcase had been delivered from the airport. He picked it up and followed Janice up the steps and waited while she opened the door. He stepped in and looked around. Her place was beautiful, elegant and tastefully done. He was turning around, when suddenly he was engulfed by arms, and lips and warm proximity and that was the last chance Jake had to study the decor for some time…..

Jake awoke to bright sunlight streaming through the bedroom windows. He turned over and felt Janice's warm body beside his. He kissed her on the neck and she gave a little sigh of contentment and then she rolled over and opened her eyes and looked deeply into his eyes.

"That was wonderful, Jacob Campbell Mackenzie, it was just what I had dreamed it would be," They embraced and enjoyed a long passionate kiss.

"And I didn't even know you knew my middle name, Janice Elysia Barnes." They both laughed.

"I guess we need to get moving. The camper Uber will be here in 90 minutes," Janice reminded.

Jake rolled out of bed, and once again felt the extraordinary weight that Earth had restored to him. "Oh boy, I feel like I weigh 500 pounds," Jake exclaimed.

"No 100 yard dashes for you any time soon," Janice smiled.

They had a light breakfast and packed sportswear for the camping trip. Everything else would be provided by the camping Uber. Promptly at 9, the Uber showed up and wisked them away. It was about a four hour drive.

Jake couldn't get enough of the scenery and particularly when they left the coastal plain and began ascending into the Sierra Nevadas. They oohed and ahhed as they passed several gigantic sequoias and finally arrived at their campsite. They unloaded the camping equipment and food supplies, checked that they had everything they needed and then discharged the Uber. They watched as it slowly descended the hill and disappeared from sight.

It was early summer and the temperature was a comfortable 70F. They started pitching their tent and had several good laughs as they flubbed the tent raising procedure.

"How many PhDs does it take to raise a tent," Jake quipped.

"Four," Janice responded. " One to screw it up, and three others to shake their heads in academic detachment," They both laughed.

Eventually they got their campsite in order and got a small fire going in the fire ring. They went through the freeze dried meals that had been provided and selected two and heated them up on the camp stove.

They spent the evening chattering and enjoying the sounds and smells of the forest. When it got late, they pulled out the provided sleeping bags and were gratified to learn that they could be zipped together. And that's what they did.

The next several days they would hike for most of the daylight hours. Each day, they carried a picnic lunch and would usually find some scenic promontory to stop at. Jake found that the exertion helped him shake off pretty quickly the months of lunar gravity. After several days, he felt like he was back to his old self.

For Janice and Jake, at the start there had been an underlying tension. They both realized that this was their first time to really find out if their thing was real. Each of them had been so convinced that this relationship would work that the possibility that it wouldn't was a little frightening.

But very quickly that underlying tension evaporated. When you find yourself with someone that you enjoy being with every moment of the day, there is no place for tension. Within days, Jake and Janice knew their bond was real and the exhilaration they felt was intoxicating. So this time they had together in the mountains was simply......magical.

At the end of the week, their Uber vehicle showed up and they headed back to Palo Alto. Janice had insisted that Jake would stay with her throughout his Earthside deployment and he of course agreed.

They talked about their current plans. Janice had somehow been able to stay in the good graces of the dean of the Geology/ Geophysics department , despite being stretched very thin during her work as spokesperson for the pyramid project. Now that things seemed to be winding down, she needed to throw herself back into her research projects and updating her class outlines for the next semester.

She suddenly got this big smile on her face and said "I have this amazing idea.

It just came to me. Dr Wilson has contacted me several times about working at Coba this summer. What if you and I both worked there? I know Dr. Higgins would be thrilled to have you there!"

Jake was surprised. He'd never even thought about such a possibility but he had thought about how he and Janice could make the most of this 6 month leave he'd been given. He had been concerned that Janice would be so busy that their time together would be limited. And if he was really being honest, the whole pyramid project had opened the world of archeology to him. The thought of a summer at Coba sounded terrific. Janice came behind Jake, put her arms around him and ran her tongue slowly along the nape of his neck.

In a husky voice she said "And don't forget the moonlit Yucatán beaches"

He spun her around and kissed her and said "Let's do it!"

Remarkably, this impulsive idea was greeted by all concerned with great enthusiasm. Dr Higgins indicated they had ample budget and housing facilities to accommodate Jake and Janice. Dr Wilson, who was still in charge of the Coba site, was also thrilled.

Arrangements were finalized quickly and within three weeks of Janice's brainstorm, she and Jake were on a plane to the Yucatán.

When they arrived, Jake and Janice had to once again overcome their rockstar status situation. While academics tend to be less starstuck then others, the archeology team at Coba still went through a phase of requests for pictures alternating with awestruck silence.

Jake didn't seem all that fazed by it and after a while he was just accepted for who he was.

Dr Higgins was thrilled to see Jake again. To him they were practically brothers. Dr Higgins initially proposed giving Jake a manger level job. But Jake refused, noting he wasn't really qualified and finally accepted a position as simply a dig team member.

Janice enjoyed seeing many of the team members she had gotten to know the year before and many of them took time to show her some of the things they had unearthed during the previous year.

The highlight of course was when Dr Higgins took both of them to the sealed vault and showed them a number of the Mayan Glyphs that had rocked the world of Mayan archeology. And of course he saved the biggest stunner for last when he showed the glyph that had been the key to determining that the Rhojani were earthlings. Jake recalled the excitement of that night and still felt a thrill when he saw the Mayan figure.

Chapter Thirteen

The next six months witnessed an explosion of research, debate, discussion and even commercialization on all things Rhojani. The collection of 8 discs were now officially referred to in academic circles as the Codex Rhojanus.

The machine learning translation programs had relentlessly pursued ever more accurate characterizations of the Codex Rhojanus to the point that translation accuracy was assessed to have exceeded 95%. The visual files that had initially resisted their efforts also yielded up their secrets. That opened up the entire Rhojani world. Soon people were viewing videos of Rhojani announcers describing some event or accomplishment. The Rhojani voice was slightly musical in tone and generally pleasing to the human ear.

One of the first lines of discussion was among archeologists and paleontologists about how they had completely missed any findings of the Rhojani society in the archeological record. The presence of a pouch on the female suggested that the Rhojani may have been part of Diprotodontia, the largest extant order of marsupials. The oldest known fossil record for this order only reached back about 28 million years, so clearly that was the most logical explanation for this mystery. But nonetheless, it seemed unbelievable to many. It made clear that someday humans could disappear without any trace. The flip side question was even more vexing. How had the symbol of the Rhojani survived to be found and venerated by the Mayans. Here no one had an answer.

The next line of inquiry among scientists focused on the search for additional confirmations of the earthly origins of the Rhojani. The star charts were compelling but scientists reasoned that there should be other confirmations in the Codex Rhojanus.

This line of inquiry soon yielded overwhelming results. Records of Rhojani timekeeping and calendars yielded the 24 hour day, the 365 day year cycle. Rhojani meteorology yielded seasons and heating and cooling weather periods. Measures of distances to the sun and the moon matched our own. This line of inquiry soon died. The evidence was simply overwhelming. The Rhojani were Earthlings.

Another line of inquiry was driven by those who were convinced there were technological jewels to be harvested. These people became known as the Disc Seveners, focusing on the one disc that seemed to be strongly focused on technology.

Many things were just variations on technology that humans had also perfected. The Rhojani were as advanced as humans with regard to self driving vehicles, and had also developed transportation on demand, rather than individual vehicle ownership. Telecommunications were also well advanced, quite parallel to our own society. But then some things started to emerge that generated a lot of buzz.

The Rhojani had developed the first prototypes of teleportation units. They had advanced to the point that personnel could be transported hundreds of miles in the blink of an eye. They hinted that teleportation between celestial bodies was on the horizon.

The Rhojani had advanced medical transplantation well beyond our own capabilities. Heart and lung replacements were quite common.

They had also perfected fusion energy reactors, but scientists who studied their designs believed the enhancements they had perfected would provide a 50% improvement in energy efficiency for our own reactors.

Rhojani organic farming had advanced to a degree we hadn't attained yet. Pesticides and other chemical agents were unnecessary due to advanced seed hybridization.

The absence of meat in the Rhojani diet raised questions about their nutrition. They seemed to get most of their protein from legumes. They didn't find any documents that explained why the Rhojani were vegetarian.

It wasn't anything the Rhojani felt needed explaining- it's just what was natural for them.

The list went on and on. Disc Seven truly was an amazing gift from the Rhojani to the human race.

Of course social scientists wanted to understand the nature of this ancient society. They were immediately mystified by the absence of any references to laws and regulations. In the historical record, a series of event descriptions started to paint a clearer picture.

One citation told of a citizen who murdered a citizen in an adjoining town. The citation went on to describe how the entire citizenry of the first town delivered gifts to everyone in the second town. The perpetrator was instructed not to ever do that again and was sent home. There was no discussion of a trial, or incarceration or laws violated.

This same kind of scenario was found in other places in the Codex Rhojanus. Individual transgressions always led to a collective response, collective atonement and individual punishment was never discussed.

The same kind of response could be seen in territorial disputes. Two countries in Pangea each claimed a certain peninsula as their own. In human history this would have been the launch point for war, with the attendant death and injury. In this case, the Rhojani convened a negotiating body, and worked out a compromise.

No where in the Codex Rhojanus was there any mention of weapons. No guns, grenades, mines, machine guns, poison gas, battleships, nuclear bombs, nothing. Scientists found this incomprehensible and wondered if a disc was missing. The Rohani provided no explanation because they had simply never learned to commit violence against their fellow citizens.

And of course there was even more. There appeared to be no ownership of private property. People certainly lived in villages, but where they dwelled, ate and slept was somewhat fluid. If someone decided to go on a trip, they were automatically welcomed and sheltered wherever they went. If someone decided they liked the house next door, they just moved in and people would make accommodations to let them fit in.

Children spent the first six months in their mother's pouch, but after that they became the collective responsibility of the village. They could live or sleep where they wanted, but were always under the vigilant eye of multiple adults.

Jobs and occupations followed the same pattern. Showing up for work was encouraged but the need for mental health breaks was understood. A child could choose any profession and could stick with it as long as they chose, or could change their mind and do something else.

All necessities including food, shelter, clothing, medical care were provided to all without any regard for ability to pay. There was a common focus on the greater good.

In the arts, the Rhojani had developed a host of musical instruments unlike anything seen before. A Rhojani symphony was as melodious and impressive as a human symphony but *different*.

These results of the social scientists' inquiries drove people crazy. How could a society have possibly survived and flourished under such conditions? Humans had known throughout our recorded history that man was inherently evil, inherently stupid, and completely incapable of sublimating his own selfish desires to the good of all. So now we're confronted with an ancient society that did it all differently.

Reactions were all over the map. Some argued that this society resembled in many ways the Huron-Wendat-Iroquois nation of the US Great Lakes, but others simply dismissed it as the Rhojani painting themselves in a positive light.

Much of this had to be construed because for the Rhojani it just was how they lived. It would never have occurred to them how different another culture could be.

There was also much interest in the Rhojani as physical beings. The statues in the pyramid had depicted them as 10 feet tall. So how tall were they in reality?

At first the answer to such a simple question proved elusive. The Rhojani had never thought to actually write down their physical size. But one scientest studying images of the Rhojani noted native vegetation in the background for which there were extensive fossil records. From that, knowing the size of the plants, they were able to confirm the physical stature of the Rhojani. Yes, the Rhojani were in fact 10 feet tall, and the

174

statues in the pyramid were life size.

The physical differences between the Rhojani and humans were examined in considerable detail. The large pointed ears suggested the Rhojani's hearing acuity might be better than humans. The ostrich like legs and oversized thigh muscles was speculated to be a better design that might avoid afflictions like osteoarthritis seen in human seniors. The large eyes pointed to probably better night vision. But all agreed that the physical differences were really minor compared to the physical similarities.

Questions of life span also interested the public. This was easier to extract. The Rhojani had provided public health data so it became clear the the average Rohani lived to an age of 85, fairly comparable to human life span.

Paleontologists were interested to find out what fauna and flora existed 300 million years ago. This period was deemed the Carboniferous Period. Disc 2 provided a treasure trove of data on the natural world of that time.

They had long theorized that the most important plants of the Carboniferous period were the ones inhabiting the large belt of carbon-rich "coal swamps" around the equator, which were later compressed by millions of years of heat and pressure into the vast coal deposits we use for fuel today. Countless pictures from the Codex Rhojanus confirmed that theory.

The Carboniferous period was the heyday of the giant dragonfly *Megalneura*, the wingspan of which measured up to 2.5 feet, as well as the giant millipede *Arthropleura*, which attained lengths of almost 10 feet. Imagine the thrill when a paleontologist actually saw these creatures alive and flying. Several videos depicting the fauna of that time were found.

One of the earliest reptiles paleontologists had identified, *Hylonomus*, appeared about 315 million years ago, and the giant (almost 10 feet long) *Ophiacodon* around the same time. Live videos of these creatures were also found in the Codex. Scientists were gratified that the Rhojani records suggested their analysis of the fossil record had not been far off.

Geography enthusiasts were drawn to the mapping information provided by the Codex.

Bostonians marveled about how they would have been able on a clear day to see Casablanca. Others marveled at how they could have driven from Brazil, through the Ivory Coast and into southern Florida all in a single afternoon. The Rhojani road system was extensive and virtually identical to modern interstate highways. There were no signs of border controls at country borders.

There were a number of big cities in Pangea. The photographic records from the Codex depicted a number of them in great detail. Tramon was a large port city, located in what would have been modern day France. Preledon was another large port city, located on the west coast of Pangea, near what would be Guadalajara in Mexico. Most of the big cities tended to be around the outer perimeter of the super continent. Images in the Codex from the interior of the continent gave the impression that there were some very arid regions with large dry deserts.

Another section of the Codex that garnered much attention was the historical accounts of Rhojani heroes.

The Rhojani had certainly had their share of plague and disease. The historical record described a global pandemic that wiped out over half the population around 500 years before the "modern" era depicted in the Codex. One of the heroes was Xander Petard who discovered the pathogen driving the global pandemic and developed the vaccine that brought their society back from the brink.

Another hero was Traddie Molechi, who solved the riddle of the great wasting disease that caused young babies to shrivel and die in their mother's pouches. Again a scientist held up as a hero.

Finally, there was Plade Gorhani, who solved the two cities impasse with his negotiating skills with what was described as an enlightened solution. This was the first hero found for a public disagreement and noteworthy that it ended in no violence.

So the human world learned incredible amounts about the Rhojani civilization and with virtually no exceptions everything they had learned depicted the Rhojani as a noble race of beings, worthy of our respect. Indeed, we were in awe of these people. When we thought about the literally millions of people, soldiers, civilians, innocent people who had perished in the endless stream of wars that depicted our history, we couldn't help but wonder if we could have done better.

Meanwhile , as news has a habit of doing, sometimes things percolate for a while before a salient question suddenly occurs to someone.

"So what happened to the Rhojani.?" Someone sitting in a bar said to his fellow drinker.

"Well that's a really good question," His bar mate replied

And it was. Soon that question was resounding through the blogosphere. And no one knew the answer.

The answer eventually started to emerge. Disc Eight, the final in the series, yielded things that no one had expected. The disc started off with reports of sudden efforts to accelerate the space program. While the Rhojani had already made substantial progress in colonizing the Moon, this section of the Codex reported on a crash program to finalize development of pulse ion drive technology. As had already happened often with the Codex, initially the sheer volume of information sometimes made it difficult to assign context to what had been found. Someone working on the translation was the first to see the term "extinction event" and immediately recognized the potential importance. It turned out that Disc Eight contained a number of references to an extinction event.

The disc chronicled the identification of a planet threatening risk, one that had been identified by their leading astronomers. Just as we had recognized that the Chicxulube crater marked an asteroid impact that had extinguished almost all life on earth, the Rhojani had documented similar strikes in their past and as a result had organized a sophisticated monitoring program for large asteroids in both our Solar System's asteroid belt and the Kuiper Belt.

The **asteroid belt** is a torus-shaped region in the Solar System, located roughly between the orbits of the planets Jupiter and Mars. It contains a great many solid, irregularly shaped bodies, of many sizes, but much smaller than planets, called asteroids or minor planets.

The **Kuiper belt** is a circumstellar disc in the outer Solar System, extending from the orbit of Neptune at 30 astronomical units (AU) to approximately 50 AU from the Sun. It is similar to the asteroid belt, but is far larger—20 times as wide and 20–200 times as massive. Like the asteroid belt, it consists mainly of small bodies or remnants from when our solar system formed. While many asteroids are composed primarily of rock and metal, most Kuiper belt objects are composed largely of frozen volatiles (termed "ices"), such as methane, ammonia, and water.

And as we've seen, once every 100 million years, on average, a 10-kilometer asteroid like the one that did in the dinosaurs will strike Earth, unleashing 100 million megatons of energy and causing a mass extinction. That's what the Rhojani were confronted with. They recalculated, they examined, they reconsidered, but the numbers always came out the same. They had about 30 years warning, but in the end, they knew there was no escape.

They weren't a society that would just go quietly. They worked on their accelerated rocket technology development plan, they looked for a new home in the cosmos and they thought about how to preserve for all time a record of who they were, who they had been, and what their legacy would be. That last part became the pyramid. Knowing that their planet was doomed, the Rhojani felt this fierce desire to leave a record of their culture, history and technological achievements, in a place and in a way that would ensure this record survived for millions of years. And they succeeded.

So then the Rhojani pursued their last option for survival of their species.They recognized that in the time remaining they could only launch a small number of people on a colonization effort. They had to struggle with some critical technology gaps, but in the final disc, they reported that 3 craft, bearing a total of 510 souls had been launched toward Proxima Centuri B, an exoplanet orbiting the habitable zone of the red dwarf Proxima Centuri.

When the word circulated around the globe about what had happened to the Rhojani, there was this amazing outpouring of grief that in some ways made no sense.

Everyone knew the Rhojani were gone. Everyone knew that there would be some explanation for why that was true. But when the explanation did come out, everyone felt the incredible unfairness of it all. These noble people simply wiped out by a mindless rock careening through the cosmos. The present-day world had become attached to the Rhojani and mourned that they were gone.

The record stops shortly thereafter. It was presumed that the expected extinction event had occurred and the Rhojani were no more. All of this came out to the public in bits and pieces and it was an emotional journey for many.

Jake and Janice were lying on the beach in Yucatán, wrapped in each other's arms, processing the latest info that had come out about the Codex and what it revealed about the Rhojani's ultimate fate. Through the pyramid project, they had developed this feeling of oneness with the Rhojani, and now they felt a dark emptiness about what had happened.

"Wow, Jake! Do you ever think about what a roller coaster ride we've been through? I can still remember looking at the anomaly on the gravimetric scan. Can you believe where this has gone? In my wildest dreams, I could never have predicted this course of events. And now I'm melancholy for a race of people who've been dead since before dinosaurs roamed the earth!" Janice looked in his eyes and said. "Did we just dream all this? Is this real?"

"I know, darling, I know. I feel exactly the same way. But I try to remind myself that we were within a hairs breath of never learning the Rhojani's story. I'm thankful that the story of these noble people finally came out. I think what we've learned about them may have some transformative powers in our human society."

"Oh I know you're right Jake. I just have to try and stay positive. But don't you have to wonder if they made it?"

"We'll never know," Jake replied.

The final disc caused lots of attention to be focused on Proxima Centuri B.

Proxima Centauri b, sometimes referred to as Alpha Centauri Cb, is an exoplanet orbiting in the habitable zone of the red dwarf star Proxima Centauri, which is the closest star to the Sun and part of the triple star system Alpha Centauri. It is approximately 4.2 light years from Earth in the constellation Centaurus, making it, Proxima c, and Proxima d the closest known exoplanets to the our solar system.

Proxima Centauri b orbits its star at a distance of roughly 4.2 million miles with an orbital period of approximately 11.2 Earth days. Its other properties are only poorly understood, but it is believed to be a possibly Earth-like planet. The planet orbits within the habitable zone of its star. It is, however, not known whether or not it has an atmosphere. Proxima Centauri is a flare star with intense emission of electromagnetic radiation that could rip an atmosphere off the planet.

It was never clear where the idea first originated, but at some point the question was asked. "Why don't we send a message to Proxima Centuri B and see if we get an answer?"

Then a second question was asked " And why don't we send it to them in the Rhojani language?"

The proposal generated lots of discussion . Some were opposed, saying if the Rhojani had been successful in their colonization effort, by now they could dwarf us technologically. A signal might bring them to us with unfavorable consequences. Some said it was just a waste of time, whatever the fate of their colonization effort, they were certainly long since extinct. And the last school of thought said "Why not?" We know who this race is. There couldn't be a more gentle race in the universe.

The people at SETI were all in for the idea. The chance to send a targeted message in the language of the recipient to their last known interstellar address seemed absolutely too good to be true.

 It was debated at length in the UN. Finally it was agreed to proceed. But ultimately deciding what exactly we wanted to say ended up causing some delays.

SETI was given the task to compose a simple message of good will, written in the Rhojani language

And the message read:

"We send greetings to the Rhojani people from Human Beings (Homo Erectus) who live on your home planet that we call Earth. We found the record of your civilization on the Moon. We have translated the discs left behind by your race. We feel affection for your people and hope your long ago journey to Proxima Centuri B or Trantor was successful."

Including the name of the Rhojani's destination planet was the final delay. It took a little research to definitely identify what the Rhojani actually called their destination planet.

180

The signal was sent by SETI personnel. This after all was their particular area of expertise. The real expertise of SETI is receiving signals, and they prepared to monitor a broad array of incoming frequencies. But there wasn't any hurry. Proxima Centuri B was after all 4.2 light years away. So the soonest an answer could come was.... 8.4 years.

It was kind of an inescapable truth of radio transmission that had been lost in people gushing about communicating with the Rhojani. So after this, things kind of calmed down and the examination of the magnificent record left by the Rhojani became an academic exercise with a longer term focus.

So after a period of high adventure and amazing moments, Jake and Janice saw things start to go back to normal. They had an amazing summer at Coba, and then Janice had to be back at school for the Fall semester.

Jake and Janice had had lots of opportunities during the summer to think about and talk about their future. Janice knew that the position Jake had been offered by the Western Consortium was a big opportunity, one that could ultimately lead to senior management. But Janice also knew it would have him away for long periods of time. And of course there were also the risks of lunar work that needed to be considered. But Janice had not voiced any of that with him. She wanted him to decide for himself what was best, without any pressure from her.

They were sitting on Janice's veranda on a fine September evening. Jake turned to Janice "Could we talk for a minute about my job?" "Of course," Janice replied.

"I've been thinking about the job, and what it will require, and how much it will force us to be apart and I'm just not sure I want to do it. I want us to be together!" Jake said with feeling.

"So what do you envision for yourself professionally?" Janice asked.

"Well, I recently visited with Dean Fage of the archeology school and had a very interesting discussion. It looks like if I just picked up a couple of archeology classes, I could then pursue my PhD in Geoarcheology. The pyramid project really turned me on to archeology. It's a lot more interesting than refining rare earth metals. Dean Fage thought I could probably finish in under two years. He even indicated he could bring me

181

on as a teaching assistant. That means that at least for the next two years, I could leave work every day and be with you!"

He picked her up in his arms and swirled her around .

"You don't think you'd miss the thrill of lunar work?" Janice asked breathlessly.

"I thought maybe I could hedge my bets on that. I was thinking I would propose that the Western Consortium keep me on in a consulting capacity to advise the Lunar Artifacts Commission during the project to turn the pyramid site into a lunar memorial site."

Jake watched Janice for a reaction.

Janice hesitated for a second. She realized this was a big moment in their relationship. She wanted her response to Jake to be just right.

"I love it!" She cried out with exuberance. "I can't tell you how sad it has made me to think about sending you back to the Moon. I haven't wanted you to feel pressure. But I think your plan is wonderful."

And so that's what they did. Initially, Mike Murley was surprised and just slightly offended, but he had grown to like Jake. He agreed to Jake's consulting proposal and looked forward to working with him on the pyramid project.

Janice got back in the swing of things in her Stanford professorship while Jake reentered academic life and found he enjoyed it. It was a little amusing for him that he still had a hint of rock star status among the students. While teaching classes, he would occasionally get questions about the pyramid and he always tried to be generous in sharing with the students what it had been like.

The normalcy of Jake and Janice's day to day lives became a source of great joy to them. Every day after classes they would share their experiences.

The Fall semester slowly passed by. One day in early December, Jake was sitting in the kitchen, when Janice came in with a bagful of groceries.

After dinner, Jake came out on to the veranda with 2 aperitifs.

Janice smiled at him warmly and said "I think I'll skip the drink tonight. And I have some news for you."

Jake sat down and took both of Janice's hands in his and said "So tell me your news my love. Did you get a call from the Nobel committee. Did you get appointed dean of the geophysics department. Did you …"

Janice interrupted him "Nope, better than all that- I'm pregnant!"

Jake sat in stunned silence for a second and then finally reacted "That's wonderful! Oh my god, I'm going to be a father! When did you find out? When are you due?"

Janice smiled at Jake, enjoying his reaction. "Just today. And the doctor estimates late August."

They spent the rest of the evening talking about babies, and baby showers and baby names and how much they loved each other and whether they guessed it was going to be a boy or girl and how this would change their summer travel plans and all of the other things that two people in love and having a baby talk about.

Chapter Fourteen

D r. Hans Schmidt of NASA's Planetary Defense Coordination Office was sifting through a large set of positional readouts from the Minor Planet Center.

The Minor Planet Center (MPC) is the single worldwide location for receipt and distribution of positional measurements of minor planets, comets and other irregular natural satellites of the major planets. The MPC is responsible for the identification, designation and orbit computation for all of these objects. This involves maintaining the master files of observations and orbits, keeping track of the discoverer of each object, and announcing discoveries to the rest of the world via electronic circulars and an extensive website.

Dr Schmidt saw that the computer report had flagged 2003 EL61. He remembered that that was the designation for Haumea, unusual dwarf planet orbiting the Sun in the Kuiper Belt beyond Pluto.

Showing up on this report indicated that some perturbation had been detected in Haumea's orbit. Dr Schmidt decided to order a scan of the region of the Kuiper Belt where Haumea was located using the wide-field telescope camera system. The wide-field telescope camera system monitors thousands of stars simultaneously to see if a Kuiper Belt object passes in front of any of them. Such an object would diminish a star's light for only one-tenth of a second while traveling by, meaning a camera has to be fast in order to capture it.

The camera picked up a blip where none was expected. Dr Schmidt picked up the phone and called the Jet Propulsion Lab.

"I need to request a scan by the James Webb Telescope II of a region of the Kuiper Belt. Here are the coordinates." He read out the numbers and the technician read them back "That's right. How soon do you think I might be able to get that? Ok, that's great"

The James Webb II was the second generation space located telescope. After the spectacular successes of James Webb I, this second generation satellite was launched in 2060, and just like the first, it sat in orbit some million miles from Earth. The first telescope had primarily focused on the infrared, but the second generation featured also enhanced visible and UV light imaging.

Dr Schmidt came in the next day and saw that his report from the space telescope had arrived. What he saw was concerning. Haumea had been the subject of several investigations including one deep space fly by that had produced excellent images of this strangely shaped dwarf planet. The images from the James Webb telescope captured Haumea. The larger moon of Haumea called Hiʻiaka was also plainly visible. But there was no sign of Namaka, the smaller moon of Haumea. Namaka is only 1.5% as bright as its parent dwarf planet Haumea and is about 0.05% its mass. It is about 170 km in diameter. And it wasn't there. It looks like the perturbation picked up on the positional readouts was caused by Namaka being ripped away from Haumea.

That was quite extraordinary. He looked at the larger field of vision photograph from the James Webb report and saw an object that could be it. He entered the coordinates back into the Minor Planet Center system and requested tracking on this object.

The following day, Dr Schmidt checked the Minor Planet Center Report. He checked for his newly added object, and was alarmed to see that it had been added to the Potentially Hazardous Asteroids report. The system modeled orbits of asteroids out several years. Dr Schmidt pulled up the modeling program to see what was shown for this object. He saw that in 36 months it would pass relatively close to Saturn. He decided to push the model parameters out for a longer time period to see what happened   He only had to go out to 60 months and there it was. This runaway moon approximately 100 miles in diameter would strike Earth at a velocity of around 22,000 miles per hour. Dr Schmidt felt the perspiration running down his back. He must have made some mistake. He ran the extended simulation again. Same result.

"Oh my god, this can't be." He called up a colleague at JPL and asked him to run the same simulation. As he waited on the phone he heard an "oh my god" on the other end and knew he already had his answer.

He hesitated for a second, then picked up his phone and dialed the number for his big boss, the Planetary Defense Officer. The phone immediately went to voice mail. Dr Schmidt thought to himself that this probably wasn't the best thing to leave a message about. He walked down the hall, found the Defense Officer and gave him the news.

Jake was sitting in his office at the Lunar Pyramid complex thinking he needed to give Janice a call.

"Hi Darling, how are you doing? Has the little guy driven you crazy yet? Jake could see Robbie playing in the background.

"He's been fine!" Janice replied "He got a gold star today at kindergarten for his dinosaur drawing- pretty good looking triceratops by your son!"

"I miss you both Darling. I'm just going to be here another two days and then I should be home. Today was the dedication for the Pyramid Marriott, so naturally Mike Murley was here. I think my consulting work here is going to dry up pretty soon, which is fine with me."

" Come say Hi to daddy ,Robbie." Robbie wandered over to the monitor and gave him a big smile and yelled out "Daddy!"

"Hi there buddie, are you being good for Mommy? I'll be home soon."

Robbie wandered back to his favorite fire truck.

Janice came back in view. "Sorry, love, I'm going to have to go. Got a doctors appt for Robbie, just a routine checkup."

"Ok love you honey"

"Love you too, bye."

"Hello this is Dr Helmut von Braun from the Planetary Defense Coordination Office. I need to talk to the NASA administrator."

The NASA administrator came on the line and Dr von Braun told him that they had found an object that was projected to strike Earth in a little over 5 years. The administrator seemed less then impressed until he was told that the object in question was a little over 100 miles in diameter.

"Oh my god, that would be an extinction event" the administrator cried out.

"Yes sir, that's correct"

"We need to go see the President immediately. Can you be in Washington by 1600?"

"Yes sir, I can."

The head of NASA and the Planetary Defense Office administrator were in the Oval Office at 4 pm. Also present were the Director of National Security, the Chairman of the Joint Chiefs of Staff, the head of the FBI, the CIA Director, the Secretary of State, the Commerce Secretary and the Vice President. President Sarah Landon arrived a minute or so later.

After the NASA administrator briefed the group, the president said. "So what are our options?"

Dr von Braun spoke up "We did a pilot study years ago when we crashed a spacecraft into an asteroid to see how such a craft could alter the orbital path of an asteroid. The test was successful in slightly modifying the asteroid orbit but that was with an asteroid about 100 meters in diameter. The object coming at us is more than 100 miles in diameter. We probably need to consider trying to hit it with a major yield nuclear warhead. But there are no guarantees. An object of this magnitude possesses enormous inertia that makes it very difficult to change its trajectory. However, we have 5 years so even a very small change now could make the critical difference. The bottom line is that time is of the essence. We must launch a warhead as soon as humanly possible."

"So are there technical issues we have to overcome to do that? " the President asked.

Dr von Braun responded. "We have the technology to deliver a high yield nuclear warhead to the asteroid. We just need consensus from scientists and engineers concerning how to detonate the warhead to achieve the greatest chance of success. Options include high velocity

187

impact right into the asteroid, use of multiple lower yield warheads, space burst detonation and others. The subject has been studied already at some length so I would expect the expert community to come to a rapid consensus."

"What's your best estimate of how soon we could launch such a mission?" the President responded.

"I think 3 months would be aggressive but doable," Dr von Braun said.

" And how long to get to the asteroid?" The president asked

Dr vonBraun continued "So we're looking at a distance of over 4 billion miles. At the velocity that most of our flyby missions to the outer solar system achieved, the trip would take several years…"

There was an audible groan in the room.

"But with creative use of the sun's gravitational pull, we could vastly increase the vehicle's terminal velocity. My guess at this point and it is only a guess, is that we might be able to shorten the trip duration down to 6 month."

President Landon resumed " So you're saying in a best case, we could strike the asteroid in 9 months"

"Yes, Madam President."

"And how soon would we know whether it worked?"

"Approximately 8 hours," Von Braun replied. "Just the time it takes for light to travel from the Kuiper Belt to Earth."

"So is there any chance that you're wrong? How has this finding been verified?" Now the President was beginning to sound apprehensive.

"We ran the findings by JPL's top people on celestial navigation and they all concurred: Earth strike in a little over 5 years."

"Any dissenting opinions?"

"No, Mr President."

The President sat back in her chair. "So when word of this gets out, people are going to lose their minds. Do you think we can keep this mission Top Secret?"

"Well, we kept the first atom bomb secret, but I'm not sure it makes sense to go that route. By being open from the beginning, we can maximize global collaboration. But if we do that, we have to ensure swift response and not be engaged in protracted debates," Dr von Braun asserted.

"Global collaboration means world leaders can reassure their citizens that the plan is sound. The world markets will definitely tank after the initial announcement, but hopefully will recover once a plan is announced," Dr von Braun continued.

Several of the meeting attendees weighed in.

"We should notify police forces across the country to mobilize units in preparation for possible rioting," the head of the FBI recommended.

"We should send top secret communications to the G9 heads indicating what we're going to be announcing," the Secretary of State pointed out.

"If possible we should delay the announcement for 12 hours to come after Friday's market close," the Commerce Secretary interjected.

"We should brief the House and Senate leadership," the Vice President offered.

"I agree with all your recommendations. Please proceed," the President responded.

Friday at 4 pm, the White House issued a press release which stressed the very fine work of the Planetary Defense Coordination Office in early detection of the threat from this asteroid. The release stressed the seriousness of the situation but reassured that US and international partners were being marshaled to aggressively attack this threat, and that the 5 year advance warning guaranteed we would be successful.

Within a short time, investigative reporters had learned that the asteroid had a name, that it was over 100 miles in diameter and that a strike would without question be a global extinction event. Soon headlines around the world screamed out **NAMAKA is coming!** News outlets came up with terrifying comparisons: the Tunguska asteroid which flattened almost a million trees over an 800 square mile area of Siberia in 1908 was about 60 feet in diameter. The Chicxulub asteroid that struck in the Gulf of

Mexico 66 million years ago and wiped out the dinosaurs was about 6 miles in diameter. And Nakama was HOW BIG ?

The hysteria produced by the announcement was as bad as everyone feared. Major riots erupted in a number of cities around the world. Several world leaders claimed the US had been premature in putting this out. The Chinese asserted that their results showed less likelihood of an impact. A number of religious sects pointed to this as the final days and claimed they had accurately predicted it. The NYSE closed Monday after the Dow dropped 22,000 points in an hour. A mass shooter took out 17 citizens in a Texas mall. Applications for a spot on the next Mars mission increased by 700% in just hours. Grocery stores all over the US sold out of toilet paper, batteries, peanut butter and bottled water within hours. Long lines were seen at ATMs until the cash ran out. Tabloids labeled it all as fake news and told their viewers it was a Democrat plot.

Within days, scientists and engineers from around the world were meeting in Switzerland to hammer out a plan of attack to bring against this global threat.

There had been considerable work done on this topic since early in the century. The Chelyabinsk meteor, which struck Siberia in 2013 had been a wake up call for world leaders.

The US established the Planetary Defense Coordination Office in 2016 as a branch of NASA. NASA's Planetary Defense Coordination Office (PDCO) is responsible for:

Ensuring the early detection of potentially hazardous objects (PHOs) - asteroids and comets whose orbits are predicted to bring them within 0.05 astronomical units of Earth's orbit; and of a size large enough to reach Earth's surface - that is, greater than perhaps 30 to 50 meters;

Tracking and characterizing PHOs and issuing warnings about potential impacts;

Providing timely and accurate communications about PHOs; and

Performing as a lead coordination node in U.S. Government planning for response to an actual impact threat. (Citation from NASA)

Over the ensuing 50 plus years, this office had worked with astronomers all over the world to establish a monitoring system to identify and track

190

celestial objects in near earth orbit. The work of the group had largely been successful. There had been no major asteroid strikes during this period. There had been a few surprises, near misses that mostly occurred from near earth objects coming at earth from the direction of the sun, a direction that presented optical challenges.

Early in the century, the DART mission (Double Asteroid Redirection Test) was launched. It involved crashing a 1200 pound spacecraft into the smaller (160 meters) of two asteroids (Dimorphos) that formed a binary system with Didymos (780 meters) at a velocity of approximately 14,000 miles per hour.

Precise measurements were made of the orbital period of Dimorphos around Didymos and remeasured after the satellite collision. The experiment had shown that it was possible to impact the orbit of an asteroid, but what that foretold with regard to Asteroid Namaka was unclear and hotly debated. Namaka had a mass over 3 million times larger than Didymos, so clearly a much larger force would need to be brought to bear. Hence the decision to go with a nuclear warhead was made virtually from the start.

The selection of an orbital window was a complicated timing question. If they could launch within 2 months, then the sun could be used to speed up the vehicle tremendously and the 8 month flight duration quoted to the president could be achieved. However beyond 2 months, Earth would begin swinging around the sun to a point where any gravitational sling shot effect was no longer feasible.

Some scientists questioned how an asteroid that until recently had an orbital period of 283 years could suddenly be threatening earth within 5 years. A recreation of orbital motions for the month prior revealed the answer. An unusual conjunction of Neptune and Haumea had caused a major gravitational effect on Namaka, causing it to be torn away from its orbit around Haumea and sending it spinning wildly through space and sharply degrading its orbit. That in itself wouldn't have been enough, but in an encounter that was astronomically improbable, Namaka was, based on its current trajectory, going to be pulled into the gravitational influence of Jupiter, accelerated substantially and then propelled onward in the direction of Earth.

The question of selecting a launch vehicle was relatively simple.

Earlier in the century, the Russians might have been the choice, but in the last 20 years, the US Saturn X rocket had become dominant in the colonization of Mars. The rocket boasted huge lift off capability and could be coupled with the third stage ion drive propulsion system to result in the maximum available flight terminal velocity.

The question of how to initiate the nuclear blast was complicated by the very rapid orbital rotation speed of the asteroid. Hitting the asteroid squarely would be complicated.

Many of the scientists were leaning toward the space blast approach in which the rocket would simply draw abreast of the asteroid and then detonate. The drawback to this was the tremendous kinetic energy of the rocket traveling at 50 or 100,000 miles per hour wouldn't be utilized The reason for this approach is that no current nuclear weapons could remain functional with the extreme deceleration and casing destruction that occurs during a direct impact.

Jake and Janice, like everyone else on the planet, were in a state of shock. The discovery of our own extinction event on the way just a few short years after finding out about the tragedy of the Rhojani left everyone numb. Many relieved the stress by convincing themselves that nothing could withstand a nuclear bomb even though leading experts put our chances of success at no higher than 50/50. Others simply tuned it out.

Jake and Janice decided they were going to find something meaningful to do with the remaining time. They owed that to their son Robbie and their unborn daughter who would arrive soon. It certainly was a natural thing that world events made them think about the pyramid. It had been a big part of their lives for several years and the undeniable parallels between the fates of the Rhojani and humans caused them to have an inspiration.

Jake started first "I think we should put the discs back in the pyramid, seal it up and bury it."

Then Janice weighed in. "And right beside the pyramid, we should install our own vault that details the human race on Earth. Leave behind our own fused quartz discs with our story."

Both knew immediately they would pursue this. They talked late into the night, brainstorming how to bring forth a proposal, how the project could be completed in time, what the human facility should look like and contain.

And they decided the first person they would talk to was Mike Murley. They both agreed that he was one cantankerous SOB, but a guy who, once he was on your side, would move heaven and earth to make it happen.

Mike Murley listened to their proposal. The more they talked, the redder his face got. Finally he couldn't take anymore.

"Have you lost your minds? You want me to take the pyramid where we've just invested 50 million dollars and reseal it?"

Jake picked up the question. "The main work immediately would be for the construction of a human vault to perform the same function as the pyramid but for the human race. We would put together a similar facility, which will survive the human race if Namaka strikes Earth. We believe that even if we somehow avoid extinction, preserving a record of who we are is a noble and worthy mission."

Janice jumped in. "And we could wait until after the missile strike on Namaka for the go/ no go decision with regard to resealing the Rhojani pyramid."

Jake resumed " We all were greatly moved by learning the Rhojani story. Do we want to take the chance that our own story may be lost forever?"

After considerable more discussion, Mike Murley was finally on board with the idea. He discussed it with Dr Monroe from the Lunar Artifacts Commission. He argued that politicians would resist embracing the idea since the rationale for doing it was failure of the mission to change the asteroid's trajectory.

Mike Murley recognized that Dr Monroe was probably right. But his counter argument was that getting people around the world to focus on how to capture and document the history of the human race would give them something besides impending doom to think about. Politicians might well see the diversion it provided as much needed relief from the daily drumbeat of articles about Namaka.

Dr James Monroe presented the proposal at a meeting of the UN Security Council. The council seemed to adopt Mike Murley's counter argument. After numerous sessions where extinction was the main event, participants jumped at the chance to talk about some positive action. After a short debate, the Council allocated 100 million dollars to fund the Human History Preservation Project. Mike Murley was put in charge.

Worldwide reaction was predictable. The English tabloids screamed headlines **UN Knows Rocket Won't Save Us**. The mainstream media depicted it evenly, noting it could be seen as a hedge against failure but also arguing that preserving a record of our heritage as the Rhojani did with their pyramid was a noble mission that people should support.

Now that the whole idea was approved and funded, Mike Murley knew he had a tiger by the tail. Everyone was going to have their own idea about what the project and the facility to house the project should look like. Dr Murley's challenge was to open the design phase to widespread participation but manage the process so the hard deadline they faced could be met. And deadline it was. The term was a little unfortunate .

Dr Murley assembled a team to coordinate the process. They included some of his own staff from the Western Consortium, architects, engineers and personnel with lunar experience: Jake, Janice and Jim Stefano.

He then drew up a list of leading academics, statesmen, industry leaders and religious leaders and invited them to participate in an advisory council. Overall acceptance rate was high. Dr. Monroe was appointed to head up this advisory group.

Meanwhile, Mission Namaka was on schedule. NASA working with private contractors had been able to prep the Saturn X rocket for launch in record time. The mission plan had been hammered out. In addition, a second rocket would be launched to place a high resolution camera within 25,000 miles of Nakama to film the nuclear explosion. The camera might play a crucial role if this first attempt was unsuccessful. After considerable debate, the final decision was to go with a space blast. This would allow for precise positioning of the warhead prior to detonation.

Jake was sitting at his desk at the university thinking about the Human History Preservation Project. The more the working group had explored the idea of mimicking what the Rhojani had done, the more the differences between the two species became apparent. The racial diversity that was a hallmark of human society seemed to be something that was totally absent for the Rhojani. There certainly were multiple cultures and languages with the Rhojani, but they seemed to be one very homogenous race. So having statues of 2 humans in the building to be constructed just wouldn't work. We needed to have something that displayed that diversity. "Maybe we need to have a line of statues of various races all mixed together and holding hands. It could convey that while there were different human races, we lived in harmony."Jake liked the mental image and thought he would bring this up the next time he met with Dr Murley.

Dr Bartlett, who first downloaded the Rhojani fused quartz discs, was working on trying to duplicate the Rhojani's technical achievement of 5 dimensional super compact permanent data storage. The idea of using fused quartz as a storage medium had been around for quite a while. And the ability to etch the quartz using 5D laser etching which employed 2 optical and 3 spatial dimensions had also been around a while. The problem was etching rate. With current lasers, Dr Bartlett calculated that they could match the volume of data the Rhojani's included in their 8 discs *in 300 years.*

Dr Bartlett was working on using a technique called parallel writing which allowed simultaneous writing from multiple lasers. His last experiment had shown a 5000% increase in writing speed. He felt confidant that they were going to solve the technical issues, but the time pressure was enormous.

A team of architects were studying the problem of how to place a storage vault on the moon that would withstand meteor bombardments and provide long term stability for the storage vault contents. In the end, they found it almost slightly embarrassing to realize that their design criteria ended up with virtually the same building that the Rhojani had built 300 million years ago. They couldn't exactly match the titanium alloy the Rhojani had used, but they came up with something of comparable strength and structural integrity. And of course the pyramid shape proved to be optimal for a structure that would be buried under megatons of lunar regolith. So the ultimate design recommendation was to be build a second pyramid adjacent to the Rhojani pyramid.

Dr Murley's advisory council was rapidly becoming a problem. This group was charged with ultimately committing the history of man to the fused quartz discs. And of course that threatened to turn into an endless battle. Do we tell the story of the colonial oppressors or do the oppressed

195

also get a voice?. Do we allow the history to only be written by the victors, or do the defeated have a voice? Were Jim Bowie and Colonel Travis heroes of Texas Independence or slave traders bent on keeping the slave trade alive?

This went on and on. The council reported back to Murley and he blew a gasket.

"Either figure out an answer to resolving this or I'll find a new council that can get the job done. For god's sake ladies and gentlemen, we're talking about leaving a record that runs to 10s of terabytes! Give everyone's view, the oppressor, the oppressed, whatever. Just remember if you don't get moving, then you may well end up leaving nothing behind." Mike Murley blasted the assembled group.

If Jamison had been present , he would have opined that there's nothing like a Mike Murley ass chewing to break up project log jams!

Chapter Fifteen

On a warm summer morning at Cape Canaveral, the entire world tuned in to watch the launch of the Saturn X rocket that was intended to save the human race from Namaka. The launch was picture perfect and the announcers noted as successive rocket stages burned correctly, that everything was "nominal" Of course there were those who thought that the term hardly applied. There was nothing "normal" here. When had we ever launched a 100 megaton bomb from a space launch facility?

The launch occurred within the 2 month window that allowed for the sun trajectory to accelerate the payload, so the original 9 month arrival estimate was still achievable.

A week before, the camera that would photograph the meeting of the nuclear missile and Namaka had been launched, again with no problems.

For many, it was kind of anticlimactic once the launch was complete. No issue resolution, just 6 months of waiting to look forward to.

Unfortunately, there was no shortage of people claiming to know what was going to happen.

There were a small number who had real expertise. They were physicists, some of whom had worked on nuclear weapons design and knew things about explosive yield and shock wave magnitude or they were astrophysicists who had studied the motions of planets and asteroids. But most of these experts weren't saying much, because they didn't really know whether this would work. So in the absence of real experts who could reassure the public, there were a large number of people looking to gain fame or notoriety by making pronouncements about what was going to happen. And pronouncements about success don't win people much viewership, so the majority of these marginally qualified prognosticators predicted doom.

And so for the next six months, the world was in limbo.

Mike Murley and his project team were working hard on the Human History Preservation Project. The plans for the pyramid were drawn up. The building would sit adjacent to the Rhojani pyramid. There would be an obelisk to mark its location. A new Rhojani obelisk to replace the one destroyed by a meteor strike was being fabricated.

The advisory committee had agreed upon a sizable percentage of the information that would be recorded on the fused quartz discs from a history perspective. Considerable progress had also been made with regard to the technological accomplishments of the human race. Agreements were in some cases required to ensure protection against patent infringement if extinction didn't occur. Attorneys liked to joke that was a win-win for the companys providing the design information.

The project seemed to be moving along at a pace that would assure timely completion.

And 6 months passed with agonizing slowness and then the world held it breath.

The photographic probe was in position, 25,000 miles from Namaka. A feed was being relayed to Earth and on Earth it was being televised around the world. Everyone understood that there would be a delay of over 8 hours between the time engineers detonated the bomb and when the image of the explosion showed up on our screens.

Engineers in the Jet Propulsion Lab in Pasadena were using the photographic probe to confirm the positions of the asteroid and the nuclear armed missile. The extremely high terminal velocity of the rocket that had been necessary to keep the travel time to the Kuiper Belt below 6 months also meant that the missile would close very rapidly with the asteroid. This meant that the timing of the detonation had to be extremely precise. Rather than try to manage the detonation decision remotely, engineers had programmed the missile to track the asteroid, to navigate for a flyby within 2 miles and to initiate detonation when the 2 mile distance was achieved. So the JPL personnel were really just observers.

The JPL flight director announced "We have flyby in 2 minutes and counting. 30 seconds. Detonation."

But of course nothing was visible. Everyone all over the world stopped. Then everyone waited. Approximately 8 hours later, the radio waves transmitted from the photographic probe reached Earth. Even at 25,000 mile distance, the blast looked huge. In the vacuum of space, it was perfectly round and appeared to engulf and entirely obscure Namaka. People around the world cheered wildly.

"Take that Namaka! Nobody messes with us Namaka!"

After the initial explosion the nuclear cloud continued to expand and the flame and bright orange color gradually faded. Within a few minutes, Namaka was clearly visible again. There was nothing to see that showed any change, but the public had already been told this would be the case. They understood that scientists would have to re-plot the orbit of Namaka, run their projections and see if the nuke had nudged the asteroid enough to change its orbit and avoid hitting Earth.

So once again the world waited to hear the verdict. An hour passed.

Finally, the JPL flight director came on camera. The ashen color of his face told many what the answer was, but they still waited to hear it.

"The asteroid Namaka is still on track to strike Earth. There is no indication that the nuclear weapon affected Namaka's trajectory."

Everyone knew this was their last hope and those hopes had been dashed. There was no Plan B. There had been discussion about trying to investigate a colonization effort to another planet. Everyone remembered that the Rhojani had done that when facing this same threat. But we just weren't there yet. The technology to really make interstellar travel feasible was probably still thirty years away.

The reactions this time dwarfed the earlier responses of people. There were untold thousands of suicides worldwide, mass suicides, terrible riots, looting and lawlessness on a massive scale, meetings of doomsday cults, people just walking off their jobs or not showing up. There was just nothing left to feel hopeful about.

199

Dr Murley had been watching the JPL announcement with his project team.

"Ok people, there it is. Now we know our work is critical. I know it's hard to keep going, but let's use the time remaining to make a difference." While he rarely did so, for a moment Mike Murley waxed poetic "Do not go gentle into that good night. Rage, rage against the dying of the light" quoting the famous Dylan Thomas poem.

Mike and the entire team redoubled their efforts. Time was slipping away.

Namaka was just under 4 years away.

The construction on the second pyramid got under way within another 3 months. First the 30 meter thick regolith was removed with large lunar bulldozers. Automated ore haulers were loaded, one every two minutes and the lunar material was dumped in a new slag heap. Once the underlying lunar bedrock was exposed, drilling rigs were brought in to drill bore holes which were then packed with explosive and detonated. The pulverized lunar bedrock was then bulldozed up and loaded into the ore handlers. Pilings were driven into the ground around the perimeter of the site to hold back the excavation walls. After several months, the site was ready to begin pyramid construction. Much of the heavy assembly work was performed by robotic machines. It was just not feasible for men in space suits to do much of this work. Within a year, the framework of the pyramid was in place and the work began on installing the tungsten alloy sheets that would form the walls of the pyramid.

Meanwhile, Dr Bartlett had made that breakthrough he needed in laser etching speed. He was now on track to have the fused quartz discs ready in 2.8 years. He felt like they had accomplished miracles but Mike Murley pushed them to shave still more time off. Dr Bartlett promised to try.

Jake and Janice supported the project as best they could, given their other responsibilities. Jake was awarded his PhD in Geoarcheology. His good friend Dr. James Higgins was there to celebrate with them. Janice, Robbie and Amanda, now 3 years old, cheered for dad as the Dean gave him his certificate.

Janice had served as a part time spokesperson for the Human History Preservation Project, doing a few of the talk shows and other promotions.

Jake had continued consulting on the pyramid project, helping with logistics planning.

And time continued to pass through the hourglass. Namaka was now 2 years away.

And just when everything seemed to have settled into a predictable downward spiral, when the swirling of the water rushing down the drain was becoming deafening, when the extinction event was starting to feel exceedingly personal, something unexpected happened.

The SETI monitoring station picked up a signal. The diligence of the SETI personnel in executing their monitoring tasks had been waning the last few months what with "oh I don't know, how about the end of the freaking world."

So it was almost by chance that the signal was picked up. At first, the signal seemed unintelligible, but then one of the SETI folks was reminded of the message that was sent to the Rhojani some 4+ years previously. He pulled up the Rhojani translation key and shortly he was sitting looking at the first message in the history of SETI from an alien civilization. Well, not exactly alien, but close enough.

The message read "Greetings to the Human Beings from the Rhojani people. We received your message. We are happy that you found the record of our people. Our trip to Proxima B long ago was successful. We would like to meet the Human Beings. We are sending a ship to visit. We come in peace."

The SETI representative looked at the message in front of him. It was the most exciting thing he had ever experienced and something he had spent years working for. He tried to decide who he should notify first.

Within hours, the President had been informed, and the message was shared with other world leaders. The message posed a difficult question for its recipients. Since radio messages required an 8 year round trip, would the arrival of the Rhojani occur too late? Would they arrive only to find a lifeless world, ravaged by the impact of Namaka? The message gave no clue as to when the Rhojani were coming. Scientists argued that the 4 light year distance to Proxima B made it unlikely that the Rhojani would arrive in time. But did it really matter? Hard to play host while simultaneously doing an extinction. Scientists also found it inexplicable that we had received an answer so quickly. Did the Rhojani have some capability for faster than light communication?

There was discussion about how or whether to respond. Finally, it was decided not to send anything. Any possible response from the Rhojani would be after the impact date.

But the word that the Rhojani were alive and that we had heard from them was another shot heard round the world. People buzzed about it. Some wondered if a society that had escaped earth 300 million years ago might have become technological giants. Maybe the Rhojani could help us. Most viewed it as wishful thinking.

So life moved on and the momentary excitement waned as the inescapable grim reality returned.

The level of chaos in the world reached a fever pitch. Global supply chains were in tatters. Virtually every organization, corporation , military unit faced more than 1/3rd of their personnel simply dropping out, staying home huddled in bed frozen by the enormity of the coming event. Nothing worked any more. The internet became more and more unreliable. Power outages became the norm. Store shelves featured more and more emptiness.

Governments pleaded with people to stay the course, but people weren't buying it. What was the point? Some saw the asteroid as the opportunity to give into their basest instincts. There were Woodstock size orgies, armed bands terrorizing the countryside, and just about every other depravity man could conceive of. But even that didn't work after a while. Breweries, distilleries and drug dealers are supply chains too and all of these things were soon unavailable.

The Human History Preservation Project teetered on the brink. Dr Murley wasn't sure they could hold things together long enough to make it work. Even his project team started having more and more defections.

And then one day, out of nowhere, without fanfare or advanced notice, the Rhojani arrived. They approached us carefully, first stationing their spacecraft in Earth orbit about a million miles away. They broadcast video signals which were seen all over the world. There on the screen were the faces the whole world recognized. The pointed ears, the large eyes, the warm smiles. The message they sent arrived in 10 different

202

Earth languages and conveyed warm greetings from the Rhojani. They proposed to send a delegation to Earth and requested our recommendation for the best place for the delegation to go. After a global conference call of world leaders, a message was sent back in their language recommending that the delegation arrive at the United Nations in New York the next day at 1300. An emergency session of the UN was called. Extraordinary security precautions were organized on the fly. No one knew what to expect.

The world was stunned. Many felt a sense of embarrassment that the visit came at a time when our whole social fabric was being rent asunder. We would like to have acted as gracious hosts, but our dilemma was similar to receiving a visit from an old friend when you're deathly ill.

For many it came as a last gasp hope.

"They came here from a planet four light years away and they did it in months. They've got to have technology we can only imagine." This was a common refrain.

The plans for meeting the Rhojani were rapidly put together. A group of dignitaries, many from the UN, plus the President of the United States, plus an assorted group of other world leaders were assembled. Somehow, Jake and Janice and Mike Murley made the list. As persons who had played a key role in excavating the Rhojani pyramid, it seemed appropriate. A private jet whisked Jake and Janice to the event.

As a sign of our affection, a large banner bearing the symbol that had been found in the pyramid and in the Mayan glyphs was displayed.

Speeches were prepared. We did our best to play gracious hosts. And we waited.

The next day, at 1300 hours, the assembled dignitaries, flanked by the heaviest security ever put in place for a UN event, were all looking skyward, trying to catch a first glimpse of the spacecraft.

No one was ever sure who first looked down from the sky and noticed the golden shimmering disturbance in the atmosphere right in front of the reviewing stand, but soon everyone was pointing to it. It gradually became more and more substantial and suddenly there they were.

The Rhojani had arrived; a group of five. They stood for a moment looking around, acclimating themselves to their new surroundings

Somehow the etched glass statues hadn't done them justice. They were as tall as we thought, but their skin had a buttery bronze color that was complemented by their incredibly colorful shimmering robes. They wore some kind of clear helmet that appeared to be providing breathing air. They looked around for a few more moments, getting adjusted to the bright sun light.

The US President, Sarah Landon approached them first, bowed and said in the Rhojani language "On behalf of human beings, welcome home."

One of the Rhojani stepped forward, looked at the president and said in perfect English. "Thank you for your warm welcome. For the Rhojani people, it is an event of indescribable joy to once again set foot on the planet of our forefathers. We look forward to making a lasting friendship with our successors, the human beings. And we are moved by your display of the Trisom, the symbol of our people.

After the initial exchange of words, the Rhojani were invited inside the UN, where the assembled guests had an opportunity to mingle with their visitors. The people arranging the event didn't know much about the Rhojani's eating requirements, food allergies, drinking habits, etc. so with the catered foods and drink, each was accompanied with a detailed description in the Rhojani language of what the food was and what it contained.

Once the Rhojani were inside, they removed their clear helmets. One of them was asked about it. In perfect English, the Rhojani said "On Earth back when the Rhojani lived here, the oxygen content was 31%. With the current 20 %, we can get by, it just leaves us feeling a little tired."

Another member of the UN delegation asked. "How can you speak perfect English?"

The Rhojani answered "We have a program that converts everything you say to us to our language. And when we speak, everything we say is expressed in your language." Our translation program includes some 30 of your current earth languages."

Jake was excited to have the opportunity to meet and talk to the Rhojani delegation. He started to speak. "My name is Jake Mackensie and I ...." He was interrupted by one of the Rhojani " Mr Mackensie we know your name well. As we approached Earth, we briefed ourself on recent events. As a result we know that you played a key role in the discovery and subsequent excavation of our pyramid, as you call it. We are grateful for what you have done. You have allowed us to reconnect with our ancestors."

Jake blushed a little. He hadn't expected that the Rhojani would know anything about him or his role in discovering the pyramid.

"Thank you for your kind words. It was the honor of my life to have been involved in bringing the story of your people to light."

The groups mingled just like social events since time immemorial. The UN members soon learned that ethanol was also enjoyed by the Rhojani.

The Rhojani gingerly tasted some meat products and declared them tasty, although no one explained to them exactly what a cow or chicken was.

The Rhojani carried no weapons and were curious about some of the sidearms worn by security personnel. Explaining their purpose proved to be difficult, since inflicting injury on other living beings was an unknown concept to the Rhojani.

Several people were curious about Rhojani space technology. They asked how was it possible that the Rhojani had arrived here in less time then it took for light to travel from Proxima Centuri B to Earth.

The Rhojani explained that their current space technology involved the mastering of worm holes, which allowed them to warp space time and take short cuts through the universe, making travel faster than the speed of light possible.

Jake asked one of the Rhojani the significance of the Trisom, and explained how remarkably an ancient group of indigenous peoples had referenced the Trisom in their religious documents. The Rhojani explained that the Trisom was the chief symbol of their race and that at the same time that the original pyramid was being constructed they had reproduced 100's of copies of the Trisom around the planet as another attempt to leave a permanent record of their society

After this pleasant meeting, the President explained to the Rhojani that the UNSecurity Council included representatives from the entire world and asked if they would like to address this body.

The Rhojani responded that they would be honored. The Security Council reconvened at 1600.

The UN Secretary General, Javier Lopez de Santa Ana, spoke to the group and introduced the Rhojani Speaker.

"Ladies and Gentlemen, it is my great honor to introduce Lander Trovari, the leader of the Rhojani Delegation. In the history of this august body, we have never experienced anything like this. We all know the amazing story of the Rhojani from long ago, but now after the passage of eons of time, we have standing before us the modern day descendants of that race. They come to us in peace."

Lander Trovari strode to the podium. His extreme height forced a minute of microphone adjustment. He looked around the room and began. For a good percentage of those present, they heard Trovari speaking in their own language, which all found amazing. Normally, the audience would hear a translator translating the speaker's words.

"My dear Human Beings, it is my extreme pleasure to stand before you today. We left this planet eons ago and suffered immeasurable loss of friends , family, indeed our entire society. We struggled across the cosmos and eventually found a new home in the planet you call Proxima B. Initially it was a struggle for us, but it finally became home to us. We left a record of our society here , with the hope that one day life would return to this planet. And return it did. We were very gratified that you found the record we left of our society and we hope that you found positive things in that record. We applaud you as the new custodians of planet Earth, as you call it. We look forward to getting to know the human beings and we feel that there is a permanent bond between our two peoples that we hope will last. We are aware of the existential threat that you are currently facing and we could not feel more empathetic to your situation. Our ancestors knew the impossible situation that faces a society confronted with such an event. A small group of our ancestors escaped that fate, and every since that time, it had been a central premise of our society that we would never let such a thing happen to us again. We developed the technology to protect ourselves, and we have been successful in protecting our planet. And my message today is to tell you that we will not let this existential threat destroy your planet. We are your brothers and we will not let this happen."

The Security Council sat for perhaps 10 or 15 seconds in absolute stunned silence. Then all hell broke loose. Wild applause, laughter, hooting and cheers. They almost couldn't grasp the Rhojani message. But they believed it and instantly the stress of the last 5 years evaporated. The press covering the speech ran for the exits to immediately get the story out.

After the presentation, Lander Trovari and the other Rhojani spoke with the assembled dignitaries. President Landon wanted to make sure there was no misunderstanding.

"So you have a way to divert this asteroid headed toward us?" She asked.

"No, not divert it," Lander Trovari said, "we will eliminate it."

"Does your ability to eliminate it have a good chance of success?" The President followed up.

"There is no chance of failure. We will eliminate it." Trovari responded.

"Is there something you need from us in return?" the President asked.

"Just your friendship." Trovari responded.

The President exhaled deeply. The incredible feeling of relief was the first positive feeling she had had in months.

After this, the group descended into small talk. The Rhojani were asked what they would like to see during their visit.

They expressed interest in seeing the pyramid on the Moon as well as the adjoining pyramid that human beings were installing. They explained that the pyramid was a last link for them with their long extinct ancestors.

Meanwhile, another shockwave shot round the planet. People wanted to believe that the end of the planet had been canceled, but after so many emotional ups and downs, no one was totally sure how to feel.

President Landon, with the UN Secretary General at her side, broadcast a message around the world telling everyone that they thought this was real, and that they believed the crisis was over.

Within a couple of days, the Rhojani tour of the pyramid was arranged. Jake was asked to help lead the tour because of his ability to describe the whole process, including how the pyramid was originally located.

Jake discussed the arrangements with Lander Trovari. Lander told him, they had their own spacesuits and simply needed to agree on a meeting time. When ready to start the tour, the Rhojani would simply teleport themselves to the site.

So that's what happened. Once the Rhojani delegation arrived, they all descended the shiny new elevators that had been installed. Naturally Dr Mike Murley was there too. He felt a lot of pride in what they had done here. Jake hadn't been in the pyramid for quite a while. Dr Murley had asked him to lead the tour. He described for the Rhojani the process by which the pyramid was found, As they entered the pyramid, you could see that it evoked a reaction in the Rhojani. They studied the etched glass statues of their ancestors and also studied the two dimensional map of Pangea. They walked all through the pyramid, sometimes running their hands over the wall etchings, sometimes just slowly reading over them.

The Rhojani listened intently to Jake's story about how the anomaly was first detected and how the pyramid was gradually revealed.

The Rhojani pyramid looked quite different now then when Jake and his team first discovered it. Numerous pictures and videos from the Rhojani quartz discs had been set up in display cases around the interior. They had been put there to enhance the experience of human tourists, but they had an even more profound effect on the Rhojani. Jake learned that getting a little misty eyed was also a Rhojani thing. He was surprised to learn that the original colonists of Proxima B didn't take a copy of the fused discs with them, so some of the images they saw today had never been seen by them before.

The Rhojani were also given a tour of the new adjoining pyramid, even though it wasn't quite ready . Jake felt proud of what they had accomplished and he thought the Rhojani appreciated our taking their concept and making our own version of it. Jake thought the human etched glass statues had turned out nicely. The Rhojani studied the different races and remarked on the diversity of the human race. Jake hadn't seen the completed wall etchings until now, and was fascinated by our own version of a dictionary to teach some future race our language.

On Earth, people slowly started to come back from the abyss. The typical mindset was something like being told that there's no trace of your cancer but still being a little hesitant to make any long term plans. Until some team of astronomers actually confirmed that the threat was ended, some would still feel that a cloud was hanging over them. There were also the more cynical types who were waiting for the other shoe to drop. "OK,". They said. "The Rhojani are going to save us, but what's it going to cost? Permanent enslavement? Our first born children?" The idea that another race could do something so monumental and not expect a reward was something they just couldn't believe.

Jake and Janice were having a difficult conversation. The love they felt for each other was real and constant and shaped every decision they made.

"So how did this whole thing come about Jake? Janice asked

"The head of the Rhojani delegation talked to me during the pyramid tour and raised the possibility of a delegation of human beings returning with them to Proxima Centuri B and becoming familiar with their world. Lander Trovari said that they desired to establish a lasting bond with the people of Earth, and they saw a delegation from Earth visiting them as the first step toward achieving that. They have talked to me because they would like me to be in that delegation. They want the man who found the pyramid to tell the story of its discovery."

"How long would you be gone?" Janice asked

"They estimated the round trip would be about 6 months," Jake said quietly.

"We both know what the answer is, Janice said. "You can't possibly not do this. My god, I would make you take me too if not for the kids!. This will be the most amazing experience any human being has ever had. Do you have any concerns for your safety?"

"None at all." Jake replied. "We've seen what amazing beings the Rhojani are. I'm sure everything will be fine."

"I love you madly, Jake and I'm so proud of you."

Chapter Sixteen

The Rhojani communicated to the UN Secretary General that they were ready to proceed with the mission to eliminate Asteroid Namaka. They proposed that a small group of humans accompany them on the mission. They reasoned that the people of Earth had been very traumatized by the events of the last several years and that having eye witnesses to the asteroid's destruction would ensure that everyone knew it was really gone.

The President of the United States decided she should be part of that delegation. After a protracted argument with the Secret Service, President Landon finally just told them that she was going and that was that. The selection of the remaining participants turned into a major debate as so many people came forward with arguments for why they should be included. Finally, the list was boiled down to the UN Secretary General, the Prime Minister of England, the President of the Peoples Republic of China, and three ordinary citizens from Germany, South Africa and Australia.

The arrangements proved again to be exceedingly easy. The Rhojani indicated that they should be given a listing of the names and locations of the people who would accompany them, and at the agreed date and time, they would be teleported to the Rhojani space craft.

Having the fate of so many heads of state in the hands of aliens would have earlier been unthinkable. But trust builds rapidly when that alien culture is the only thing between you and annihilation. So the process went smoothly and soon all of these human delegates found themselves circling Earth in a Rhojani space ship.

It wasn't so different from current space craft used for current Moon and Mars flights. The seats were naturally larger to accommodate the Rhojani stature. The atmosphere was very fresh with the increased oxygen content that Rhojani were accustomed to. The flight controls were complex and exotic, with astral navigation shown on large clear freestanding screens.

The delegation were warmly greeted by the Rhojani. Lander Trovari greeted President Landon with an extended hand. The Rhojani had been taught our custom of shaking hands and now did that as a sign of cultural respect. All of the delegates were fed a meal of Rhojani food. Just as we had done, the food choices were accompanied with descriptions of what each item was written in the multiple Earth languages of the delegates. The guests were then shown comfortable seating for the planned space flight. They were given a description of what they would experience during the flight. Basically, the flight would only last a few minutes, the screens that were currently showing a view of the Milky Way would go blank for a short interval and then the screens would once again show stars, but now the ship would be in the vicinity of Jupiter.

The delegation viewed the interior of the Rhojani spacecraft with a mixture of wonder and awe. The control panel for the ship featured luminescent screens that responded to the Rhohani's touch. There were individual pods in which each passenger would ride during the warp jump. The front of the craft featured a command console where the Rhojani pilots would operate the ship. Several of the delegation asked Lander Trovari to give them an overview of how the Rhojani ship operated. He graciously explained that the ship featured what he described as a warp drive which essentially could generate a worm hole in front of the ship which the ship would then enter. The key to successful faster than light travel, Trovari explained, had come when the technology to control the worm hole exit point was perfected. Now it was possible to go from our current location to virtually anywhere in the universe.

"So are there any limitations on how far you can go?" President Landon asked.

Trovari responded "There is one substantial limitation. Long jumps across great distances produces a dilation in time, meaning time on the ship passes more slowly than for others. So for example, when we made the jump from Proxima B to Earth, the Rhojani on Proxima B would have experienced the passage of one month, but for us on the ship, only a few minutes would have passed. A jump for example across the entire Milky Way galaxy would involve perhaps a week of ship time, but meanwhile on our planet, 5 years would have passed. So you can see this becomes an issue of major import when intergalactic travel is involved."

The Australian observer asked "So how about the trip today. How much time will we gain?"

Trovari smiled. "Today's trip will only move the earthly clock ahead by an hour versus a minute or two here on the ship."

They all relaxed in their pods. Lander Trovari kept them advised about when the "jump" was going to occur. When it did occur, it was as smooth as riding on an elevator. There was hardy any sense of motion at all. As they had been told, the screens had gone blank for a few minutes and then suddenly the stars reappeared. And dominating the middle of the screen was this rolling grey mass that everyone in the delegation recognized immediately. There it was, the agent of their destruction, the cause of so much anxiety in their lives the last several years: Namaka

Lander Trovari invited everyone to once again leave their seats. He proceeded to explain what was going to happen. "We know that from your own astronomers and physicists you are aware of the existence of black holes. Your physicists also postulated the existence of worm holes, although I don't believe you have advanced to the point of being able to create them or manipulate them."

"Black holes are everywhere in the galaxy. Our own scientists estimate that there are as many as 500 million black holes just in our galaxy. They come in all sizes. Through the technology we have developed to manipulate worm holes, we have learned how to warp the space time continuum both for the purpose of faster than light space travel and for manipulation of black holes. In the trip you have just taken, you have traveled through a worm hole. On this trip, you traveled over 2 billion earth miles in just a few minutes. We will position our ship approximately 25,000 miles distant from the asteroid you call Namaka. That will place us close enough to observe what happens but still at a distance far enough to ensure our safety.

213

"What you will see now is the use of a worm hole to retrieve a small black hole from interstellar space. We have previously located a black hole of the appropriate size. We need to find one large enough to swallow the asteroid, but not so large that it will draw in other nearby celestial objects or our spaceship. When we're ready to proceed, we will produce a worm hole that has one end in space-time near our selected black hole and the other end in space-time near the celestial object we are targeting. "Ordinarily a black hole drawn into a wormhole would simply oscillate back and forth inside the wormhole but never exit. We learned how to eject the black hole at the point in space-time we select. In this case, the black hole will be released in the vicinity of this rogue asteroid. The asteroid will be drawn into the black hole, crushed beyond anything we can imagine and disappear. Then we will create a second worm hole and the black hole will be drawn into it and conveyed back to deep space." Lander Trovari completed his description.

The delegates listened with fascination. "So how big is this black hole?" President Landon asked

"It is about the diameter of one of those grapefruit you showed us," Lander answered. "And it has a mass of approximately 10 Plant Earths."

"Can anything go wrong?" the Chinese delegate asked

"We have done this thousands of time without incident" the Rhojani leader answered. "Let us begin."

A Rhojani crew technician began manipulating a complex control panel.

The delegates stood transfixed, watching the image on the screen of Nakama, rotating rapidly and looking lethal. There was a tension on the ship that was palpable. Until the Rhojani made good on their promise, nothing had changed. Suppose they changed their minds? Suppose something malfunctions?

"If you look just to the left just above the asteroid, you can see a faint shimmering. That is the worm hole that will soon deliver the black hole." "Ich sehe es! I see it!" the German delegate cried out.

After a few minutes, the worm hole became more and more distinct. It reminded some of a funnel cloud laying on its side.

Lander Trovari spoke again "Now we'll initiate discharge of the black hole from the wormhole"

It was very faint, but within a short time a shadow appeared to pass in front of the shimmering wormhole. The wormhole seemed to fade away.

"Now the black hole has been ejected by the wormhole and is drifting toward the asteroid. Watch closely, things will move quickly now"

And in the blink of an eye, the asteroid was gone. There was a flash of light and for a second the tiny black hole was framed by that light.

And that was it.

"And now we will create a second wormhole to remove the black hole."

The delegates could make out a second shimmering worm hole. The black hole was difficult to see. Landar Trovari gave a running commentary."The black hole is approaching the worm hole and... now the black hole has been sent back into deep space."

The group of delegates couldn't help themselves. They let out a big cheer. They chattered like school kids all the way back to Earth, hardly believing what they had witnessed.

Once back in earth orbit, one by one the delegates bid goodbye to the Rhojani. On that day, the Rhojani also learned the human custom of the hug, which they found to be very nice. Of course it was a little awkward and they had to kneel down on one knee to make it work.

The delegates were then teleported back down to their respective countries.

Soon the word spread "faster than a prairie fire with a tail wind."

In popular lore, man has talked about epic parties that featured man's ability to throw a celebration, but none of those came close to what happened next on Planet Earth. It was the greatest celebration of all time. For a solid week, people danced, hugged, drank, called old friends, made new friends, buried hatchets, resolved long standing disputes, shot off fireworks, loved their neighbors, refrained from road rage, had barbecues, picnics, parties and pretty much tried to forget about the asteroid and all the anxiety it had produced.

World leaders held an international conference and in an unparalleled display of global cooperation, developed a set of measures intended to restore the world economy to full health. Import duties were suspended. Interest rates for the Fed and the IMF were reduced. Employers were offered tax incentives designed to reward companies that rapidly increased production. Before long the economic picture brightened.

The Rhojani were invited to a variety of events where various groups and countries wanted to express their thanks, but they politely declined. Each of the delegates who had been present for the asteroid's destruction became a media star. Everyone wanted to hear the story over and over of the black hole devouring Namaka.

Amazingly, life started to return to normal. For some who had burned their bridges there was a need for heart felt mea culpas. But people were in a forgiving mood and the near breakdown of society soon started to fade from memory.

While the Rhojani had demurred when it came to attending ceremonies to receive public thanks, they soon made it clear that there were lots of things on Earth they were interested in seeing.

For several months, the media carried one event after another where Rhojani faces could be seen towering over the crowd. Wimbledon, Formula One racing, American football, European football, sessions of Congress, tent revival meetings, Dixieland jazz, rock concerts, surfing competitions, skydiving, and on and on. The Rhojani seemed to enjoy soaking up human culture and everywhere they went, the people expressed their love and gratitude.

Finally, the Rhojani let world leaders know that they would be heading back to their home planet soon. The selection of persons to return with the Rhojani had been going on for some time. The Rhojani had indicated that they could accommodate about 20 people. At one point, the selection committee tried to bump Jake off the list and the Rhojani quietly objected, so Jake stayed on the list. The criteria for who would go was weighted heavily toward engineers and scientists because all believed that this partnership with the Rhojani offered an unparalleled opportunity to advance human technology. But there were also a couple of social scientists because the way the Rhojani thought and lived was so different, and maybe we might just learn something there, too.

Jake and Janice did their best to prepare for the trip. They had never been apart this long in years. The last month before departure, Jake spent extra time with Robbie who was now eight and Amanda who was five. He told them that he was going to be gone for a while but of course it didn't fully register with them. He told them where he was going and the kids found that hard to grasp. His work had wound down with the Human History Preservation Project, so he just had a couple classes he was teaching at Stanford. He got a graduate assistant lined up to fill in for him.

He and Janice made sure to carve out some quality time for each other. They had another sunset dinner at the restaurant in Pacifica. After dinner, they sat on the restaurant's veranda and held hands as they watched the sun sink into the Pacific.

"I saw it!" Janice cried out

"Saw what?" Jake asked

"The green moment!" She smiled

"No way!"

"Way!"

They laughed and kissed passionately. That night, after they put the kids to bed, they made love and lived just for a while in the moment.

"What do you think it will be like, Jake?" Janice asked.

"I think it will be a lot like what we saw in all those videos of the ancients but the technology advancements will no doubt be dazzling. Similar to what the delegation who accompanied the Rhojani to the asteroid reported. Can you imagine a people who can use black holes like giant vacuum cleaners?" Jake stopped and looked deep into Janice's eyes. "But let's not talk about them. Let's just talk about us. Are you ok with this whole thing?"

"I'm fine darling," She replied. "I know the time will pass quickly and then you'll come home with stories of your amazing adventure that will be with us always. I can't wait to hear them!" They cuddled for a while longer and then drifted off to sleep.

Jake and the rest of the Earth delegation were paraded on the world stage prior to their departure. They were interviewed and featured in online stories and asked how they felt and they all did their best to respond, but they really didn't know how to feel or even how to prepare. Living in a totally new, totally foreign culture could end up being a wonderful experience or it could be very difficult. Only time would tell. The group, however, felt optimistic because the Rhojani visitors to Earth were in every case great individuals and during their visit they had all become immensely popular.

The day came for the departure and a brief ceremony was arranged at the United Nations. The Rhojani spoke and assured a safe return of all involved and the Earth delegation head spoke and promised that they would do their best to ably represent our planet and then with almost no fanfare, the Rhojani teleported them to their ship and they were gone.

Janice threw herself into her work to make the time pass more quickly. Her research over the last several years had been very productive. She had developed a new technique for predicting earthquakes and had had several recent notable successes. She had been invited to present at the next International Geophysics Congress and she was excited about that.

Robbie and Amanda gradually missed their daddy more and more. They had been used to his occasional trips to the moon, but he had never been away from them so long. Janice took them to the park frequently and tried to keep them busy.

The Human History Preservation Project was completed and the facility dedicated. Both the Rhojani Pyramid and this new Homo Sapiens Pyramid would remain open to the public, but both facilities were designed so that they could be sealed up at some point in the future if another extinction event threatened earth. Now that the human race and the Rhojani were linked together, that risk seemed far less.

Scientists continued to explore the tremendous volume of information that the Rhojani quartz discs had provided. Some argued that the data was less useful, now that we had access to the living descendants but others argued that the disc data was as relevant as any other archeological record. There was lots of debate among social scientists about the absence of violence in their society. Some argued that testosterone was probably not part of the Rhojani male body chemistry, hence the absence of testosterone fueled rage. Others argued that had human society modeled itself after the Hurons, we might much more closely resemble the Rhojani. Had private ownership not driven greed and competition then maybe we would have been a more peaceable society. No one had the definitive answer but all agreed that the modern Rhojani seemed to be just as gentle and peace loving as their ancestors.

So time passed and one day, a radio transmission from the Rhojani was received saying they were once again orbiting the Earth and were returning with our delegation. The message said they would return 1300 tomorrow in front of the UN.

At the specified time, an army of reporters and spectators were waiting This time they knew not to look up. The brief golden shimmering that now was recognized as the Rhojani teleportation waves was replaced in an instant by all the Earth delegates plus five Rohani.

A microphone had been set up and Paul Singleton, the leader of the Earth delegation, stepped up to it and began speaking.

"Thanks to all of you who came out to welcome us home. I think I can speak for all of us when I say that our experience visiting Trantor exceeded our wildest expectations. The Rhojani people were the best hosts you could ever imagine and they have shared much with us about their world and their people. In the days and months ahead we'll be sharing a lot more about what we learned, but suffice to say we look forward to a long and productive partnership with our Rhojani brothers. And now I'd like to ask Predur Matura to say a few words.."

A Rhojani female stepped up to the microphone and began speaking

"Greetings to our brothers and sisters of Earth. We have been honored to share our world with your delegation. The five Rhojani you see here will be visiting you for a few months and then if there is interest among the human beings, we will take another delegation to come to our planet. You heard today from Paul the name Trantor which is what we call the planet you know as Proxima Centuri B. Thank you for receiving us today. Peace and Prosperity to all!"

And so began what would become a long and productive relationship between 2 planets and 2 races bonded together by a common origin. The Rhojani proved to be the type of partners that one can only dream of. Generous, sharing of all they had, accepting of our shortcomings, technological giants, and a warm caring race of beings.

As a result of the first delegate mission, the team came back with technology to make teleportation possible, with the preliminary specs for creating and controlling worm holes, with vehicle levitation technology that would allow three dimensional vehicular traffic, and a single pharmaceutical agent that would cure all cancers. All of these things would require additional human development but the basic technology was in our grasp, so it was just a matter of time until these things became part of life on Earth.

The delegation members talked extensively about their experiences. The Rhojani had been wonderful supportive hosts and had always tried to respond to anything the delegation requested. The group had been the focus of much public attention on Trantor and Paul Singleton had given an address to their equivalent of the United Nations. Jake was much in demand with the Rhojani and gave his talk describing the pyramid project something like 10 times during the visit.

Jake arrived back in California the next day and received endless hugs and kisses from Robbie, and Amanda and of course Janice. After things had quieted down, dinner was over and the kids were in bed, Janice looked at Jake and said,

"So, tell me all about the trip and don't leave anything out!"

Jake began "The hype you've heard about the Rhojani and how great they were is all absolutely true. The Rhojani are warm, generous, open minded and they went to great lengths to make us feel welcome and at home."

"Each of us was billeted with a Rhojani family. I stayed with the Orouda family. They were a Mom and Dad and 3 kids ranging in age from 3 to 13. They were terrific people and I spent many nights talking to them 'til the wee hours. They were very interested in learning about humans. They also wanted to know lots about our planet. They have an oral history about Earth that paints a very idealized picture of it, and they wanted to know what it's really like."

"Their lives are surrounded by technology we have only dreamed about. Teleportation is used on the planet to get everywhere so people can commute to work on the other side of the planet or down the street. Their vehicles can cover ground like a car, or levitate like a helicopter, so their cities are really 3 dimensional with many high rise buildings. Their robotics are far advanced over what we have. Most of their daily chores, cooking , cleaning are all done by housekeeping robots, that seem almost human. From a health perspective, they also are very far advanced. While we learned that the ancient Rhojani had an average lifespan of 85, their descendants live to an average age of 120. Cancer is totally curable. Organ transplants are almost routine."

"Their diet, as with their ancestors, continues to be a vegetarian diet, They have a protein source they call Wala which seems to be a tofu like product that they eat a lot of. The Earth delegates found we could eat most things that the Rhojani offered us, but there were a couple of things that made several of us pretty ill at least for a short while."

"The Rhojani routinely receive implants that give them phone and Internet access without requiring any external device. Some times it was almost disquieting to see one of our hosts close their eyes for a second and then report back on something they just searched for."

"Wow, Jake, just incredible stuff. So what was Proxima Centuri B like?"

"It's certainly different from Earth. For starters, it has a year that's something like 11 earth days. The sun it rotates around is a red dwarf, which is a lot smaller than our sun and really looks quite different in comparison. The distance to the sun there is something like 1/20th of the distance between Earth and the Sun. The radiation levels on Proxima B are pretty intense. We needed to stay out of the sun or use shielding to protect ourselves. The atmosphere was perfectly breathable, maybe a little higher oxygen content then we're used to. The planet seems pretty arid. Given my choice, I'd stay on Earth."

"How about their politics," Janice asked. "Did you learn anything about that."

"Because they all started eons ago as a single colony, they have evolved as a single country. Their population today is only about 50 million total. They have what appears to be a democratic government with elected representatives, someone who seems to function like a president, but no evidence of a judicial branch. Consistent with what we saw with their ancestors, they appear to not have laws. I asked my hosts how disputes are settled if their are no laws. They indicated that they have things like product and equipment specifications which provide guidance as to how to build a product, but that laws to make people do certain things just weren't thought to be necessary. They felt their ability to conduct thorough and logical debates on questions facing them allowed them to come to reasonable solutions. One of the things that may help make that work is this absence of private property in their society. I asked my hosts who owned the house they live in and they indicated it was the city. I asked them if they paid rent to live there and they didn't know what rent was."

Jake continued "The Rhojani are actively exploring their region of the galaxy. Their ability to warp time and space means that large sections of the galaxy are within their reach. I asked them if they had encountered other intelligent beings and they responded that the galaxy is teeming with life. I asked them how they would defend themselves if they encountered a predatory race bent on galactic conquest. They found the question puzzling and said that so far human beings were the only race they had encountered that routinely turned to violence."

Janice just shook her head.

Jake resumed. "I asked them why they were willing to help us if we might be a risk to them. They said our common bond was too important to turn away from."

"The Rhojani in general seem to be remarkably happy. The delegates talked among themselves about how we never saw Rhojani get angry or argue or even get just a little snippy. We found it truly remarkable. I asked one of my hosts about it and at least for a while it was a struggle to communicate what I was asking. My host said. "What does getting angry mean" I tried to explain as best I could. They finally responded that they just never feel the need to do that."

"The delegates met regularly during the trip. We all agreed that the people of Earth stood to benefit greatly from their relationship with the Rhojani."

"So where do you see that relationship going from here?" Janice asked

"I'm not sure." Jake replied. "So far it has been kind of one sided, with all the benefits of the relationship accruing on our side. The Rhojani seem to be inherently generous, but at some point it might be good if there was some more tangible benefit that they derived from this relationship."

"So far they've never really asked us for anything, right?" Janice asked.

"That's right," Jake replied.

"So maybe you should ask them. Janice said.

"Ask them what they want?" Jake asked.

"Well perhaps couched a little more artfully. Maybe something like "After all you have done for us, is there something we can do for you?" Janice said

"It's a good suggestion. I think the next time I see Predur Matura, I'll ask her," Jake said, giving Janice a warm smile.

The opportunity arose more quickly than Jake expected.

A few days later he got an invitation to the world premier in Hollywood of the documentary film "Nakama" which purported to tell the whole story of earth's brush with extinction. The trailers for the film claimed to have exclusive footage of the actual destruction of Namaka and the Rhojani delegation had been invited to attend.

Jake decided it might be fun to attend, and he talked Janice into coming along and taking a couple of days off from classes.

They decided to do it up properly. Janice bought a lovely cocktail dress and Jake dressed up in his Sunday best with the moon rock bollo tie he loved. When they arrived, the movie director, cinematographer and producers were having their photos taken in front of a Step and Repeat banner. When several of the Rhojani arrived, they graciously consented to have their pictures taken with the director. One of the producers spotted Jake and came running over and convinced Jake to join the photo op.

Finally everyone filed into the theater and the director took the stage.

"Hi Everyone, I'm Werner Herzog III. Welcome to the world Premier of Nakama. We are incredibly fortunate tonight to have several of the

Rhojani delegation with us."

He was immediately interrupted by thunderous applause as everyone in the theater stood and cheered . The Rhojani seemed appreciative of the recognition.

"I'd also like to point out that several delegates just back from their trip to Trantor are here tonight, including Dr James Melville, Derek Williams and a name we all know- Jake Mackenzie."

There was a second standing ovation. Janice was beaming and Jake just looked uncomfortable.

"With the help of a number of world leaders plus assistance from the Rhojani, we have captured the whole story of our near extinction. Without further ado, let's begin."

The film was very well done, narrated by Herzog himself, of course. Jake was surprised to see that the producers had actually secured film from the Rhojani that captured the moment Namaka got eaten. When that occurred, the whole room erupted again.

After the film, there was a Q and A session with lots of people asking questions.

Later folks were milling around in the theater lobby. Jake saw the heads of several of the Rhojani towering over the crowd and worked his way over to them.

Jake greeted them warmly "Hello Everyone, Predur, how are you? Have you been enjoying your time here on Earth?""

Predur, dressed in her glistening robes, turned and smiled when she saw Jake.

Jake thought to himself that Predur was very attractive; he could see why Rhojani males would find Rhojani females alluring.

"Jake, so nice to see you. Yes we've been having a marvelous time. I've discovered I'm a natural at wind surfing. And California is so beautiful!"

Jake saw this as the time to ask that question "Predur, could I speak to you privately for a minute?"

"But of course," Pradur responded graciously.

They found a conference room and went in. Predur of course had to duck as she entered.

Jake looked at Predur and began "First let me say that no one in authority has asked me to do this. This is just something that I personally want to ask you."

"Please Jake, you know you can ask me anything you want," Predur smiled warmly.

Jake hesitated for a second and then started. "So after coming back and saving the life of every human being on our planet, isn't there anything that the people of Earth can do for the Rhojani?"

"Oh my goodness Jake, that is so sweet, thank you for asking! " Predur beamed at Jake. "But you know we didn't help your civilization to reap some reward. We did it because we could and because it was the right thing to do."

"I understand," Jake smiled back at her. "But I'm asking you to tell me something that we could do that would bring pleasure to the Rhojani people." Predur smiled and hesitated for a second. "Well, there is something that some of my fellow delegates and I have discussed, but we have been hesitant to bring it up."

Jake smiled again "Please tell me, Predur. Maybe I can help."

And she told him.

And Jake thought to himself "We could do this!" He felt the rush of excitement that comes with realizing your next big adventure is about to begin.

And he repeated what he had just thought out loud to Predur.

"We could do this!"

Chapter Seventeen

O h my god, Jake! That's incredible!" Janice exclaimed.

Jake had just told Janice the results of his discussion with Predur Matura.

"So tell me again how she responded," Janice said.

"Predur told me that both groups of Rhojani who visited here had found themselves totally in awe of the huge oceans. Proxima Centuri B is a dry rocky planet. While their folklore about ancient earth had described the large oceans, none was mentally prepared for how magnificent they were. They felt that their roots are in this wonderful ocean covered world and being back here had awakened primordial memories of those roots."

Jake continued. "They had talked among themselves and with the leadership of the Rhojani about how wonderful it would be if they could establish a permanent base here. They envisioned over a period of years how millions of Rhojani would make the trip to visit here. They have been hesitant, however, to broach the subject with humans. They don't really understand human attitudes about private property, so they were concerned that such a question would offend humans."

Jake added. "They seem to have a well developed concept for what they would really like to build here. I'm just not sure what it would take to make it happen."

"I think we could help them, Jake"

"What do you mean? Jake asked.

"I mean that they were right to be hesitant to broach the subject with humans. Presented in the wrong way, people could react negatively, see it as the start of the Rhojani takeover of Earth. Many humans might be supportive right up until they got the idea that the Rhojani wanted *their* land. I think we could help the Rhojani to navigate the minefield infested waters that are human sensibilities. What if you and I met with the Rohani delegation and helped them put together a proposal that we thought the human race would accept." Janice looked at Jake questioningly.

"It seems like an awfully big thing for the firm Barnes & Mackenzie to take on," Jake said with a warm smile.

"I know what you're saying. I don't disagree. But if we simply worked with them to develop the starting concept, we could then help them present their proposal to a larger audience which could then make an even larger pool of planning resources available to them. I just feel like they'll never make progress without some initial assistance," Janice looked at Jake with that serious expression that he knew and loved.

"Ok, you've convinced me. I'll propose you and I get together with the Rhojani delegation. I'll explain to Predur what we're thinking. Do you think we should involve anyone else?" Jake asked.

"Right now I think the number of people involved has to be kept really small. If word should leak out prematurely, the whole thing could be doomed. But it wouldn't hurt to have maybe one other person involved to make sure we're not going down a wrong path. What about Paul Singleton, the delegate lead for your trip to Proxima Centuri B?" Janice asked.

"I think that's a good suggestion. Paul impressed me. He represented us well during our trip. If I shared this whole idea with him and he was supportive, it would give me greater confidence that what we're doing can work," Jake said.

So Jake went to work on their idea. He was gratified that Paul Singleton was immediately on board and supportive. He then contacted Predur Matura and she also was supportive of his proposal. Jake made arrangements for all of them to meet in New York City in a week.

Jake thought to himself later how easy it is to think you know more than someone else... even if they come from a race of technological giants.

So when Jake and Paul and Janice sat down with Predur and the other Rhojani delegates, they were stunned with the complexity and sophistication of what was being proposed.

In a nutshell, the Rhojani proposed to build a facility that would serve as a Rhojani tourist destination and a technology transfer center. They wanted to find a temperate location on the ocean. They envisioned a facility that could accommodate up to 10,000 Rhojani visitors a year plus 2,000 human engineers annually who would come there for advanced technology training. They would be open to the construction at a later date of additional facilities if either tourist traffic or technology transfer demand showed it was warranted and they were requested to do so by Earth governing authorities.

They would perform all the construction themselves, with the facilities being totally independent in terms of energy, food and water production.

They went on to describe how the facility would be modeled after their own cities and would utilize the same technologies- levitating vehicles, teleportation, high rise living quarters. They noted that the design of the city itself would give human city planners and architects the ability to study their designs . They indicated that human tourists would also be welcome there and that design of facilities would take into account the differences in stature between humans and Rhojani. They put up a number of concept drawings that brought the whole idea to life.

They indicated that they would only proceed once they had the full permission of governing bodies, and that they would end the venture on Earth if at any point in the future were requested to do so.

Both Paul and Jake, having lived in and seen Rhojani cities, could visualize what the facility would look like. They both knew that the interest among companies around the globe in Rhojani technology was intense.

After the Rhojani completed describing their vision, Paul Singleton spoke first. "I think your idea of combining these two different purposes is very good. I envision that the technology transfer part will win over some who might otherwise be resistant to the idea of Rhojani tourists on Earth. One thought I have is that we, meaning human beings, may need to pass some additional laws that place any technology you share with us in what is called the "public domain", which means the technology is available to all without restriction."

Paul continued. "The one issue which may produce controversy is the initial selection of land for this facility. As you know, we humans have a long history of private property rights which may cause some headaches. But I think that's an issue that can be solved."

"Another thought I have is that it might make sense to consider whether there may also be a tourist market in the other direction. Having been to your planet, I can tell you that I think many human beings would have great interest in being able to visit and experience your culture."

Before the meeting started, Jake had the feeling that the Rhojani would meet stiff resistance to a proposal to establish a Rhojani colony on Earth.. After listening to their concept, Jake's opinion changed completely. He now thought that the biggest issue would probably be different countries arguing over who got the Rhojani facility.

Janice had listened carefully throughout the meeting and now finally spoke up. "I think this can be done." Turning to Jake and Paul she said "So what do you see as the next step?"

Jake responded " I think we, meaning everyone here today, should request a meeting with President Landon and get her reaction."

The proposal was discussed and agreed to by the group.

Afterward, they were all talking and Predur approached Jake. " We hadn't really considered that human beings would be interested in making vacation on our planet," she said.

Jake responded. "For many human beings it would be the adventure of a lifetime. It certainly was for me."

Predur smiled, appreciating the complement to her home. "Our people would certainly welcome it."

Jake called the White House after the meeting. He didn't really have any experience with such things and wondered if setting up such a meeting would be difficult.

He spoke with 2 different staffers who immediately escalated his call and soon he found himself talking to the President's Chief of Staff.

"So you, Paul Singleton and the Rhojani delegation would like to meet with President Landon, is that correct?"

"Also, Dr Janice Barnes.

"And what would be the purpose of the meeting?" the Chief of Staff asked.

"The Rhojani have a proposal they would like to discuss with President Landon. Do you think that would be possible?

"Frankly Dr Mackenzie, if the Rhojani said they wanted to meet with the president to talk about the weather, that would still be fine. After saving the world and taking President Landon along to watch, these folks can meet with the president anytime they want. So yes, to answer your question, that would be possible."

"Thank you," Jake stammered.

They proceeded to set up an appointment for the following week.

A week later, Jake found himself along with the other meeting attendees, ushered into the Oval Office.

The President greeted the Rhojani delegation warmly, greeting each one by name and shaking hands with them. Jake and Paul had met the president when they went on the mission to Proxima B, and she also greeted both of them like old friends. Then she turned to Janice smiled and said " And who do we have here?" Jake said "Madam President , I'd like you to meet Dr Janice Barnes."

President Landon smiled and said " I remember you Dr Barnes. You were all over the airwaves when the pyramid project was active. I think I saw you on at least 2 talk shows"

Janice laughed and said "That was me. My 15 minutes of fame."

"So let's all sit down and talk." The president waved everyone toward a couch.

The Rhojani proceeded to give their presentation about the tourist and technology transfer center.

Jake watched the president closely, trying to detect how she was reacting to the presentation, but her body language gave no real hint.

Finally, when Predur finished speaking, there was an awkward pause.

Paul Singleton spike up "Madam President, we know this is a lot to digest. Our thought in seeing you today was to get your initial reaction and if you were at all favorably disposed to this idea, to get your advice about how best to move it forward."

Finally the President spoke. "The whole topic of Rhojani technology and how to best take advantage of the Rhojani generosity with regard to that technology has been a hot topic within my administration. The solution you offer here of a Rhojani built site to facilitate that technology transfer strikes me as one more sign of the wonderful intentions of the Rhojani. To also have it function as a tourist destination for Rhojani visitors seems like the very least we can do for the people who saved our whole planet."

"So Dr Singleton, returning to your comment about getting my initial reaction, my reaction is we should do this, we can do this, and we will do this," the President said, looking directly at the Rhojani delegation.

"I have a couple of minor suggestions. We need to pass a "Global Public Domain Act" so everyone shares equally in technology. My other suggestion is that the proposal contain provision for several additional facilities to be located around the globe. I predict the big issue is going to be countries arguing over who gets the first facility," the President said.

"With the agreement of this group, I would propose that this delegation make this presentation at the UN Security Council. After you make your presentation, I will also address this body and express my support for the proposal."

And the rest is history.

Epilogue

The Rhojani and the Human Beings lived ever after in harmony.

The first great Rhojani center was built on the Texas gulf coast in 2085. It was wildly popular among Rhojani visitors, and human engineers benefited greatly from state of the art training facilities.

Within a few years, hovercraft became ubiquitous in world cities, and building design began to reflect the new accessibility options. Teleportation facilities were introduced around the world and soon became the preferred means of travel for most trips over 100 miles.

The first spacecraft built by humans featuring warp drive capability was produced within 5 years. On its maiden voyage, it traveled to Proxima Centuri B to deliver the first group of human interstellar tourists.

Additional Rhojani tourism and design centers were added in Calabria, Italy, Saigon, and Tahiti in 2088. The Rhojani couldn't get enough Calabrian pizza.

Surprisingly, despite their differences in body chemistry, the anti cancer technology of the Rhojani also worked for humans.

The Rhojani performed several more asteroid interdictions over the following 10 years, but none on the scale of Namaka.

The Rhojani lunar pyramid remained a favorite stopping off point with Rhojani connecting with their past.

Janice's research on earthquake detection was made redundant by the Rhojani technology that both detected and halted the progression of earthquakes.

Janice and Jake both went on to long and productive careers. They revisited often in their conversations the great lunar pyramid adventure. And of course, many more adventures awaited them.